# ETERNAL CITY

Also by Mark Thompson

*Dust*

MARK THOMPSON

# ETERNAL CITY

Red Door

Published by RedDoor
www.reddoorpress.co.uk



ISBN 978-1-915194-07-7



A CIP catalogue record for this book is available from the British Library

Cover design: Patrick Knowles
Typesetting: WatchWord Editorial Services
Printed in the UK by CPI Group (UK), Croydon

For Liz

. . . and to the memory of
my wonderful mother and father,
who I hope live anew

昔のことは水に流せ
むかしのことはみずにながせ

*mukashi no koto wa mizu ni nagase*
let old things drift away on the water

*Japanese proverb*

# prologue

Let me get something straight. I should not be here. The others should be here. Just not me.

Shelley and Keats and Gramsci and all the others that ended up here. They should be here, but not me. I should be sitting in the rooftop bar at the Knickerbocker in New York City, or having dinner at Quaglino's in London, or slumped in a deckchair at the mock beach by Checkpoint Charlie in Berlin drinking cocktails with Hannah. I should be glancing with pride at my wedding ring, as we stroll hand in hand. Most definitely of all, I should be anywhere but here.

They say that accidents can happen anywhere, any time, to anyone. It is the mantra of the health-and-safety brigade who make a cosy living in this modern world where fear outweighs delight. I mean, I jumped out of an aeroplane with twenty-five pounds of silk and cord and a gut-wrenching fear, only to be filled with a sense of pure elation ten seconds later, five thousand feet above a daisy meadow, that two grams of cocaine and a lottery win could not possibly match. Play safe long enough and you will still end up dead. There's this idea that if you live life eating only health foods and abstaining from alcohol, cigarettes, narcotics and dangerous pursuits you will live longer. Maybe you will. Chances are you won't. Wasted. Bored. Gone.

The combination of things in everyday life, their very order, determines outcomes. Some foreseen and others unforeseen. Looking left instead of right crossing the street in an unfamiliar road system in an unfamiliar country can get you gone. Let's say you replace a broken wire inside an electric guitar amplifier. You connect it to the negative as you should, plug in your guitar, turn on the amplifier and play a tune. Job done. Let's say, though, that you connect the new wire to the positive by mistake, through error, carelessness or lack of knowledge. You plug in your guitar, switch on the amplifier – and join me, and Shelley and Keats and Gramsci and the others.

Now, if I had come here with my camera earlier in that fateful day, climbed up the side of the tower taking good account of the loose moss and fractured stone, held on tight until I was balanced securely, then focused down on Shelley's tombstone, clicked off a series of shots, then gone to meet Hannah at Masto, eaten lunch and drunk those great wines, I would probably be sitting in Madrid or Bogotá or some other capital city right now, reading my brief for a magazine or book cover shot. Instead, I am stuck here, forever, with a bunch of poets, religious maniacs and Romans.

The reason I am here is a combination of things put together in the wrong order. The irony being that I had put things in the wrong order many times, but never had such a bad result. Life, as they say, is what you make it. Then I found, aged twenty-eight, that death has to be what you make it. My advice? Live it while you can.

# the flight now boarding

Four words I had never imagined speaking. Four words which, when placed in a particular order, can change a normally unconcerned person's destiny, priorities, role, status, standing, and just about everything that has gone before. Four words which change lives forever. For better, for worse. For richer, for poorer. In sickness and health.

Four words can mean everything, or nothing at all, depending on the order they are placed. Order-created meaning. Honour. Your. Guilty. Not. Four words carrying differing weights. Honour. Such a hefty and regal weight. Defined as it is as *high respect; great esteem*, and *the quality of knowing and doing what is morally right*. But adding one extra word can change the idea of what is right to something else. From something laudable to something evil. Killing, for example. *Honour killing*. I ask, where is the esteem, the morality in that? Guilty is a word which really shouts. Or maybe not. Those four words placed in a new and meaningful order can change the course of a person's life. 'Not guilty, Your Honour.' Not a sentence I ever had to say. But adding a single word after guilty can change it to something to relish. *Guilty pleasure.*

Let your hair down. Do not pass Go. Paint the town red. Throw me a line. Stand by your man. I want you now. Somebody call the cops. You are so beautiful. Tomorrow is another day. And the winner is. Your card was declined. You let me down. Live and let live. Keep off the grass. The flight now boarding.

And there I was, passport and boarding pass in hand, travel and camera bags at my feet, with Hannah embracing me, when, as she kissed me goodbye and leaned back smiling to look into my eyes, four jumbled words formed and jumped into my mind like party fireworks, all cracking and sparking and flashing so bright they lit up the world.

'Hannah?'

'Yes?'

Then they formed in sound as I let them fall whispering through the air.

'Will you marry me?'

# last call

*Last call for British Airways flight BA one seven three to New York. Would any remaining passengers please make your way to Gate B thirty-five where this flight is about to depart.*

I am now running from security to the gate, grinning wildly as Hannah's reply, 'Yes, oh yes, yes!' repeats in my ears. I had uttered those four simple words. I received four words in response. Well, three of them were the same word, but they were words of gold. I am elated, bursting, positively divine. I am man. I am Superman. I am a god. My mind is filled with sun, rainbows, waterfalls, and the sounds of Beethoven and choirs and angels on clouds with harps. Keith Richards just blew kisses to me. I am kneeling to be knighted. I am a Nobel laureate, and the discoverer of a vaccine for every ill. I am an Oscar-winner. I am an astronaut. Everyone surrounding me is mortal. I am the saviour of mankind. I still feel her soft lips on mine, and our lips are honey and silk and gossamer and myrrh. I never felt this good. Not ever. Not when I signed to Lewis & Horwood Agency. A licence to print money. I was signed aged twenty-six, which made me the youngest photographer on their books, anywhere in the world. A fact recorded in blogs, photography magazines, and even a side comment in the *New Yorker*. I am not even American. A pretty good achievement by anyone's stamp. And now I am blessed. Now I am immortal.

An oft-employed wry look and strained smile. 'You just made it.'

'I just got engaged!' I say excitedly, showing my passport and boarding pass to the attendant, who hands them straight back after a practised glance.

'Congratulations!' she calls, genuinely smiling, as I dash towards the boarding bridge, waving my documentation as I had to Hannah when I'd passed through to security ten minutes earlier.

I apologise to the middle seat passenger as I slide into my seat by the window. The pilot announces that our final passenger, me, is now on board, 'which completes checks, so we shall shortly be departing for New York.' The seatbelt sign comes on, and the cabin crew begin a safety demonstration, which is easier to watch on the screens in the seat-backs. I ignore the demonstration. I've seen it all before.

My travelling companion, a sour-faced man in his fifties, says a slightly weary, 'Good for you,' when I tell him, bursting with pride, that I was late to board as I had just proposed and been accepted. The biggest moment in my life, the gloss of it only momentarily dulled by his additional sour comment. 'I hope you both know what you're doing.' Not a question. A chastisement.

The sound of a doorbell chiming and *Cabin crew, seats for take-off* announces our departure, then comes the part I love most as we race along the runway, and the painted distance-markers pop up quicker and quicker until they blur into an indefinable on-off like a strobe light, and then a hard bump as we lift into the air and my stomach stays attached to the tarmac below. Then, after what feels like only a couple of seconds, the click of wheels folding up, and a sudden quiet and that initial feeling that the engines have stopped and we are about to be the opening headline on news stations around the world. Of course we are not. I am going to die, just not yet. Unexpectedly, but not yet.

We are still climbing, and I watch London fall away as we bump, bump, bump through changes in air pressure passing up through wisps of cloud. Suddenly we are above the cloud, in brilliant blue, as another doorbell sounds, and the simultaneous click of a pair of seatbelts unlatching heralds a stock announcement that the seatbelt signs are still illuminated and we, the flying cattle, should remain in our seats as the cabin crew whirr into practised motion. I am feeling euphoric and wish I could call Hannah to express my joy, but content myself with looking down on patchworks of farm fields, and the rare sight of a turquoise rectangle, a lone swimming pool, as we head across Oxfordshire and out towards Wales and the Atlantic Ocean beyond.

# in love with everyone

My travelling companion is a man practised at social isolation. As I try to engage him in friendly conversation, he nods inattentively then reaches into a Ralph Lauren bag he has fished out from below his seat, pulls out a set of earplugs and eyeshades, pushes the plugs into his ears and slides the shades up on to his head, then drops his seat back, to the obvious displeasure of the lady in the seat behind. He is an ignorant bastard. I look for something redeeming. Maybe he has just been seated on too many flights next to a younger man, or woman, who just got engaged, and he is weary of the self-loving jubilation of others. Or maybe he really is just an ignorant bastard. But then again, maybe he's just a man with much on his mind, such as failing health, maybe cancer, or an impending prison sentence, or worry that his wife has been sleeping with his best friend, or his best friend's wife, while he has been away trying to clinch a business deal that will make his unhappy wife happy and keep their kids in their prestigious school, or get them all far away on that trip they talked of to Hawaii or Japan, or Vietnam where his ageing father had fought as a nineteen-year-old. Maybe he is just tired of life. Imagine. Imagine being tired of life. What would Dr Johnson say about that?

I stare out at the ocean far below, watching for tankers or cargo ships as my thoughts flit from my beloved Hannah to the sea, which I have always loved for its beauty and power and mystery. I cast a sidelong look at my neighbour and start to feel the milk of human kindness draining away from me, leaking mysteriously out through the hermetically sealed window to run along the length of the wing and fall to the mysterious depths below, but then a stewardess catches my attention, leaning over the slumped body of John Doe, offering me a silver tray, on which is a small bottle of champagne and a flute glass, together with a plate of chocolate mints.

'Congratulations on your engagement, Mr Chambers, on behalf of British Airways, Captain Amos and the crew.'

She beams down at me. She is beautiful. I am thrilled. I radiate joy. She sees that in me, I'm sure, and adds, 'Just press the button above your head if you need anything.'

I am in love with her. I am in love with everyone. I am even inclined to give my travelling companion the benefit of the doubt. I want to wake the miserable bastard, just to make him envious, but I satisfy myself with a photograph of the champagne on the tray, and then a grinning selfie with the fizzy flute to my lips, which I will send to Hannah when we land to reinforce just how special this day has been. I mentally thank the departure gate lady who has arranged this. I love her too.

# the sea makes them free

I am excited. I am drumming my feet on the aircraft floor, quickly but quietly. The first officer announces the weather at JFK as we begin our descent, then I stare out of the window, looking down on to Long Island, at the mansions and countless swimming pools of the Hamptons, then we are across the Rockaway Freeway, and touching down. Immigration, as ever, takes a lifetime. My work visa is scrutinised as though it contains some secret code which the officer knows is there but cannot decipher. He looks at me as though I have brought some deadly disease with me which may kill him, then says, 'Enjoy your stay in New York, Mr Chambers,' but he does not mean it.

A yellow cab after a wait in line. The driver introduces himself as Tariq, then, beaming, asks me how to get to the Roosevelt on Madison in heavily accented English. I guess he is Indian. How would I know? Only in America could you be expected to pay a king's ransom for a taxi ride and have to schedule the route yourself. My sense of humour tempts me to ask if he would like me to drive the cab while he takes a nap, but sarcasm would dull my sense of joy.

He saves the day by resorting to technology and sets off following a route on his phone. We join the traffic heading for Manhattan. Jamaica, Queens. Armageddon. The stark contrast to anything my country has to offer. My countrymen revel in knocking the imagined decline of their society, but the fear of crime vastly outweighs its reality. They should come to Jamaica, Queens for a reality check. Subconsciously I pull my shirt-sleeve down over my watch as we wait at a crossing light, and Tariq rolls up the windows and presses a lock button. The soft click of the door-locks shouts of danger. He had slipped off his fake Rolex as we approached the stop light. Nobody wants to die for the sake of a ten-dollar watch. Shop-fronts are padlocked metal shutters covered in sprayed graffiti with a rectangle cut out where the transaction takes place. Like a twenty-first-century take on the check-window at a 1920s Speakeasy, now a hole in a steel wall where dollar bills are slid across for a tube of toothpaste, gum and a pack of Marlboro, or Peter Stuyvesant on promotion with a dollar-off coupon. Bills first, then goods and change. I wonder how the shopkeepers get their cash to the bank. Maybe, like the gold-miners of the Old West, they have a tunnel that leads to the bank basement. The only way to guarantee not being shot dead by some spaced-out crackhead with a gun.

I am soberly reminded of a statistic I read in the in-flight magazine about a small-arms survey. There are, apparently, over one hundred and twenty guns per hundred people in the good old US of A. That equates to hundreds of millions of guns. Number one in the list. My country is one hundred and twenty-seventh on that list. You have probably as much chance of being hit by lightning as being murdered by a handgun where I come from. Tariq was wise to hide his watch.

Peter Stuyvesant, immortalised not as the last Dutch governor of 'New Netherland', now New York and New Jersey, but as the name on a pack of cigarettes with the boast *the international passport to smoking pleasure.* Stuyvesant died in 1672, aged eighty, in an era when life expectancy for the likes of Jamaica, Queens' low-life was about twenty-five years. If they were lucky. I doubt Peter Stuyvesant was a smoker. Not even a spliff.

Tariq's nephew is to be married in Bangladesh in three weeks. He and his wife would love to go. Driving a cab in New York City does not pay for long-haul flights. His son is going to become a doctor. He is fourteen and studies every night and, apart from baseball practice on Saturdays, studies all weekend. He is determined not to drive a cab like his father. They are blessed to be in the United States. His wife is the best cook outside Bangladesh. Even better than his mother, although he would not tell his mother so. On days off Tariq likes to drive out to Brighton Beach, just to watch the sea, and the ships sailing into New York. He tells me he has an app on his cell phone that has the name and itinerary of every ocean-going ship. It fascinates him to think of the distances that ships travel, and he wonders where the crews are from and how many of them are criminals wanted in their home country. According to Tariq, many Bangladeshis fleeing justice take to the sea. A reversal of historic piracy, when the criminals took to the high seas to plunder, not to hide. Tariq, his wife, and their children, the doctor-to-be and two younger siblings, occupy two rooms and share a kitchen and bathroom with another Bangladeshi family in an apartment in the Starrett City housing complex, Brooklyn. They sub-let it from a Hispanic dentist. That place has some history. Donald Trump's father Fred Christ Trump owned a lump, and left some to the idiot child. Tariq says that the apartment is crowded and both families walk on eggshells around the other, but that he saves every dollar he can to get the deposit together to fund a move so they can have an apartment to themselves. He tells me that is why he loves to watch the sea, where he can talk to his wife without whispering, and he can see as far as the horizon. He says the sea makes them free. They buy Russian snacks as they stroll the boardwalk, then make love in his cab as they have no privacy at home. He is amazed that free movies are shown all summer long in the parking lot just along from Brighton Beach at Manhattan Beach Park. Free movies to have surreptitious sex by. Only in America.

I tip him generously. He is a likeable guy and I regret my initial impatient thoughts with him. I hope he adds my tip to his apartment deposit, and treats his wife to a night of sex by the sea. I also hope he buys condoms with some of the money. Three children are enough in his situation.

Tariq toots the cab horn as he pulls into the late afternoon traffic and waves his arm from the open window, his fake Rolex sparkling in sunlight. There are no tickets in his hand.

I check in, drop my bags in my room. I am relieved. A tenth-floor room. Always book a room lower than thirteen. It is a beautiful afternoon. My shoot is not until the following morning, so I do what pleases me most in New York City and walk to the Knickerbocker for a cocktail, before making my way to the Empire State Building, where I love to look across the city from the viewing platform. The Knickerbocker is busy with business types, and the idle rich. Women who shop and lunch and work out and spill their tired tales of insecurity to shrinks who charge by the minute. Pot-bellied self-made men with fou fou wives, who have replaced the first and second wives, and who may themselves be replaced as the errant husband makes more and more money (they too may end up on the shrink's couch wondering where it all went wrong). Third-rate actors and fading and rising sports stars. Music producers and scriptwriters and investment bankers and the kinds of drug dealers who do not sully their hands with parking lot exchanges, but whose tainted money moves them ever closer to the Hamptons. Property developers lobbying crooked councillors. Drug lords turned property developers lobbying equally crooked councillors. Photography here is discouraged *for the privacy of the clientele*. In reality it is discouraged so that no innocent photographic record on antisocial media can place criminals and sex-cheats with their illicit companions and come to bite them in divorce and corruption scandals.

I decide on a Manhattan. It seems an appropriate drink in the circumstances. I stand out on the terrace and marvel at the view. Although it is late in London, maybe one in the morning, I call Hannah, who has sent me a message of dozens of emoji hearts and kisses. We whisper as though others can hear. Sweet words of tender love. I am reminded of Tariq as we say our goodnights, and hope he finds that apartment soon. I hope his son becomes a doctor and finds a cure for coronavirus, malaria and the common cold while he is about it. I want everyone I see to be golden. To touch their god and see a world where war is unknown and life is rich and bountiful. I want the husbands to love their fou fou wives and the shrinks to become gardeners as their clients no longer need them. I want love for everyone.

I take another glance around the bar, and head to West 34th Street. The queue is short and then I am into the Empire State Building. The elevator is from another world. It is silent and perfectly still as it rises, counting floors in groups of ten. In seconds we arrive at the eighty-sixth floor. My stomach, as in take-off a few hours earlier, is still on the ground.

## the restless city

I am a moth. My flame is lights. New York City. I close up my jacket as the wind, I know, will take on a sudden chill as nightfall creeps. A Canon hangs around my neck like an old friend on a drinks night, welcome and reassuring. My go-anywhere-and-shoot digital with 24–72 equivalent focal range. It does the job for me as Finn Chambers, tourist.

A family from Chippewa Falls or some far-blown town jabber excitedly, pointing out the great cathedrals of this fabulous city. If I have one sight which never fails to excite me, apart from Hannah's smile or come-to-bed look, it is the towering majesty and symmetrical beauty of the Chrysler Building seen from here. It is beautiful, and perfect. Better than any catwalk model or rose tree.

The tower sways. It's unnerving that this steel and brick monument moves with the wind, and it's uncomfortable, feeling it sway so slightly, when everything about it seen from the ground suggests that only a force greater than nature could move this Colossus; that only a bomb, or an aeroplane smashing through it, could cause it to fall. I have seen many an excited, confident person panic and grip the guard rail, only to laugh off that instant of unexpected fear, as this mighty giant flexes to remind its visitors that nothing built by man is forever. To remind them of their frailty, of their flesh and bones. To remind them that they are not designed to fly or leap from heights or race motorcars or be shot by guns. That they are designed only to fall on grass and yielding earth. A lesson I will come to learn at my cost.

Building lights appear like a billion stars, slowly filling the expanse of this magical city. Unseen hands turn switches on and off, and timers click to light entire floors and stairwells in a thousand skyscrapers, as daylight fades and nature attempts to cloak the Earth in night but the restless city refuses to be hidden. Car lights form rivers of red and white a thousand miles below. The constant faraway sound of horns blaring causes me to think of Tariq, and his cab, and his wife naked below a floating dress, eager for their clandestine lovemaking. I wish them well, and make a further wish that their children excel, lifting them out of Brooklyn and on to the Hamptons. I wish for happiness for the world, which spreads before me, as I view my kingdom.

I click off a series of shots, staged evenly through the evolving cityscape where time passing rewards the patient spectator with breathtaking images, as an artist paints a canvas in slow real-time, adding darkness to silhouettes and bursts of light like fireworks exploding until the night and the city call a truce, where stars are set in the blackness of night and the city beats with a vibrant heart, spilling light from every window, and streams of traffic bear witness to the existence of people arriving and leaving. The city giving birth as if to children of the night. The family from Chippewa Falls left long ago, although their excitement stays behind as though this building, this very platform, holds on to the energy created by its myriad visitors; as though they have no right to take away their gasps and wows.

# something small to focus on

Breakfast in motion. I sit silently reading in the rear of a limousine which has collected me from the Roosevelt. I place my cardboard coffee in the armrest cup-holder, and chew through an apricot Danish while I read my brief. I have read this through so many times that I know every detail, but I always see the same typo, which jars. The only typo is my name. Finn Chalmers. I try to put this down as an autocorrect error, but struggle with the idea that a computer does not recognise the word *chambers*. As in *a typical revolver has six chambers*. Catacombs have chambers. A judge has chambers. City Hall has chambers. I read on, euphoria allowing me to forgive the creator of the brief, for I am Superman. I am the luckiest man alive. I am engaged to be married to a goddess. I am Cupid, God of love.

I am to photograph X and Y for an exclusive for a British fashion magazine. The magazine will pay them a king's ransom for their *love story* about how they met and fell in love on a film set, and went on to win Oscars for best male and female lead in the movie, which swept the board, taking more statuettes than any other. Theirs is an Oscar-scripted story of multicultural and multi-racial love.

In truth it is a story of infidelity and betrayal and lies and deceit. The unfortunate and cast-aside Mrs X and Mr Y are noticeable only by their invisibility in this world of glitz, of happy vacuous fodder, where lives and actions are viewed not through a microscope, but through a kaleidoscope where the value of advertising revenue and copy sales obscures, spins, and distorts the truth. I am newly enthroned as king of all I survey, and I find their cosy projection difficult to swallow. Lucky for them I am their photographer and not their interviewer. Not their interrogator. Not their judge. The magazine will syndicate the story, and my photographs, to every country on Earth for a colossal profit. I will do well. My name will be seen in every country too. I make a mental note to ensure I am credited correctly as Finn Chambers. The abandoned Mrs X and Mr Y may sell their stories to the *National Enquirer* for six-figure sums, but thereafter they will appear only on third-rate talk shows or *Celebrity Skating on Dog Shit* or some other mindless garbage until, within months, they are forgotten by everyone but their ex-spouses' lawyers, who will make a final offer of a gagging-clause deal with a sum too large to turn down but a mere fraction of what they probably deserve. X and Y meanwhile will decorate red carpets and the covers of magazines for years to come.

We arrive in hermetically sealed air-conditioned silence at Trump International New York. There is a sudden burst of noise as my door opens to the living heat-embroiled city and the driver flashes the briefest of smiles, fishes a card from his breast pocket, taps a finger on the cell number and instructs me to call when I am through, before handing me the card and wishing me a good day. He has not asked me a single question about who it is I am heading to this prestigious location to shoot. Maybe he is used to stardom, or maybe just used to people shooting people in New York City, both metaphorically and actually. Tariq would have asked a million questions, in between giving me his family history.

Starrett City and this hotel. Two worlds apart whose only connection is one name: Trump. It strikes me as ironic that the hotel initials spell *tiny*. Like the former hands on the levers of power.

As I step into the entrance a bellhop leaps across, offering to carry my camera bag. My livelihood is in this bag, so I politely decline and he flashes me a genuine smile. His *Let me take that for you, sir* was courteous and accented. I guess him to be Puerto Rican by his look and accent. He probably lives, like Tariq, with two families in a one-family apartment, maybe even in Starrett City, so I tip him twenty dollars anyway. He beams at me, thanks me with sincerity, and bows slightly before slipping the note inside his uniform pocket. Perhaps he recognises me as king of the world.

The fixer strolls across to meet me, hand outstretched with absolute confidence. She is about my age, late twenties, elegant in a *strictly business* way. Her teeth are perfectly straight, and veneered in a shade of nuclear fission blue. She has no discernible accent. Her smile disappears as quickly as it appeared, as though a clapboard has been snapped down after the clapper-loader's call: 'Boring Life – Unimportant Person – Take 100'.

The suite I am ushered to has been well chosen. It has wall-height windows that look out across Central Park, giving the impression that all is open and that windows are empty space. Initial introductions where X and Y are blessed with the opportunity to shake the hand of the king of the universe, a living god. I unpack my tools of trade. Light meters, filters, digital and conventional SLR cameras, tripods, iPad, notepad and pen all to hand, and straight on to the job. I snap X and Y, his arm around her shoulder as she hugs his waist, looking into each other's eyes, then back at me, then both looking wistfully at a light switch across the room, giving them something small to focus on. Central Park is framed distantly as though they are standing on the entrance porch to an English mansion and their backdrop is hunting woods, created for the kings of England.

They change clothes several times, each attended to by personal aides, as Miss Nuclear Teeth checks her watch and her cellphone with a frequency that reminds me of a pecking farmyard hen. She makes frequent calls, checking God knows what. She eyes me coldly whenever I steer a change of setting from my brief, such as when I suggest the pair be shoeless and barefoot, that X should lose his tie and unbutton his collar and the cheating lovebirds lie together on the teal chaise-longue that features along one wall. They appear to love the idea, although MNT does not.

MNT shuts down my part in the proceedings by beaming at everyone in the room and reminding X and Y that they have a lunch appointment. She asks if I have everything I need, and makes me as irrelevant as possible by calling me Phil. I assure her I have more than I could have hoped for, remind her that my name is Finn as in the shark soup, and thank X and Y for being such great sitters. This is a professional courtesy. They both smile as though they mean it, and shake my hand again, not realising what a privilege it is for them to have had a true living god in their midst.

I am in the elevator and down to reception in seconds, where I call the limo driver. He takes me to the Roosevelt, and waits double-parked while I collect my few things and check out. There follows a silent drive to JFK during which I dearly wish for Tariq and his honest open chatter and friendliness, and his stories of Bengal and Brooklyn. I am in luck and have changed my return for an earlier flight. I have a yearning to get back to the loving embrace of Hannah, to lie barefoot entwined with her on our sofa and stroke her golden hair.

Feeling as I did when I took my first flight as a kid, I am both excited and nervous. I pray to a god I do not really believe in to ensure that the aircraft will not fall screaming into the sea. I now have something all-consuming to live for. I am to be married. To a goddess.

# slow suffocation

Be careful what you wish for in life. My return flight to London is my worst nightmare. Changing flights has meant I no longer have a window seat to gaze from, but find myself stuck in the centre between two of the kind of morbidly obese men who should, in all fairness to other fee-paying travellers, be required to purchase two adjacent seats. I disappear between folds of human. I have asked the smiling stewardess who welcomed me on board for a change of seat. The flight is full, but she will see what she can do. In the meantime I crank up the volume in my headphones and listen to a recording of a stand-up comedian. I am finding it difficult to laugh. Not that the jokes are not worthy of a guffaw, but my ability to breathe is seriously constrained. I miss the miserable bastard from my outbound flight.

The initial bump and sway ends and the *fasten seatbelts* sign extinguishes, to my relief. I decide that the way to make best of a bad situation is to stand at the rear of the aircraft. Seven hours standing has to be preferable to slow suffocation. I struggle out from captivity, and ask the same smiley stewardess if it is okay if I stand by her station. She says she sympathises, as she starts a practised routine, loading containers into ovens, and assembling a drinks trolley with her colleague. I am starting to relax when a ding-dong bell sounds and a brief announcement tells passengers that the captain has switched on the seatbelt sign and for everyone to return to their seats. I groan inwardly and request the aisle passenger to grant me access to my seat. He grimaces as though the effort is too much, which in truth it probably is, as he staggers to stand in the aisle. I feel the aircraft floor lurch unsettlingly, as though this one person moving may flip the plane into a screaming sideways dive straight down into the Atlantic Ocean. My sole reassurance is that the counterweight in the window seat has balanced this out.

I sit in my seat by pushing against a wall of fat, and as I am about to reach for my seatbelt the aisle passenger slumps back down, thereby sealing off my seatbelt from view. He is breathing as though he has run a marathon and sweat pours from his brow, which he then mops with a silk handkerchief decorated with lobsters and crabs. Food is never far away.

Just as I am losing the will to live, praying that this journey will end so that I can be within the loving embrace of Hannah's silken arms, the seatbelt sign switches off and the stewardess answers my prayers, leaning around lobster man to beckon me. She moves away to allow him to fight himself upright as I slide past him like a prisoner who has forced cell bars apart. 'I couldn't bear seeing you so uncomfortable,' she says diplomatically. I take my bags from the overhead locker and follow her forward. She leads me through a curtain into business class, where one seat remains unoccupied. She asks if I would like a drink. I thank her profusely for her kindness, and request a gin and tonic.

'You deserve it,' she says, laughing.

I am in love with her. I am in love with all the smiling people of Earth.

I spend my time reviewing shots of X and Y on my iPad, and then, as though time has suddenly been freed from bondage, the welcome announcement: *Cabin crew, seats for landing*.

Bump, the roar of reverse thrust then sudden quiet and clicking belts, then I am out of the aircraft, thanking every crew member I can. I look around for Miss Smiley but cannot see her. Presumably she's stuck at the rear of the plane, levering my former travelling companions from their seats.

Hannah is standing in the arrivals hall with a three-foot-square white card, the outer edge of which is covered in large red stick-on hearts and in the centre in scarlet lipstick is written: *Welcome home, fabulous man!* I laugh so much my face burns as I rush towards her. Passers-by stare at me, wondering who I am, and why such a beautiful young woman would be waving a banner for someone as ordinary-looking as me.

We kiss for an eternity, Hannah dropping her sign as we embrace, then we scoot out to take the Tube home. I hold on to the retrieved sign, which I intend to keep forever. I adore this girl. Hannah makes plans as we roll, talking excitedly about wedding dresses and wedding venues, and stating that she only needs the simplest of rings, and the simplest of ceremonies. She is beautiful, and happy, and kindness itself. I ask if she would like to choose her engagement ring in Rome. The agency had messaged me an offer to shoot a magazine cover involving a couple of nights in the Eternal City. A simple brief, photographing iconic poet Percy Bysshe Shelley's tomb, which I had read and accepted in the departure lounge at JFK before I became the filling in a human sandwich. Hannah's eyes widen with delight. She kisses me again, staring into my eyes as she did when I had proposed, and repeats what she had said then. 'Yes, oh yes, yes!'

My neck is stiff by the time our train reaches Turnham Green. Hannah receives and answers a text from her mother as we leave the station, no doubt letting her know I am safely back on home ground. I feel like a precious commodity. I am hoping to undress her as soon as we open the door to my flat, but as we enter the ink-dark hallway she clicks the light on and I am surrounded by my mother, father, brother, Hannah's mother and father and countless friends, and everywhere there are gold balloons saying *Congratulations* and *Engagement Party*. The dining table is overflowing with food and drinks and suddenly everyone is hugging and kissing us both as champagne corks pop. Joyous. I am elated, as though these feelings will go on increasing until I simply float into the air.

Four days later, after a series of rushed visits to bridal shops and online searches for venues for intimate weddings, interspersed with work at my studio to process shots of X and Y to submit to the magazine, I, Finn Chambers, king of the world, take my seat next to Hannah on the Tube back to Heathrow airport to jet to Rome.

# brighter than the sun

There should be a time for everyone when life, and everything we see, feel and experience in it, shimmers; where our hearts and souls combine to produce a feeling so immense and all-consuming that we are breathless with ecstasy, unable to hold any more joy within. I have that feeling as I look around from our table outside this homely corner restaurant in Piazza Margana. I see my life as brighter than the sun. I am truly the luckiest man on Earth. I beam at every passing stranger and, without exception, they return my smile. I am king of all I survey. I raise my glass to toast Hannah, who is the source of all joy, and who will soon be queen of all we both survey, joined in marriage, forever. We shall be kind and benevolent rulers, just and wise, and we will spread love like the sun's rays across this troubled globe. Tomorrow I shall shoot Shelley's tomb, before taking Hannah to Via del Boschetto to seek out an engagement ring fit for my queen. I am the envy of every living man. I am touched by hands unseen, by the moon and stars, by a pure essence, by absolute love. I am divine.

# a dangerous combination

The day dawns bright, a beautiful late summer day in Rome, warm as an English heatwave. Not a care in the world. Beautiful Hannah is brimming with excitement. Hannah has rings on her mind. No one could imagine anything horrendous happening on a day like this, least of all me. But it does. That the lure of fabulous food and great wines could kill a man is something beyond imagination, but, unbelievably, it can. Killed by ham, cheese, olives and wine. Quality. Killed by quality. I ponder the idea that there cannot be many people killed by quality. Maybe just me.

Talk about putting a foot wrong. Literally. Great brief. Fly to Rome, stay three nights in Piazza Margana surrounded by restaurants, beautiful sights, beautiful people, and take some photographs of Shelley's tomb for a magazine cover. Getting paid a significant fee for doing something I love in this fabulous city, and taking along my beautiful fiancée to buy her a diamond ring – what comes better than that? How many people get those opportunities? Not many. Most people get the mediocrity of punching in with *good morning* and punching out at the end of a same-old same-old day with *see you tomorrow*.

Plan set. Brief read countless times. Walk to the English Cemetery, gain some height above Shelley's tomb, take some shots, adjust the settings to differing shades as though the time of day is shifting, apply some groovy colour filters, fire off some moody black and white images, then lunch. Job done. Except that the combination of things in everyday life – their very order – can determine outcomes unforeseen. That is how I came to be killed by quality. What ifs? Life is full of them. If onlys. Life is full of those too. Decisions and consequences. Indecisions and consequences. Opportunities and consequences. Missed opportunities and consequences. For everyone killed by some Jihadi or anti-government nutcase or even the crazy on the bus, there are many people who, for decisions made or not made, or opportunities missed, would, but for those determiners, have been in the right place at the wrong time.

If we had just walked past Rita's, I would not be here now. There is something about the scent of hot food on a stove, the sound of people-babble and the sight of smiling happy people drinking wine that draws me like the Dance of the Seven Veils. Of course a man is no longer allowed to fantasise about the removal of layers to a hidden delight, as that, too, like the health-and-safety circus, is to be decried, as our biological nature faces moral castration in the hideous hypocrisy of modern life. A life in which the propagators of social acceptability – the students and religious zealots and politicians and journalists – behave in one form, and denounce in another. We are driven to destroy the reputations of our predecessors and erase whatever they achieved in their time, as though we have a God-given right to judge those who went before us, with no recognition of their achievement within their time; without objectivity. Social media makes everyone an expert. Truth be told: social media facilitates those who have nothing to say, but who will nonetheless say it. Everyone has a voice. As a child I wondered why my father would occasionally hold a finger to his lips and whisper *silence is golden*.

In my love of talking to strangers, I ask a security guy, smart uniform and holstered gun, standing outside the bank in Via della Marmorata where I stop to take lunch money from a cash machine, for the quickest way to the non-Catholic cemetery. I ask if he speaks English. In that halting way when someone has been put on the spot, he says he speaks a little, and asks me if it is the English Cemetery I mean, then proceeds to give me precise directions, sending us along Via Galvani. If I want to place blame for dying, I could lay it on him, for sending me past Rita's. Then again, that would be churlish, blaming a pleasant-mannered man for trying to assist a stranger with a shy smile and a story to tell his wife when he got home safely from his shift, assuming he had not been shot by some bank robber. Maybe I died from my own faults. This is something to consider. Maybe if I were less gregarious, or less lazy by nature, and had got my map from my pocket and looked at the route, I would not have taken the shorter route provided by the guard, but instead followed the more obvious one on the map, and never passed Rita's and had Rita kill me. Decisions and consequences. Cause and effect. Actions and result.

We stroll along Via Galvani. Hand in hand. Sunglasses to dull the searing light. A cloudless sky. A perfect day. An average-looking street with unremarkable buildings that frankly could be in any city anywhere. Rome. The Eternal City. Stunningly beautiful, but even cities as beautiful as this have mediocrity. Streets that have nothing of immediate attractiveness about them. The streets I fear as a place to live. Streets that remind me of battery hen enclosures, where hundreds of lives run quietly adjacent to one another, like a printing press stamping out handbills for an unremarkable event. Lives that mean something, or possibly nothing, to those living them, but which, for sure, have no interest to a passer-by such as me.

Until we pass Masto. Sometimes life throws out unexpected surprises, which makes living it that much more enjoyable. Masto is one such surprise. Hanging hams, and racks of shelving stacked rich with wine, throw out unseen arms which wrap around us and draw us into the interior; air thick with scents of rosemary and hot oil. As seductive as any dimly lit cocktail bar in Manhattan or Bombay.

Inside, a bunch of American students takes up three sets of tables, drinking wine, and their guide, a good-looking forty-something guy who reminds me of Michael Hutchence, is talking at zed volume. Really loud. He spies my T-shirt and immediately bangs out a statement about the Haight Ashbury Music Center, as though he has known me all his life, to the point that he does not actually address me with any form of conversation opener. I don't know whether to regard this as rude or overly familiar or just the way a guy trying to be *down with the kids* acts to make himself more interesting to his entourage. I decide it's the latter and smile. I make some throwaway comment about it being a great store and how I visited recently and was delighted to discover it was still there after all these years. I offer this up because the students are all looking at me, waiting for a response to their temporary guru's bonhomie. Hannah is studiously studying the blackboard specials, no doubt thinking thoughts about loud tour guides. I guess he is Italian-American and teaches at the American Institute, as his Italian is faultless and his English, American. Turning away, I then try to drown him out by examining the menu, but it is hard to avoid the self-loving booming of a man like that.

They leave with a series of *ciao*s and waves, and quiet descends like nightfall. I notice a bicycle high up, fixed to the back wall where in any other local restaurant there would be a bad painting of the Colosseum or fields in Tuscany, and feel suddenly at home, as though all my life has been spent searching for this place. It strikes me as I look at Hannah, who just raised her eyes from the menu to look at me, that home is not a place, but a state of mind. Being here, or anywhere for that matter, with the woman I realise I truly love more than life itself, is home.

Rita comes over to our table with a shy smile and earnest expression, and in her halting English, overhearing our conversation, asks if we would like prosciutto and cheese. She tells us that she travels all Italy sourcing the best artisan products for her customers. Rita has that rare quality: passion. It shines out through her eyes, which expand as she describes the care and love with which independent producers imbue their craft. Quality. Passion and quality. I never imagined those things as such a dangerous combination.

I spy the bottles along the shelves. Bewildering in array, and beautifully presented with inch-perfect placement, and every one so inviting. I ask Rita for her recommendation and she suggests tasting one which she thinks we would love. She returns moments later with two small plastic dishes, one containing tiny cubes of chopped prosciutto and the other tiny cubes of cheese. She pours a generous amount of red into our glasses to taste. We both smile and nod, two Pavlov's dogs showing approval, as Rita tops them up, and moves away. We look at each other and start to laugh quietly, thinking that these small dishes are a joke but at least the wine is wonderful. I make a comment about the chalkboard description of prosciutto and cheese assortment as a 'feast' and am laughing again, shaking my head in wonder, when Rita reappears, placing a platter of riches before us. The plastic dishes were simply a master class in hosting, something to test against the wines as a courtesy while the chef prepared our banquet. Heaven.

Heaven. Now there lies a concept. Rita reappears to ask how we like the platter, and describes each item with love-coated words. She fills our glasses and moves off to attend to another group of American students and their guide. Thankfully, this guide is a quietly spoken Italian woman, who tells her entourage that Masto is the lifetime dream of the owners, who have built a business which locals and tourists alike regard as the gem of Testaccio. She spouts on about there being a host of restaurants in the area but Masto is her favourite; that the passion of the owners is what makes the place.

There it is. Passion. Everyone has heard of crimes of passion, but crimes of quality? Only in the concept of goods being fit for purpose, and the old adage that *you get what you pay for*.

Rita pours the remainder of what was not quite a full bottle into our glasses, and, as we drain them, offers a sample of another gem. I am keen for a taste, and, as Rita moves away, I glance out through the open doorway to check the light. Perfect. Rita brings two glasses of ruby delight. I sniff the wine, appreciating the heady scent which promises a taste of liquid joy. I take a sip, savour the rich round flavour, sling my camera bag over my shoulder, kiss Hannah and tell her I'll be back in twenty minutes or so, snatch a chunky piece of ham, and scoot out of the door with a backward glance and a smile to Hannah. I wave the ham as she waves to me.

# open but unblinking

I am aware of a Japanese tourist looking down at me. She is shrouded in Tyrian purple and shimmers with light. She babbles words I cannot understand to another Japanese woman who I take to be her mother. She is distressed, so I stand up. Her shimmer fades. They are both distressed. They shuffle away from me.

Soon after that, two cops – a woman, young, very good-looking in that classic Italian way, and her colleague, a slim, athletic man of about mid-thirties – stand looking down at me. I look down at me too, then back at them. I am confused that I can see me and that I appear to be injured. I must be concussed. I think they make a fine couple. I imagine her in a low-cut ballgown, sipping champagne, her arm through his at a black-tie party, with the Rome night sky lit by fireworks behind them. I am aware then of Hannah running towards us, crying, clutching her new handbag, bought yesterday: red, white and green, the colours of the Italian flag.

I rush towards her, arms open to grab hold of her, to embrace her and tell her that I am okay, that I will mend, that

I should not have had that one extra sip of wine, which I am now intent on returning to Masto to finish. She runs through my open arms, as though I am not there, and starts babbling in broken sobs like Morse code, supported by the male officer while the striking lady cop tries to calm her. I shout to Hannah to stop fretting and start to laugh. I stop laughing when I realise the three of them are looking at my body, lying on the ground, crumpled like a Guy Fawkes mannequin made of straw and sacks, my skin pallid with blood drying from a rivulet coming from a gash to my head which is seriously dented where my skull has been smashed; my eyes open but unblinking, clear like the eyes of fresh-caught sea bass. I realise that I, too, am looking at my body. I look around me to see people. People who had not been here when I'd climbed the side of the tower to gain height to shoot Shelley's tomb. When I climbed, there were only three other people in my section of the gardens: the two Japanese ladies, and an Italian gardener weeding between headstones over towards the visitor centre, plus a small group of visitors way down in the old part by Keats's grave, too far away to be discernible as to origin. Now, they were all gathered around me.

# handshakes all round

The female officer ushers Hannah away, holding her around the shoulders to calm her grieving sobs. I feel unable to move, so I call to Hannah to stay, then stand watching them as they move towards the main gate. They appear not to hear me, so I scream out, 'Hannah! Hannah!' then they are gone from view. Most of the suddenly present others melt away as though out of respect, or uninterest, as though the show is over and they are required elsewhere, but a few remain standing at a distance. Silent spectators.

The male officer takes off his hat, sits on a tomb and lights a cigarette. He gets out a mobile telephone and calls someone. He speaks quietly, smiling frequently, and I know he is talking to a woman. Or maybe a man. He sprinkles whispers of '*amore*' throughout, and ends with '*ciao*' and blows a kiss. Two men in their thirties arrive, talk to the uniformed officer, asking him what he knows. The term *accident* is used several times. The uniformed officer points to my camera which is lying against an adjacent headstone, the case smashed and the lens hanging oddly, like the broken neck of a hanged man. Two women in paper suits arrive, and all five stand discussing my demise. They are joined by an anxious, arty-looking woman who is clearly an official of the cemetery. She holds her hand to her face as she sees my supine form and turns immediately away. The detectives talk briefly with her, one making notes in a small notebook. She is clearly distressed and from my minimal understanding of Italian I understand that she will wait in her office and allow the authorities to get on with their work. I doubt she has seen a dead body before. A tear rolls down her face, and she turns and walks back towards the visitor centre, pink shoes dusted slightly from the dry earth. The forensic examiners unpack photographic equipment and examination kits, photograph my remains, examine the side of the wall, take fibres caught in the brickwork using tweezers and sticky tape, then use cotton buds to swab my head, and some bloodstains on Shelley's tomb. One of them takes photographs of blood marks and of the loose moss and broken brickwork, then, using a telescopic ladder, gains height to take shots of my body lying beside Shelley's tomb from above.

Next, a smartly dressed man of around fifty strolls up through the graves, smoking. He drops his cigarette butt and grinds it with his black leather shoe. His suit is of fine cloth, and his tie silk. His haircut is classy and expensive. The uniform officer who had seated himself on a headstone stands up, replaces his hat, and salutes the man. The detectives speak briefly with him, then walk off as the forensic women talk and point and he stands, arms folded, listening and observing intently. He could be the chairman of an Italian bank, but I assume him to be an examining magistrate. Another man arrives who chats to the examining magistrate, then, after a bunch of smiles and mutual shoulder-pats, crouches down beside my body, feels for a pulse, looks at his watch and pronounces me dead and states the time. No doubt he will be paid a decent expense to state the bleeding obvious. More grins, back-slapping, laughter, then handshakes all round and he wanders back towards the gate. *Ciao.*

What the fuck is everyone smiling and laughing about?

The forensics team pack up and move off towards the exit as a couple of funeral guys wheel a trolley along the shingle path. The examining magistrate signs a form for them and takes a torn-off copy which he then folds meticulously and places inside his fabulous suit. He passes some comment to the remaining cop and walks off towards the gate with a wave of his hand. I notice his hand is empty of ham.

The funeral men take a large black zipped bag and lift me carefully with hands encased in plastic gloves, which I note are the same shade of violet as the marzipan pansies that decorate my parents' wedding cake in the photograph on the stairwell at my home in London. They lay me inside the bag with great reverence, for which I feel sudden gratitude, zip me out of sight, then lift me on to the trolley. They confirm with the cop that I will be taken to a specific mortuary, and trundle off along the pathway with my body. As they exit the gateway I realise with a sudden sense of loss that this is the last time I will see me.

The cop wanders around some of the tombs, hat in hand. He now has sunglasses on, and has lit another cigarette. He wanders across to a grave, having stood reading a noticeboard. His uniform is immaculate.

'Gramsci,' a voice says behind me.

I spin around to see a man who looks remarkably familiar standing there.

'The Italians always go to see Gramsci,' he says. 'I could have told you that wall was a danger to climb,' he adds, grinning. 'But there again, I could not.'

He grins again, and holds his hand out.

'Percy Shelley. Pleased to make your acquaintance.'

# writ in water

I want to scream, but no sound will form. I am clearly having a nightmare. One minute in my dream I am taking photographs of Shelley's tomb. The next he is stretching out his hand. Now I know I am dreaming and any second the alarm will sound, and I will roll over, hit snooze on the phone screen and steal a few more minutes, or maybe roll in towards Hannah and try to interest her in wake-up sex. My dream state changes and I now want to laugh, but there is something about Hannah's distress and departure with the lady officer that I find unsettling and I cannot, although I want to, wake up and get on with life. Am I concussed from my fall? Have I actually *had* a fall? Am I really dreaming? I recall the sensation of brick suddenly giving way and of attempting to leap forward so that I could land on my feet, and of the speed of rush as Shelley's tomb came up at me. Then nothing. Nothing until the Japanese lady and her face painted with shock. One second she is looking down at me; the next I am standing; an observer, watching her and her mother looking at me. Or rather, watching them looking at my lifeless body on the ground.

Shit. This is unreal. I want my life back. I want to be with Hannah at Masto drinking wine and holding out my glass for Rita to fill. I want to be at the Knickerbocker, or Quaglino's, or Charlie's Beach. I want to be anywhere but here. I am aware of talking aloud, then screaming and yelling, telling myself this cannot be real.

'I am afraid this is real, my friend.'

I turn back to see Shelley still standing behind me. Although he is speaking softly, he appears to be grinning. He looks like a guy who likes to grin a lot.

'Do you have a name?' he asks, adding, 'Everyone has a name. Some here would like to forget, or have others forget. But we all have a name.'

Something leaps out of that statement and smacks me hard in the face. I know he is talking about Keats. I had wandered by Keats's grave and noted its inscription. *Here lies One whose Name was writ in Water*. I now know I am dreaming and the shadowy form of awakening is somewhere in the background, inching its way towards me, ready to burst through so I can wake and trot on down to Masto to reunite my life with Hannah's, and drink red wine.

'Your name?' he asks again.

'Finn,' I say slowly.

# chained to a dream

I am still dreaming, but my dream is becoming overcrowded. Shelley is far from alone in my dream. Behind Shelley is an array of people in costumes of different ages; they could be a scene from a magazine illustration or a slice of a waxworks museum. At this point in my dream they are standing still, watching me. They remind me of the Midwich Cuckoos in *Village of the Damned*. My dream is like a frozen screen, then, as though a hidden remote control has been pressed to *play*, they start to move about, as though interest in me has again faded and they have better things to do.

I am willing myself to wake when Shelley says, 'There is someone I should like you to meet.' He motions his hand towards a delicately handsome young man dressed in a maroon velvet jacket with white cravat. Dapper. 'John, let me introduce you to our new friend. Finn, allow me to present John Keats.'

The awakening looming just out of reach is almost tangible as I urge it on, but it just will not come. I nod towards Keats in disbelief as he holds out his hand, which I meet without any sensation of touch, just a sense of warmth. Wake up! Wake up! This is disturbing; everything feels real but obviously cannot be, and I long to wake and find Hannah next to me. I start to laugh in my dream, suddenly amused by the thought that any second Coleridge and De Quincey and Shakespeare and Mussolini will come prancing through the cemetery singing 'Springtime for Hitler and Germany' and smoking weed. Naked.

I am still laughing at that thought when Shelley starts to laugh too, and Keats smiles at me, clearly amused by my laughter, although there is sympathy in his look. My dream is starting to mutate into nightmare and I wonder if one of the American students had dropped acid into my wine when Rita paused to chat to them on her way to our table. The cemetery seems fuller, with more and more bizarre characters, as though the dead have come out to play. I think I should be panicking, and I want to scream my fury at being chained to a dream from which I cannot awake, but no sound will come. Yet I seem incapable of panic or fury, just an unworldly feeling which amounts to a mix of incredulity and interest and amusement, as though I have walked into a dimly lit car park late at night to see two naked lovers romping in their car, illuminated by the interior light.

# not equipped for this

A dawning realisation. I am not dreaming. Not possible, of course. I am dreaming, just examining my dream and my situation within it, as part of my dream. This explains everything to my satisfaction and I close my eyes in order to sleep through to the alarm. I have gone off the idea of wake-up sex with Hannah. I just want to wake up, with Hannah, then hold her to me, feeling the heat from her warm body, and the smooth sensuality of her skin, inhaling the indefinable scent of her.

I open my eyes and Keats and Shelley are still present, and from the edge of my field of vision I see the police officer walking towards the exit, having finished perusing Gramsci's grave. I watch him stroll past the main gate, as though he has nothing to pressure his time. He goes inside the visitor shop, then reappears, removes his hat, and lights another cigarette. He stands smoking, staring up towards where we stand. I imagine he is looking at us, so I wave my arm wildly to attract his attention. Shelley chuckles behind me. The cop drags heavily on his cigarette, blows out smoke, then drops it to the floor and steps on it, replacing his hat and turning to speak to the arty lady who has appeared on the tiled steps by the shop. She stands with her arms folded tightly, as though holding herself together, and the officer gestures with his arm back in our direction as though referring to the fact that his work is done. She looks in my direction and again I wave my arm and shout, 'Lady!' I shout again, louder, having found some fury from deep within, but she continues to converse with the cop, who gives a brief salute as they turn away from each other, she heading back into the visitor centre and he out through the gate. I am invisible to them. I realise as he goes that I may never see this man again, and I am suddenly hit by the realisation that I may never see Hannah again. I am not equipped for this.

I turn to look at Shelley, whose eyes glint with mischief, a half-smile on his face, but Keats looks at me sympathetically.

'It takes a while for dreams to fade to acceptance,' he says quietly, 'but that will come quickly, like a bird returning to its nest at evening.'

I mean, what am I supposed to think here? I arrive by jet-propelled aeroplane into a city I love, have some fun, loving life with my beautiful fiancée, planning the purchase of a ring and a perfect wedding, revelling in my small contribution to the twenty-first century, then, boom, out of nowhere I have two poets from the early nineteenth century, two men whose works I have read little but whose fame and influence is legendary in my time, apparently befriending me. If I am not dreaming, and am soon to awake, then the only explanation is my earlier theory: the American students have spiked my wine. Lysergic acid diethylamide. Lucy in the Sky with Diamonds. LSD.

I walk away from them. The more I attune, I see people sitting everywhere, mostly on tombstones. Others walk by alone, in pairs, in groups. I go to the west wall and stand there alone. I run through the day's events, a chronology reliving every second of every minute that the day has carried, and, every time, the order remains the same. Nothing changes. I keep glancing towards the entrance, hoping to see Hannah coming towards me, waving her new handbag, laughing, saying, *Where did you get to? I've eaten your ham and drunk your wine!*

Except, however often I look, there is no Hannah, just an empty space or a group of tourists coming through the gate, or bizarre figures strolling. I remain where I am, determinedly, as though standing my ground. The sun gradually lowers in the sky, casting shades of vermilion and mulberry across the tombstones, cypress shadows lengthening, adding drama to what, for me, is an all-too-dramatic scene. Jupiter and Venus, pinpricks of luminous silver, dot the darkening sky and are joined by patterned stars as the heavens emerge through the falling night. I must awaken. Hannah will surely have set the alarm.

# from dark to dawn

A strange thing occurs to me. I have been standing for hours. No alarm has sounded to wake me. I am alone. I have watched as day turned to night. I am not tired. I realise I have no need of sleep. I am aware that if I decided to I could simply close my eyes and rest, though I am staying alert to monitor the night. Many of the people have disappeared, but some roam the garden, for it is as much a garden as a cemetery. I am staying alert to assess the passing of time, to see whether I am tripping, dreaming, or dead.

Time appears to pass as slowly as life. I watch foxes come out, a mother and three cubs who play between the graves. It strikes me then that there are only people here, no animals or birds from another time. I listen intently, but only hear the normal stirrings of things in the undergrowth, the furtive slinking and occasional hissing of the cemetery cats, and the hum of a small group of my fellow cemetery-dwellers talking way down the gardens.

But I could dream the passage of time, surely? A dream that appears to have time passing as normal, when in fact dream-speed is racing. Do dreams occur in real time, or do they race through at the speed of light experienced as normal time? It is not a question that ever occurred to me, not ever having been faced with having to prove to myself that I was alive or dead. That is a consequence of never having had, in all honesty, to give too much thought to anything in my brief life. Just the usual stuff rolling up to twenty-eight years of age, such as choosing a university or a job or a car or a film to watch or which drink to have or whether I should be a party guy and snort cocaine or smoke green, and to wonder if I am gay. Just the usual shit.

An owl hoots and its mate responds. It is like something from a made-for-television film. A dark cemetery under a clear black sky filled with stars. A moonless night when the owl hoots and the naïve young girl taking a short cut home stops in her tracks, as though the sound of owls hooting is the portent of doom. We all know what comes next. But in reality, or what I currently think may be reality, there is no young girl taking urgent steps, eyes wide with panic. There is just me, standing where I have been for hours, counting time.

I look from ground to sky with frequency, waiting for signs of night to fade. The fox and her cubs reappear briefly then head to a corner of the gardens up the slope from where I stand, the cubs making their play-fighting fuss as they disappear into the shrubbery, the mother turning briefly to check for watchers, then she too is gone. I wonder if I imagined them.

Watching the night in a way I never had, the transition from dark to dawn is as slow and conniving as ice forming on an oily pond. Black fades unnoticed to charcoal to grey to grey-green as stars switch off one by one, as though some unseen hand operates a giant light board with a billion dimmer switches. A celestial graffiti artist slow-motion-sprays the sky.

# still clean-shaven

Darkness dissolves to light. As though evil has been overcome. Shades of blue strengthen from slate, as soft steel shades shimmer through a yellowed promise of morning, on to perfection; a blue so rich it makes me glad to be alive. Alive. Taking a good look around, and having passed a night all through, experiencing every second of the passage of time, and seeing so much apparently unhurried activity, I put my hand to my face and register the fact that I am still clean-shaven. My skin is as soft as yesterday. There is no stubble. I am dead.

That then begs the question: if I am dead, how am I thinking and seeing and hearing and evaluating? I mean, what the hell is that about? If I am dead, then I ought to be just a body now, in a mortuary, awaiting a certificate of release so that Hannah can ship me back to England for burial or cremation or whatever means of disposal my family decide is fitting for someone who was careless enough to take a header on to Shelley's tombstone and cause them all a great deal of upset and inconvenience. But here I am. Seeing and thinking as though I still have my eyes and brain and thought.

As if things could not get worse, I notice that a man in an artist's smock who looks like Rubens is lying on a tree limb above me. He waves a friendly hand in my direction, pulls his cap down over his eyes and adopts a state of repose, as though he is returning to his nap. There are people in various places – up trees, sitting on cemetery walls twelve feet above the ground dangling their legs, and one man sitting on the high tip of the angel's left wing on Emelyn Story's tomb the *Angel of Grief*, an iconic and moving sight which cannot fail to set feelings stirring in the heart of anyone who sets eyes upon it. Despite my usual ambivalence towards any non-violent irreverent behaviour, and my tendency for attraction towards bohemian and louche life, I view this with distaste. There is something about this incidence of irreverence that causes me to question again whether I am actually dead or dreaming. I stand glaring at this man and his apparent indifference to the values of the souls below.

'It takes a little time, but we all arrive at the same realisation. Eventually.'

Shelley again. Still grinning. In normal circumstances I would probably tell him to fuck off.

'How can this be?' I ask, looking past him at the assortment of history in view, the people of all ages.

'Your spirit has freed itself.'

'I don't believe in spirits, and I don't believe in God, or gods, or the devil, or purgatory or heaven, or the signs of the zodiac or astrology or fuji or mediums or the Ouija board.'

I am angry, stating as I believe. Shelley smiles kindly and says, 'Don't tell the Romans,' as he walks away.

# madness is curable

There is something about the way I move now. I walk, but without effort. I feel normal but weightless. I cross the gardens to the gate so that I can see the road outside, and I watch life going on. Cars drive along the street occasionally and a woman goes by walking a dog. A group of schoolchildren in checked skirts pass in a haze of jabber and flailing arms and smiles, tossing hair and adjusting satchels and backpacks as they walk. Normal life. Across the junction at a small car workshop set back from the road, a man in oily overalls is leaning into the engine compartment of a Fiat 500. I always loved those cars. The engine is running and he keeps tugging the throttle cable as he listens intently to the engine rate rising and falling. He reminds me of a doctor with a stethoscope listening to a patient's breathing. I hope the 500 makes it. It is a soft shade of mint green.

I am watching life for a reason. I am calculating normality in terms of time. I mean, I cannot really be dead. Dead people cease to exist. They are replaced by newborn babies and the cycle starts again. One out, one in, like a busy nightclub.

I turn to view the cemetery inmates frequently. They are the most bizarre assortment of beings, or non-beings, that I could ever have imagined. Little wonder that I cannot believe what I see. I mean, would anyone in their right mind believe this shit? I have smoked weed and mixed too much alcohol of assorted types with what another partygoer told me was Bolivian but could just as easily have been powdered citric acid or flour, which I tried to sift up my nose but sneezed and choked on. I still never saw people from another century. Just swimming lights and a swirling sense of people – people my age, from my century – getting out of my way like a herd of stampeding wildebeest as I threw up, vomiting a yellow tube in front of me. All that happened there was that some kind human, a real person, my friend Natasha, put me in a corner against the wall, fetched a bucket and a blanket, and let me sleep while she cleaned up pools of my vomit and apologised to the hosts of the party, her friends, who laughed it off. The only fallout was my need to apologise profusely to our hosts the next morning and carry my shame out of the door while a number of people I had never met before, and hoped wholeheartedly never to see again, wished me well as I made my exit. Shame. I vowed never to try cocaine again, and not to drink alcohol for as long as I lived. One out of two I managed, which is just fine. There is something life-changing about watching passengers change seats in your carriage on the Circle line on a Sunday morning to avoid the stench of a man in a psychedelic shirt stained with vomit and wine. It is particularly profound to realise that that man is you.

The day passes at what I have to accept is normal pace. I want some sign that things are fractured. Disconnected. Jumpy. Irrational. Pieces of jigsaw that do not fit. Realisation is sometimes slow, but in this case I fight not to accept the reality that is dawning little by little. I look back through the gate at the man in overalls. He is on a mobile phone chattering away, running his free hand through thick greying hair, with occasional gestures towards the Fiat. He laughs and ends the call. *Ciao*. I am determined to watch time pass through this day, as I did throughout the night, trying to make sense of it all. John Keats's words keep coming to me: *It takes a while for dreams to fade to acceptance, but that will come quickly, like a bird returning to its nest at evening.*

What is wrong with me? John Keats? John Keats has been dead for two hundred years and I think he has spoken to me. Smiled at me. I am going insane. That is what this is. I am not dead or even asleep and dreaming. I am having some psychobabble schizoid cliff-edge moment whereby my brain is rejecting reality and plunging me into a psychological nightmare. I need to go to a hospital. I need urgent help.

I rush along the path and into the visitor centre, where two middle-aged ladies, one apparently English from her accent and the other Italian, are discussing some shocking event from the day before.

I try to compose my thoughts so as not to alarm them, but babble, 'Please, ladies, could you direct me to the hospital, or call a taxi for me? I am feeling dreadfully unwell.'

They ignore me. They do not pause in their conversation, or flinch, or look in my direction. It is as though I am not here. Angrily I shout loudly to them, 'Am I invisible? Are you deaf? Can you hear me?'

The English lady turns away from her companion, saying, 'Excuse me.' Thank God! She has noticed me. But she picks up a telephone from its cradle which is ringing quietly and speaks machine-gun Italian, ends the call, writes a note on a piece of card, then turns back to the Italian lady and they continue to talk, in English now, saying what a dreadful shock it must have been for the people who saw me fall. The Japanese ladies. Poor them. What about poor me? I am the man with the broken head.

Every reasoned attempt I make to explain this ends in defeat, as though solving a newspaper crossword, confident about four words pencilled in clues across, only to work out a missing word down and find that all four answers across are wrong. Dreaming? I may have to accept that I am not. Insane? Still a possibility. Maybe I'm so psychotic, everything just so badly jumbled, that I can no longer distinguish hallucinations from reality. What if I just imagined, in my psychosis, that I had asked the ladies in the shop for help? Maybe they responded but I could not grasp the reality of their response. Maybe the telephone call was not incoming but outgoing, the lady calling for an ambulance and noting an incident reference on the card. Yes, surely that's it, I decide with a sense of relief.

I feel suddenly unencumbered at the thought that I am going mad, as this explains everything, and madness is curable. I stroll towards the gate, feeling unburdened and quite serene, to await the arrival of the ambulance.

I find with some amazement that I can simply jump up and land on my behind on top of the wall and dangle my legs twelve feet from the ground. I am insane.

## the best for others

I am sitting on top of the wall, contemplating how someone as well put-together as me, with a happy life, great job, about to be married to a beautiful woman, can suddenly fall off the edge of the world. I know it can happen. But it does not happen to people like me. This is what happens to other people. I am suddenly reminded of a comedian's quip on that view: *Chum, you* are *other people.* I laugh out loud, causing a couple passing to smile up at me. They are wearing period costume from the 1920s. Elderly. Arm-in-arm. Much as Hannah and I had been twenty-four hours earlier.

Twenty-four hours. How can that be? Am I now so mad within a day that I think I can levitate twelve feet up to a wall-top, and just as easily drop down again? I feel I ought to panic, but panic and anger seem to be deserting me, along with worry in its stronger sense. I want my life back. I want Hannah, but something underlying creates a calm which belies my desire. I don't know what to make of it, although I am not truly anxious, which feels strange, as I normally do anxiety pretty well. If anyone ever saw me running like a man being chased by muggers across the various alphabet zones at Schiphol airport, then it would translate in large clear letters for the casual observer the level of anxiety I can create over something as simple as catching a connection – a connection which had been made nigh on impossible to meet by circumstances beyond my control. That is something that some of us can state with blithe ease, and sleep easily knowing. *Circumstances beyond our control.* But some of us, me in particular, carry a level of guilt about being late for a meeting or assignment, even when it's caused by an act of God such as fog, or an act of zombie-witted negligence like a wire left off a switch by an aircraft technician which causes an alarm light to operate when there is actually nothing wrong, but which delays departure nonetheless. Actions and consequences. Like some careless photographer having his life ended by quality.

I am swinging my legs back and forth, taking in the beauty of the tomb of Caius Cestius, marvelling at such a feat of architectural engineering, when Hannah, her parents, my father and mother, my brother, plus a smart young woman and a dapper guy in a pinstriped suit, walk in through the gateway, together with the lady official from the Cimitero Acattolico. I call out excitedly, but not one of them looks up. I call again and wave. My cries go unheard. An older woman passing by glances at me as she strolls towards them, and says, with a look of sympathy bordering on anguish, 'I am afraid they can neither hear nor see you, my dear. It doesn't hurt to try, but sadly, unless they join you here, they can never hear you.'

She smiles in a kindly way, and continues on, appearing to walk straight through my mother. I jump down and follow them, hesitant in case I truly am crazy and alarm them. Wait, though. If I am just crazy, why have my mother, father, brother and Hannah's parents flown to Rome?

Hannah's father David has placed his arm around her shoulders. She is sobbing, as are her mother, Claire, and my mother. My brother has my mother supported on one side, and my father, himself now with tears rolling down his cheeks, adds his arm to comfort her from the other side. They walk up towards Shelley's tomb, led by the cemetery lady. The tape placed around the tomb by the forensic examiners has been removed, and all now appears normal; Shelley's tomb has been scrubbed by the gardener, and no trace remains now of blood. Shelley sits way off to our left, on another tomb, watching expressionless, talking quietly to Keats, who glances across and gives a brief sympathetic smile. Hannah sobs uncontrollably and seems unaware of me standing right in front of her. Her mother has pulled her close and is patting her shoulder as though comforting a small child who has grazed her knee.

I reach out to touch Hannah's face but I feel nothing. I hug her and Claire and my arms simply flow through them, like breathing smoke into steam. I rush to embrace my mother, father and brother, who are huddled together, my father attempting to maintain conversational contact with the dapper man, who it appears from their exchange is a diplomat from the British consulate. My loving arms flow through them too. It transpires that the embarrassed-looking girl is another consulate official who will facilitate my repatriation, or rather the repatriation of my battered body, back to London. The even more messed-up thing about being killed by quality is that it will be the only time I have flown as a VIP. Ironic, considering that I – that is, me, me the spirit, the driving machine – will not be taking that flight.

Overcome with grief, Hannah falls to her knees, laying her head on Shelley's tomb where a few hours earlier my smashed head had come to rest. Claire attempts to help soothe her daughter by stroking her hair, although she herself is weeping.

Strangely, I feel that I want Hannah to stand up, wipe the tears from her eyes, and smile. I do not feel the sense of anguish I ought to feel at seeing her so distressed. I feel a faint sense of guilt, but not the raging torment I ought to be wringing my hands over, sharing empathically in the sorrow of our families. I feel that I should be chastising myself for not trying harder. I want to rage and yell that I must not be left here, that they must take me with them.

I finally summon something from within my madness. From somewhere deep inside, I find my voice and yell, 'Please! Please! See me! Hear me! Hannah! Mum! Dad! Take me home! Take me home! Don't leave me here to rot!'

It's as though I'm watching a digital film, where the sound is muted. No one hears me. No one living turns or embraces me, sobbing, promising they will care for me. That they will save me. I look behind me and there are many people around, but even the spirits do not rush to aid me.

As quickly as my frantic urgency to be heard and helped by Hannah and my family had arrived, summoned from somewhere just within reach, it seems to have slid back away from me, as though I may have mistaken it for something I can't quite regain in memory. I notice that the lady in charge of the cemetery is becoming overwhelmed and biting her lip as tears roll from her eyes. I admire those eyes, and the dark arch of her brows, and start to feel drawn to her attractiveness, which had previously escaped my notice. There is something sociopathic in this thought.

Some of the residents of the cemetery look on with sympathetic eyes, while others merely glance across at this wretched scene and carry on about their lives. Their 'lives'? I need to get a grip. I try to focus on making myself heard again by calling, 'Hannah! Hannah! Hannah!' then, 'Mum! Mum! Dad!' but no one responds. My words have the weight of confetti scattered to the gentle breeze, heard only by my fellows in this other world.

Claire and David gently lift their daughter away from the cold stone. I stare into her beautiful face, tortured and tormented though her features seem now. I want to take her in my arms and kiss away her tears, to place my lips on hers and breathe joy back into that beautiful girl. I suddenly again experience anger and frustration and will myself to wake, to change what I see before me. I need to wake up: a sense of now-or-never panic comes to me, to prevent the loss of a love which was to be my life, my reason for waking every day to live with passion; to make that day and every day as perfect as I could for the girl I love. Now here I am, fighting not to accept what I, the great sceptic, may have to accept: my life with ghosts. A life that seems bereft of worry and fear, while Hannah carries on, sentenced to her time in purgatory with a cross to bear that she neither wished for nor deserves, for the rest of her living days. I consider the manifest unfairness of this: that I, the careless photographer killed by quality, have not been the victim I thought, but am the architect of this situation, the robber who has stolen his love's joy and condemned her to a life sentence of loss and misery.

# left alone

I feel the closest thing to sadness I seem currently capable of as Hannah, face tear-stained and numb-looking, breathing in short gasps as though she is running the Boston Marathon, supported by David and Claire and followed by *cimitero* lady, Italian flag handbag marked with dust from the ground, passes along the path towards the gate. I stand arms wide and close my eyes as I try to embrace her, but, when I open them, Hannah, Claire and David have passed through me unfelt and are being ushered into a sleek black car by a chauffeur, as another chauffeur stands by a second car, doors open, waiting for my mother, father, brother and the diplomats.

My mother has aged. It's only days since I last saw her. She seems to have raced ahead as time kept normal pace. Her sadness is palpable. I try to summon anguish for her plight, and that of my father and brother, but, try as I may, I cannot quite deliver. They too pass through me as I try to touch my mother's face, to brush away her tears, and catch my father's eye as he continues his dialogue with the diplomat, his way of coping. I call out to Hannah as she takes her seat, telling her that I will always love her, and I echo the same to my parents and brother as they disappear inside their limousine. All in, chauffeurs shutting doors like bank vaults, solid and dull sounding, then the cars drive away slowly along Via Caio Cestio.

I stand inside the gateway, watching the indicators then brake lights pulse as the cars pause then turn into Via Marmorata. Then they are gone. I call out, 'No! Don't go! Come back! Come back!' Left alone, I stand staring at the junction of Via Caio Cestio and Via Marmorata, praying to see both cars returning, bringing my loved ones back to me. I wait. Occasional cars pass, but the limousines do not return. The mechanic is leaning against the bonnet of a Lancia, smoking. Everyone in Italy smokes. He talks into a mobile phone and smiles often. *Ciao.* He ends the call, steps on the cigarette end and turns towards his workshop.

I sense warmth at my elbow and turn to see the same lady who had walked through my mother. She introduces herself. Lady Mary von Haast. She says simply, 'Take heart, young man.'

'I don't belong here,' I reply.

# all too much

The kindness of this stranger touches me. I smile but walk away. I wander slowly across to Shelley's tomb where, moments earlier, my love and my family had grieved for me. I look down at the stone.

*Nothing of him that doth fade,*
*But doth suffer a sea-change*
*Into something rich and strange.*

Strange alright. It does not come stranger. One minute, alive and well and loving life; the next, frightening a pair of Japanese women and turning other people's lives upside down. Clean stone, blood washed away, leaving no evidence of Rita's crime, or of Shelley's part in my demise. Sea-change. Understatement. Where is my sorrow? *Cor cordium*. Heart of hearts. Lost at sea. Drowned and washed up with Keats in his pocket. Hearts entwined. And Edward Ellerker Williams's stone beside his. Two lovers perhaps, who hid the love that dare not speak its name? I shall ask Shelley about that, when I can face his half-mocking stare.

I shall ask Shelley? Ask *Shelley*? Ask a dead poet? A few hours ago I could not have regarded a conversation with a two-centuries-dead poet as anything other than fiction, fantasy or insanity, and now I am planning to put him on the spot over two Latin words. It is none of my business what Shelley's inclinations or loves were. Or who. I am like some sordid hack from a Sunday newspaper, digging up dirt about someone of note long since gone, whose reputation I want to make a career from tarnishing. How would I feel if some bounty-hunter published a story about me, aged thirteen, climbing on to the roof of my school swimming pool to peer through the skylight on a dark winter's night to watch the mothers' swim group walk naked as they showered and changed. And let us be honest about it. Aged ten or possibly eleven, or even twelve, it would be laughed off. But thirteen? Thirteen could be portrayed as a sexual deviant starting a dangerous descent. Branded. Tarnished for life. Fortunately for me, we – for I was not alone – we, all four of us, spied and escaped, laughing into the night, undetected. But what of Shelley? His life, and his secrets, examined, dissected and cut wide open for two centuries. To be stitched up again neatly or not by the insight or motives or jerked-up logic of scholars, students, writers, historians, journalists, outers and opportunists. People. Love them or hate them. Just do not trust them.

I chastise myself slightly for thinking of mistrust. I was imbued with the notion to trust people, that they are worth investing in, until such time as they may betray that trust. Glass half full. My nature. Instilled in me by my parents for good measure, just to make sure.

A passing couple, chic and sophisticated, sporting an elegance that has rarely been bettered since the 1930s, acknowledge me with a cheery, 'Good afternoon.' They speak simultaneously, which sounds false, as though they are robots programmed to talk. The man touches the brim of his hat, and his lady, resplendent in voluminous beach pyjamas – red with cream circles, and a cream silk jacket, her hair hidden beneath a huge red sunhat – giggles and nods her head towards me.

Drawn away from staring at Shelley's stone, I move from one scene bordering on the bizarre to something which, in my attempts to rationalise my fate, my current nightmarish realisation that I am my spirit, is simply too much to take in. Below the brick tower that aided my departure from one world to the next lies ground twenty feet below the *cimitero*, where, strolling by the base of the pyramid tomb of Caius Cestius, priest, soldier, man of influence, are dozens of figures in togas. Ancient Romans.

Ancient Romans? It is all too much. Again I want to retreat into the safety of madness, where delusion and hallucination can be explained, where a few pink and blue pills can restore normality, and everyone can then go home to watch television and carry on cautiously until their next appointment.

# a roll of the dice

I retreat from my vantage point. I hear Shelley laughing, and look around to see him, Keats, a man I take to be Joseph Severn, and a small child who is toddling about, the source of Shelley's amusement. Ill-prepared for any more shocks to my belief system, I head up to the scene of my night vigil, and place myself within the bushes where the foxes disappeared. From here I am simply an observer unobserved. 'Rubens' is up a tree again. I shake my head in disbelief, but resolve to make his acquaintance should my acceptance become less tumultuous. He looks for all the world an interesting character with a fascinating story to tell. Maybe he knew the actual Rubens. I may ask him, when I am ready.

Everyone around me has something of interest about them, some from their apparent eccentricity, and others simply from their era. I have often thought of time travel, and what I would see should I be able to journey back to a particular era. It dawns on me that the lives of men and women through the ages have actually been brought to me. A truly staggering thought. Lucky me. I laugh to myself, unsure whether the laugh is one of bitterness, madness or excitement. I shall see. I close my eyes, and follow the example of Rubens, deciding to rest until my thoughts are less molecularly fractured, bouncing around looking for a positive attachment as they are. I summon strength of feeling, and pray futilely that when I open my eyes again I will be in our hotel bed, with Hannah sleeping peacefully beside me, her golden hair flowing across her pillow.

I resolve to challenge my perception, to test whether I truly am dead by spending twenty-eight entire days sitting here, one day for every year I had lived, listening to chiming church bells and singing birds, noting the comings and goings of various souls, testing time and what I see. Rubens occasionally drops down from his perch to wander. I see him fade into a tomb occasionally and figure that it is his, so I have resolved to look at his name, in order better to introduce myself.

Despite my plan to see out a routine based around a meaningful number, nothing really changes. No one bothers me, not Shelley or Keats, who I see from a distance most days, although each evening, as the light fades, Lady Mary Von Haast comes to sit beside me and talks to me about my life, and her life, and her adjustment to loss. She rolls back and forth between English and Italian as she educates me. She feels much like the loving mother I have lost. The foxes pass me every time they enter and leave the gardens. So as not to alarm them, I sit motionless with my back against the wall close to their den, which is reached by a hole beneath a shrub to my right. There is something delightful about the cubs. I think to myself that all creatures, both people and animals, are at their best at a few weeks old. Then they grow into whatever they will be: saints, sinners, moderates or monsters. A roll of the dice.

Coming to terms with the probability that my eternity will be spent confined in this cemetery is a difficult nettle to grasp. Each day as I sit, I reason that, in order not to succumb to this garden forever, I have to find a way out, to return to my life with Hannah, to be alive again, or at least to be close to those I knew and loved. Although reason suggests to me that I should accept what I now know to be true, I push and squeeze my thoughts, to send a message to my phone alarm, to allow me to wake to the sound of Hannah scrambling eggs as the scent of brewing coffee drifts from the kitchen, but nothing changes. No alarm sounds. I remain where I am. My body, head caved in, will now be back in London, a source of anguish to so many loving deserving good honest caring people. My family, friends, employers, colleagues, neighbours and Hannah. And here I am, feeling anger ebb away, as though I am becoming strangely content when my instinct should shout *Fight! Fight for your life! Fight for your love!* and I find myself only wishing for Hannah to come back to visit, if only so that I can see her if not feel her. Just to know that she is still mine. That I am still loved.

## the heartbeat of life

Feeling like the afterthought invitee to a party at which I am not truly welcome, I decide I have pondered long enough, having proved to myself that time moves as it always has. I have borne witness through twenty-eight long days now, as end-of-summer flowers, fraction by fraction, poked through the soil and grew to maturity, finally blooming with petals and stamens rich with nectar for harvesting bees, who, as the days shorten, make ready for winter as autumn stands just out of shot, waiting to sneak in. I make my way out from the shelter of the border shrubs into the beauty of the day, and head down towards the gate. Rubens looks my way and gives a brief wave with a casual calm that suggests he is either unafraid of falling from the tree, or simply cannot fall. I wave back, slowly and hesitantly. There is something about my sense of myself that reminds me of a new-born deer staggering to stand, or a drunk searching his pockets for a door key to allow him sanctuary from the street. I feel all eyes on me, some overt, some from under hat brims or sidelong. The new kid on the block. The difference between them and me? They belong here.

Everyone here has a tomb, their home. People literally vanish inside tombs, or into the ground where their stone lies flat above. Phut! Gone. Images in a magic show. Smoke and mirrors. Where do I belong here? Nowhere. Am I condemned for an eternity to rest beside a wall, behind a shrub and bushes, a discarded item, a man wrapper from a human sandwich carelessly dropped by himself?

I shake my head as though I can empty it of this thought. I need to reconcile some facts here. I need to get a grip.

I walk slowly to the gate, smiling tight-lipped and nodding to various strangers as they pass. There is a sense of courtesy about most which is reassuring. No sense of animosity towards the uninvited guest. The interloper. The foolish dead.

Claudio, for I have given him a name, is working under the bonnet of a different Lancia. I need to name him. As I have with Rubens. A person without a name is always a stranger. Shelley made that clear. I am sitting on the wall by the gate. I am still somewhat bemused, and amused, by my new-found ability to levitate. Claudio is muttering to himself indistinctly. The day is still as glass. Air probably warm judging from the sun shining brightly in an azure sky. Another realisation: I do not feel heat or cold. I have remained outside since my header, and felt no change in temperature despite sitting out through many nights. I remain comfortable in jeans and my Haight Ashbury Music Center shirt. My much prized Old Skool sneakers seem what they are now, a pretty meaningless item with a marketed mythology, the basis of all fashion perhaps being comprised of two things: human vanity combined with the driving force of earning from manufacture – human endeavour to make a buck. This kind of thought normally causes my head to ache, but now, in all truth, I really do not care. Another thing along with heat, cold, hunger, thirst. All gone.

I smile to myself as I watch Claudio struggling to undo a rusted part with a chrome wrench. Claudio has to care, if he is to be paid for repairing this motor car. I no longer have to give a damn about anything. I am starting to feel a growing affinity with my situation, which suddenly disappears as my thoughts spin to Hannah, and longing for her and our life together returns. I imagine Hannah now, at her flat, being comforted by family and friends who think through every sentence spoken with a pre-rehearsal at lightning speed in their heartfelt desire to not say the wrong thing, to avoid jarring her sensibility, to wrap her in cotton wool. I shrug mentally. There is nothing I can do to bring happiness back to her. Though I would if I could.

Claudio makes one final mighty effort, his face showing strain as he pushes hard down on the wrench. It gives suddenly and he pulls his hand to his mouth. '*Fanculo!*' Fuck you! He shakes his hand, rubs it down his overalls, lights a cigarette. He smokes with one hand, and takes a close look at his damaged hand. '*Stupido.*' He smiles to himself and shakes his hand again.

Claudio appears to be a man of few words. I would like to go across to him and learn more but I am confined to my new home, which, although reason tells me I should be resentfully regarding as a prison, I do not. Not yet.

I walk the perimeter of the cemetery, pausing to look through the spy-hole out to the street which is set in the wall to allow passers-by to see Keats's tomb when the gardens are closed. I wonder what Keats makes of that. A man who died so young, with little fame in truth, who is now fêted and celebrated, a star of the literati, and on every shelf in every library on God's earth. Keats must feel robbed of all that. Cheated. A dead celebrity. For a second I wonder if he knows about his fame; but the constant flow of adoring fans must ensure he does. Cheated by time and tuberculosis.

The light across the *cimitero* is pure. Colour abounds. Flowers coat the day with a richness of matching purity. Jasmine flowers, white as snow, and pomegranates hanging, as beautiful in shades of burnt orange merging to deepest ruby as any still life created in oil paint. It is breathtaking. I feel a contentment which should be at odds with my reality. I am dead. I have lost the girl I loved. I have lost everything and everyone I hold dear. I am a spirit. I should be wringing my hands in torment. I smile to myself on recalling Picasso's defiant statement: *I am an artist. I have no guilt*. I am a photographer. I am losing mine.

A parakeet flies chattering by and swings suddenly on to a branch above me. It is beautiful. Green as filtered light through overhanging summer branches. Another misplaced being. Born of escaped cage birds, bound for the delights of Rome. Free to fly away, but, like me, strangely trapped here. 'Fly,' I say quietly, not truly wishing it, wanting to admire the exotic beauty of this fabulous stranger for longer – for beauty, I am starting to feel, is the heartbeat of life, and of death.

The parakeet flies away at the call of another. I continue on. My thoughts turn again to Hannah, only to be interrupted by Shelley, who suddenly appears before me.

'As you seem to be staying,' he says, with a look of amusement, as though it is his best party joke, 'I am going to introduce you to those you need to know,' adding, 'unless you are resigned to your life with foxes?'

I realise he has been watching me. I suspect there are few secrets here. Little hidden from the scrutiny of others.

He takes me by the elbow to lead me, and again I feel a strange warmth. It strikes me that the only times I have felt anything since my feet slid and a rush of air announced my imminent demise was when Shelley and Keats shook my hand and Lady Mary von Haast held my elbow. Everyone else, Hannah, my mother and father and brother, simply passed through me, leaving no sense of their ever having been.

Shelley steers me along the path, introducing me as *our new friend Finn* to everyone we meet.

## already well acquainted

Shelley. I am still stunned. Percy Bysshe Shelley. Poet. Essayist. Legend. Icon. Tour guide. Shelley leads me by the arm. He misses no one as we stroll.

'Lady Mary, may I introduce my good friend Finn? Finn Chambers, Lady Mary von Haast.'

Shelley had asked me my surname as we walked, stating that formality, although alien to him, would require a surname, to avoid confusion with any other Finns in the *cimitero*.

'How many are we?' I had asked.

Grinning as usual, he had replied, 'You are you.'

'Oh, but we are already well acquainted, Percy,' Lady Mary remarks, looking radiant as she winks an eye at me. 'Mr Chambers and I are old friends.'

I bow towards her and hold out my hand, which she takes with an air of delight. I kiss her hand, as much as a spirit is able. I am grateful for her kindness towards me. Shelley beams. I blush, or feel that I am, somewhat embarrassed by my display of arse-kissing. What the hell am I doing? I have never kissed a woman's hand before – except for Hannah's as a show of affection to seal my devotion. I would have climbed inside Hannah's body if I could when she had looked into my eyes at the airport, and again in Masto. For the first time in my twenty-eight years I had felt that great love that Shelley and Keats, my new-found companions, and Byron and Coleridge and Wordsworth and Hemingway and Virginia Woolf, had felt and lived and written of. Pure love, that for an instant is so concentrated and all-powerful, with the potential of that microdot of unimaginable energy which exploded, hurling blinding light and gases outwards to create the universe; heralding man, woman, sex, fire, farms, buildings, art, music, war, society, palaces, beauty, medicine, money, pornography, infidelity, technology, corruption, literature, drugs, theatre.

'Do excuse us, Lady Mary,' Shelley purrs as though allowing her into some great confidence, then, lowering his voice, adds, 'but we have others not so charming as yourself to whom to offer the hand of our young friend.'

He raises a brow conspiratorially, causing her to laugh out loud. For a woman approaching seventy she has the bearing of a young girl, with a striking beauty that radiates from her. Her husband must have been a lucky man.

'You are such a charmer, Percy, but you know I love you. Well, I have been here since before the Great War, so I can wait a little longer to interrogate Mr Chambers further.'

Shelley too kisses her hand, then marches me away. I look back briefly to smile at Lady Mary, who blows me a kiss. Her way of saying my secret education is safe with her, although I suspect that there are few secrets held here. Shelley has no doubt observed Lady Mary's evening strolls to my solitary refuge. I laugh to myself that Shelley referred to me as *our young friend*, as though I were not twenty-eight and he twenty-nine. When I give it a little more thought, I start to defer to Shelley for having a couple of hundred years on me, but then I think, why should I?' Has he seen what I've seen? Has he seen men land on the moon? Could he even countenance the concept of transferring the entire contents of the Bodleian Library from his old university in Oxford to the Library of Congress in Washington DC in a few short minutes, without the aid of a crew of two hundred men and ships? Three thousand miles. Twelve million books. Minutes. This modern world. I have seen some shit. Shelley has only seen these gardens for two hundred years.

Keats is sitting on the headstone of Joseph Severn, who is sitting on Keats's stone. Two small children are playing together nearby, chattering kid-style. I know it is Severn from a painting shown in a television documentary about Keats. Good painting. Good likeness.

Severn is so much older than I had imagined. In my mind, he should look just like his portrait. I imagined him as of a comparable age to Keats and Shelley. And then it strikes me that the spirits here are as they were when they died. It's obvious when you consider it. And that gets me thinking about God and heaven and that kind of stuff. The stuff that keeps you up until way too late over whisky with friends. The meaning of life. The existence of God. Or not, as the case may be. I shake hands with Severn, and Keats catches me staring from Severn to the children and back again to Severn.

'If I may read your thoughts for a second,' he says with a wry smile, 'we stay as we were.'

I turn to Keats and, not having seen myself reflected, ask, 'So do I have scars?'

'The beauty of the spirit is that it manifests the body as it was prior to whatever caused its death. No scars, bloodstains, guillotined bodies carrying their heads in the crooks of their arms for eternity. Nothing you may have imagined.'

I am relieved. 'So I look normal.'

'As normal as you ever did,' Severn retorts, making Keats laugh. Severn puts his arm around my shoulder and says, flipping a thumb towards Shelley, 'Don't believe a word this bastard tells you, though. He will tell you the moon is a figment of the imagination, dreamed up by man, and he'll push his atheistic doctrine at you until you agree with him. He'll twist even what he believes as irrefutable truth for his own amusement, heathen that he is.'

Shelley grins.

'And be wary of mentioning Percy to the Reverend Mr Barrington, Finn. You may find yourself in waters hotter and deeper than those at the Bagni di Bormio. Both Oxford men, but that, as they say, is where the similarities end.' Severn grins at his own mischief. These guys grin a lot.

'If you speak of something, say of it with passion, Finn, lest your words carry less weight than Severn's and the wind blows them away.'

Shelley, being poetical.

## free to roam

My mind fluctuates. I have a sense that I should be railing and raging against my death and despairing over my loss of family and Hannah, but something overrides what I feel should be my instinct. Surely if I were now hanging by my fingertips from a cliff edge I would be panicking and desperately clawing at the rock to pull myself to safety, to save myself in order that I should not lose all that I loved, particularly the woman who turned me from ordinary Finn Chambers to Finn Chambers, King of the World? Where is my passion? Where is my fight? These thoughts slide away as I look towards Severn.

I see goodness in Joseph Severn. A man of humour, underpinned by a kindness which radiates from him. He and Keats are bonded by a shared appreciation of beauty, which, devil-may-care persona aside, bonds Shelley to them both. Shelley, however, is an enigma. I reserve judgement about him. It would appear I have all the time in the world.

The children are interrupted by Severn, who calls to them. One, a giggling baby, waves his feet and hands lying on his back, and the other, a child of about three, toddles like a half-finished toy across the daisy mat and stands before us.

'My son Arthur,' says Severn, waving his hand towards the baby, 'and Percy's son William. No doubt you will see much of them.'

Shelley reaches down with tenderness to stroke William's hair. Then William toddles off towards Arthur to resume their play. I feel a gladness which is difficult to categorise. Something that approaches relief to see children happy in this unreal world of spirits and frozen time. Time as I know it rolls forward, day into night, returning to day again, but the spirits here, all of us, are simply framed at a time before death.

I recall television interviewees who claimed to have died. Accounts of purple tunnels and bright white light. I had scoffed at such reports. I'm no longer scoffing. Time passes, but we remain as we were. Stuck forever, the same way that time seems to stand still on New Year's Eve, in a frame of frozen anticipation before the countdown to another year begins. Out of the old and into the new, time temporarily seeming locked. But time is never locked. Time, as they say, marches on. It has certainly marched on for Severn, who, at the age of eighty-five, is ill-suited as the father of a seven-month child.

As if to cement this reversal of natural order, a family stroll by, collared immediately by my tour guide who introduces them as the Kraafts: mother, father and son. The son, John Kraaft, is much older than his youthful parents. This is insane.

Keats, Shelley and Severn start a conversation about Wordsworth. I notice from the inscription on Arthur's stone that the man himself was at his christening, although little Arthur will never grow old enough to appreciate poetry. Not Wordsworth's, nor Keats's, nor Shelley's. I decide to leave them to their discussion; I know little of these people and their contemporaries, apart from their fame, and fear my ignorance will see me flounder in such elevated conversation. I stroll to the gate to watch Claudio. I want to make the most of Claudio, an ordinary man more akin to my own life, before the rains come and he is confined to his workshop, as I am confined to this cemetery. Beautiful though it is, the thought that eternity within these walls is my everyday is a fact to which I need to become reconciled. I do not belong here.

Claudio is sitting on one of two plastic chairs outside his workshop. The Lancia has gone, to be replaced by a blue Hyundai. An old red Vespa sits beside the workshop door. Claudio is jabbering and gesticulating to the person on the other end of a telephone conversation. He runs his hand through his hair. *Ciao*. He tucks the phone inside a bib pocket on his overalls, and starts the scooter. He roars off, barely pausing as he swings right into Via Caio Cestio and out of sight.

I jump up to sit on the wall, thinking of Hannah, and where she might be at this moment. I wish only good things and happiness for her as my thoughts spin to my family, only to be interrupted by the sound of a scooter engine as the red Vespa rushes back into view. My thoughts have caused me to miss the arrival of a pretty dark-haired girl who is parked in a soft-top powder-blue Volkswagen Beetle outside the workshop. How did I miss that? As Claudio parks the Vespa on its stand, she gets out of the car and walks high-heeled, skirt swinging, towards the chairs. Claudio approaches her, kisses her on both cheeks and places a hand on her bottom; they kiss again, lips to lips this time, slowly, and she pushes him away, laughing, as she moves to sit in a chair. Claudio goes inside the workshop then reappears with two bottles of beer, one of which he hands to the girl as he takes the other seat. They smoke and chatter and drink beer from the bottle. She looks at her watch, stands up, leans over him to kiss him, this time lingering as he strokes her bottom again, fishes sunglasses from her bag, then strides, polka-dot skirt swirling, to the Vespa, starts it up and drives off along Via Paolo Caselli.

Claudio lights another cigarette and takes a draining swig of beer, before collecting Claudia's bottle – I name her too.

'A penny for your thoughts, my young friend?'

Shelley has appeared next to me. Uninvited.

'Just looking out past the prison walls.'

'Where would you prefer to be?'

'The Knickerbocker Hotel in New York. With Hannah.'

'Impossible, I'm afraid.'

'I know,' I say. 'I just would love to leave this prison long enough to look inside Claudio's workshop.'

'Who?'

'The man over there – the mechanic,' I say, pointing across at Claudio, who now has the hood up on the Beetle.

'Why not? Let's do it.'

I am stunned. I had imagined myself confined, forever, within the walls of the Cimitero Acattolico. Limited.

'Can we leave here?' I ask.

'Of course,' he says looking bemused. 'Why on earth would you think of this place as your prison?'

'But no one seems to leave here?'

'This place, my friend, is their home. They choose to remain.'

I am suddenly enlivened. I can leave. I can re-join Hannah. I can see my mother and father.

'Sod that,' I say. 'Cheers, Percy, I'm off.'

I drop to the path inside and start to walk towards the gate. Shelley catches me.

'There are some things you need to understand, Finn.' He speaks gently, and for once looks serious. 'We are all at liberty to leave here, but travel to England is not achievable, I am afraid, my boy.'

'But surely, if we can leave, what is to stop me simply levitating into a taxi and out of the city on to a ship or aircraft?' I feel a sudden need, armed with this new information, to break away from Shelley's world, to go home and regain whatever life I can by watching Hannah and my family, friends, familiar sights.

'Your spirit has defined characteristics, Finn. We are all free to roam, but roam too far at your peril.'

Stuff that. Shelley and Keats and Lady Mary von Haast may be confined by their own time to ideas of limitation, but I am a child of the space age, of books acquired at the speed of light, of drones that exterminate terrorists in hidden bunkers thousands of miles from the controlling hand, of heart transplants, and sight restored. I am invincible.

'I don't think your limitations apply to me,' I say haughtily, my mocking look turned on Shelley.

He eyes me with a frown. 'Stray too far and your spirit, the thing that is now you, will dissipate into fog, then particles, then you will be gone. Forever.'

His voice is loaded. Truth. His words are truth. I want to ignore his statement, to wipe it from the air, but I sense only truth. 'What happens then?' I ask, deflated.

'No idea,' says he, shrugging. 'Nobody seems to make it that far and return. Believe me, I tried, as did Severn and Sanchez. As we started to dissolve in the air we all stepped back to safety, all of us afraid. It is the only time I have felt fear since that maddening day at sea.'

'Sanchez?'

'There are many here whom you have yet to meet. All in good time. You have a sufficiency of that. Infinite time,' he says without a hint of wistfulness. 'Let us visit your friend.'

Shelley strides the few yards to the gateway, and turns, smiling again. 'Come along. Let us see what this day has for us.'

# through the gateway

Shelley had drowned at Livorno. I ask if he is still an atheist. He smiles without reply. I press and ask him if our current situation is proof of God? Of a deity's generosity in allowing us all the grace of a better moment before death? I mean, I could be walking around like a zombie, head caved in and face dripping blood. He laughs, but offers nothing.

Passing through the gateway into Caio Cestio, I feel elated, new-born. It hits me that I am in the company of a legend, who, if he was alive now, would be an A-list celebrity. I wonder how he would feel about that: about having my vacuous plastic society's labels and values applied to him.

I pause to look left and right at the pavement edge, but Shelley does neither and marches on. He carries on unnoticed by the delivery driver who runs into him in a Fiat van. *Corriere Espresso.* In such a rush he will never know he just ran through Percy Bysshe Shelley. English poet. Icon. I catch up with him, and – just because he can, I suspect – Shelley jumps up on to the roof apex of Claudio's workshop. He sits grinning for a few seconds then drops down as I approach the entrance.

We step inside and immediately I am overjoyed. Normality. I imagined a shambolic interior. I do not know why, but I did, probably because the exterior is shabby, and held no promise. But here are workbenches, shelves, racking, all ordered, with everything seemingly in its place. A place made for each tool. The cemetery and Claudio's workshop have a lot in common. Ranks and rows of order. Nothing misplaced. An inspection pit in the floor. Tracking and wheel-alignment racking on another area of floor. Cars arriving dead, coming back to life. And then, wow! A dusty old Ferrari partly hidden under a sheet in one corner. Claudio's personal restoration project. Every Italian's dream. Red, as it should be. Little by little. One day.

I notice Shelley standing by a washbasin to the rear of the workshop, staring admiringly at a pouting raven-haired girl. A Pirelli calendar. A row of them. Every year Claudio has been in business, I suspect.

'Don't let the *femministe* catch you, Percy,' I say, wagging my finger. 'This sort of thing is frowned on these days. You're not in 1821 any more.'

'So to gaze upon such beauty is a crime? Take me back to my youth!' He laughs, then says, 'Have you seen what you needed?'

I nod by way of answer, as I take another look around.

'Then let us gather our friends and explore the day.'

Claudio is oblivious, working beneath the open bonnet of the Beetle, as Shelley walks up the wheel arch, over the roof and down the trunk. We cross the street to the *cimitero* and I dare to be hit by an oncoming car. I steel myself for impact. The Mazda passes through me without effect. I realise truly that I am dead.

# scene of the crime

Shelley calls to Keats and Severn, and another older man who is sitting on Keats's stone. They amble over towards us, leaving the children where they play on the lawn.

'Edward, I have the pleasure of introducing to you my new friend Finn Chambers.' As this elderly man in Victorian dress, complete with black silk top hat, stretches out his hand to mine, Shelley adds, 'Finn, this is Edward John Trelawny.'

Another legend. After shaking the warmth that now passes for a hand, I show my surprise that he should be here. 'Oh! I thought you died in England?'

It just comes out. Feeling the tiniest glow of embarrassment, I turn to Shelley for support, but it is Keats who saves me.

'That is the strangest of things you will find here, Finn. You may wait by a tomb, and never see the person named thereon. They are elsewhere, their spirit having signed off from the underworld at some other time and place. Then again, there are those, like Trelawny, whose remains have been brought from far away, whose spirits are evermore here, having chosen to release themselves only upon arrival at this place. And there are those who have no name here, no tomb to call theirs, who could, but for the absence of those aforementioned, roam these gardens homeless for eternity.'

'By those who have no name here, you mean me?' I ask quietly, thinking then of Keats's own inscription.

'Oh, you and Sanchez and a few others.' Sanchez again.

Trelawny is old, pushing ninety, but walks easily. Another benefit of spirit life. No aches, pains, arthritis, gout, blindness. Jesus would love it here. Sight to the blind. The sick healed. The dead back to life.

'And what brought you to your rest here, Finn? Adventure?' asks Trelawny. For an old guy he has a remarkable sparkle and air of fun about him.

'I was killed by quality,' I say, without a trace of hesitation. 'Killed by the finest of food and wine. Killed by Rita.' I pause momentarily before stating, 'Rita of Masto.'

I add my last to sound mysterious, taken up as I am by Trelawny's reputation as one of history's more creative embellishers of the truth, or, perhaps more accurately, a fanciful conman and bullshitter.

'Killed by careless misjudgement, if truth be told,' says Shelley as he puts his arm around me to reassure me that he is laughing at my misadventure, not mocking my misfortune.

'Rita of Masto?' Trelawny smooths his cavalier moustache. 'Any relation to Helen of Troy?'

We all laugh, and I get a gauge of Trelawny, who I can see is searching for some tangible figment to attach a story to. No doubt he will make it a tale about pirates and him swinging from the masthead before leaping from the burning ship to be rescued by mermaids, who he will imply loved him in positions that only mermaids can.

'Masto?' he says, musing. I head him off.

'It's a restaurant.'

'The quality must be sublime, for it to kill such a fine young man as yourself,' says Trelawny. 'And where on this good Earth would such a dangerous establishment be?'

'Via Galvani.'

'Then let us away.' Shelley takes my arm and leads me towards the gate.

'What about the children?' I say. 'Is someone going to watch them?'

'Whatever for?'

'Well, it's not normal to leave a baby and a toddler alone in a cemetery, surely?'

'What could possibly befall them?' says Shelley without expression. 'They are dead.'

As we reach the gate Shelley pauses and, looking to our left, calls out to a studious-looking man who seems to spend his existence lying on the roof of the gardener's store. 'Signor Gramsci!'

The man turns his head towards us.

'We are off to sample some fine delights at Masto, Antonio. Care to join us?'

It is apparent, then, that the air of mystery I wove around Rita was played with by Trelawny. I doubt there is anywhere unknown to my friends in Rome. So there we are, Shelley, Keats, Severn, fabled English adventurer Edward Trelawny, the legendary Italian communist Antonio Gramsci and me, wandering, unseen except by passing spirits, through the thoroughfares of Rome. You really could not script this. You would need serious drugs to believe this shit. The Romantics and the imagination? Some serious imagination required here.

I do not know anything about Gramsci, except that Shelley had said he was – and from the brief conversation we have had following our introduction clearly still is – a committed communist. He is a passionate man. Passion. It strikes me once again, as we approach Masto, that this is the thing that, along with humour and kindness, makes us remember people. Passionate people command respect, even from those who oppose their views, and we remember them for that. Unpleasantness, however, causes us to recall those we would rather forget.

A sudden sense of anticipation awakens within me. I expect to feel trepidation or angst at the prospect of returning to the scene of the crime; to the past life in which so recently I had a full house in my lucky hand, only to see my cards scatter in a moment of carelessness brought about by quality. If I had ever considered my demise I had imagined it would be the result of a defective parachute, or a stray bullet while shooting black and white moods in Soweto or the Bronx.

Trelawny is telling Gramsci some story. No doubt some fanciful tale manufactured to entertain the communist. From what I catch, it involves the emancipation of downtrodden fisherfolk of the Peloponnese, with Byron's name being dropped like confetti. Keats leans towards me and whispers the phrase *pinch of salt*.

As we stroll I notice two things. None of my spirit brethren rushes anywhere. The spirits we pass, and there are many, are unhurried about their business. From Romans in togas to occasional peasants in clothes of the field, none seems troubled or encumbered by deadlines or time. Time is irrelevant. Colour, though – colour is vivid. There is an iridescence to light, to flowers, to buildings, to everything. The grey cement between bricks, never intended by its creators as anything other than the adhesive of construction, is beautiful. Climbing plants flowing over high walls, so rich with colour; jasmine white as ice cream and bougainvillea rainbows hanging in reds, oranges, vermilion and magenta shades that dazzle the eye and steal one's breath. I savour this. I taste their blossom on the air, so thick is the scent.

A strange sense of camaraderie flows through me; as though I have known these figures previously, although I now know that when we die we do not come back as another being in another time, but that our spirit simply lives on. Forever. If we choose. We continue our brief walk towards Masto, cutting along Via Nicola Zabaglia. Shelley sticks his hand out at right angles as a young man on a bicycle rides along the cycle path towards us. If Shelley had anything solid about him the boy would be knocked flat, but he passes through unscathed and oblivious. There is something wonderfully cavalier about Shelley. A man who, even in this spirit world, lives life on his terms, unbridled by the limits of others. A true prince of Bohemia.

As we approach Masto, Shelley disappears briefly. I am confused by his absence, but he appears again from a third-floor window, dropping to the ground. Grinning. 'Later,' he says to me, sounding like a ten-year-old Californian kid. He winks at me conspiratorially, and places an arm around my shoulders as I pause outside the restaurant, the others waiting patiently behind me.

'This,' I say, turning to face them, 'is where quality got the better of me.'

We stroll inside. There are tables taken, and Rita is bustling from one to the other and in and out of the kitchen. The smells are sublime. I can still smell. I have all my senses with the exception of touch, which is now reduced to that odd sense of warmth from contact with my fellow spirits. It's a small price to pay, I guess. I can still hear music, smell flowers and see the beauty of the world – and its ugliness. I wonder if taste is still available to me as we take seats around the only unoccupied large table. Shelley, being Shelley, sits astride the bicycle hung as art on the wall, before answering my unspoken question by dropping to the table below the bicycle, where a smart young Italian man is holding the hand of his beautiful girlfriend, talking quietly and looking into her eyes. Shelley licks the cheese on the girl's plate then leans across and sticks his tongue in her glass of Montepulciano. He looks across at my gawping face, and gives a nod of approval. He comes to sit on the table edge.

'That was a bit disgusting,' I say disapprovingly, my face contorted. 'How on earth is she supposed to eat and drink after you licking and poking your tongue into her meal?'

'Blissfully unaware.' He smirks, and adds, clearly attempting to shock me, 'I may place my tongue elsewhere before the hour is done.'

Keats, who is without doubt a more restrained soul than Shelley, tuts his disapproval, although I am not convinced this is genuine. Keats has a sparkle in his eye and, I suspect, could never truly disapprove of Shelley. Gramsci seems unconcerned by Shelley's ribaldry, deep as he is in conversation with Severn. Trelawny is making eyes at Rita, who might have been troubled by the lascivious attentions of an eighty-eight-year-old man had she been able to see his lust.

A building realisation creates a delicious sense within me. They, all of them, the inhabitants of the *cimitero*, are youthful. Lady Mary, Severn, Trelawny, Gramsci, Shelley, Keats. All youthful in outlook and attitude. As my grandfather had said somewhat sorrowfully about becoming old: *the spirit is willing, but the flesh is weak*. I am truly delighted to learn that this applies only to the living, and not the spirit world, where an eighty-five-year-old man can vault a twelve-foot wall with no effort at all, and laugh, eyes twinkling, with his seven-month-old baby boy.

I am deluded. I thought that due to their age and origins – and, let's face it, time dead – this bunch would be staring open-mouthed in wonder at this modern farce we call the present. Particularly Shelley and Keats. Romantic visionaries. Men who wrote with such incredible delicacy about love, life, romance, beauty and the soul of mankind. I put this to Keats.

'You too, Finn, in good time, will see the evolving nature of this earthly life. Some things you'll receive with open arms, and others with a sense of dismay, although dismay is rarer than in your previous life. Has it visited you yet?'

'Has what visited me?'

'The realisation that disappointment, worry, anxiety, misery, fear, envy, longing have left you, or are diminishing, and you struggle to feel guilt about that?'

I turn suddenly as Hannah walks in through the open door from the street, blonde hair swinging. Except this girl is not Hannah. I feel no great emotion that this is not my queen, the woman I loved so deeply, and who I will never now marry and raise a family with. I should be angry with myself, but I am not.

I turn back to Keats.

'I am visited.'

# the light beyond the purple

This group of ours, if viewed by mortal passers-by, would be no doubt taken for a family of younger men with fathers and grandfathers, out for lunch, not as a collection of some of the greatest poets, thinkers and men of their age to have set bare feet on sand. It strikes me that these men, as in life, are bonded by a shared friendship, by mutual interest and questioning natures. There are many similar groups that I've seen: small friendship cliques, and families, who choose, as in their mortal lives, to keep to a circle that suits them, to mix with other like-minded people. There is much here that reflects the living world. Time, for instance, moves at the same pace. There is nothing they have not seen in their time dead. Knowledge, that accumulation of facts and experience, must overflow with my new companions. An unwelcome thought then chips into my mind: I may have nothing to contribute, so little have I seen of life, nothing to merit my inclusion within their circle.

Gramsci takes my attention from this new concern, enthusing in thickly accented words, translating, for my benefit, the values that Rita speaks of when describing the things she loves and admires about the artisans who supply this fabulous place. Gramsci hails her passion for the labours of the toiling men and women, the producers who deserve both praise and the profits of their labour for creating the finest-quality produce, out of pride in and love of what they do. Trelawny, eyes crinkling, casts them over Rita's looks and figure, and pulls a lewd face when I look at him. These are men of their time, unfettered by this modern stamp of thought-policing, honest in their views. So unlike my generation of 'modern thinkers': us, the modern stalwarts of standards, bleating sheep who thrive on reputation-destruction and an obsession with celebrity, as though some self-loving halfwit with five minutes of fame is the arbiter of what should be the aspiration of everyone. Forever apologising for the behaviour of our forebears, when we, the dead, know we are far from responsible for the sins of others. In times gone by, men traded silk, salt, cattle, rice, wheat, gold, whatever made a buck. No right thinker, living or dead, could condone a trade in people, of slavery or sex trafficking, but both things still continue, because men always have been, and always will be, capable of depravity. It is the joint attraction of those two devils, wealth and power. Evil men trade in evil. My generation now trades in guilt.

Feeling kinship with my new company, and in my desire to unburden the thought that I may have nothing to contribute, I throw in a basic invitation for observations from their perspective on whether we have, in fact, advanced at all since their day, even from that of Gramsci, the second most recent intern among us now gathered in Masto.

Gramsci responds with a simple observation about my generation. That we weigh ourselves down with First World angst and contrived individual concerns. He says the more he sees of modern life, the more inclined he is to disconnect from twenty-first-century values; from the hypocrisy of inflated values, where virtue-signalling people demand the destruction of the constructs of preceding generations while fuelling in the Third World the sickening slaughter of the poor and oppressed, who, under threat of death and butchery, are robbed of their true worth, driven to grow not food for their families, but plants that make the product that reaches the toilet stalls in nightclubs and university bars in our safe little world. I sit stunned by his observation, feeling suddenly responsible for the failings of a whole generation. My flag-waving swagger of technological pride is entirely gone.

Gramsci, seeing in my face the questioning look of someone whose iron-certain belief has rusted, changes tack to shift the ills of the modern world from my generation in general to his old enemy, the capitalist controllers of wealth. He continues by adding that the more money people have, the greater their fear of losing it. Their desperation to hang on to it reduces their connection to the true value of things, to what brings joy in working folk, like the smile of a newly born baby or the caring neighbour who, without being asked, mows the grass of an elderly couple whose once pristine lawn has become overgrown. He expands from this to the dumping of grain into the sea, not to feed the fish but to keep the price of bread, that essential of the poor, artificially high to protect the futures traders and giant conglomerate multinationals' fat profits. He describes the antics of federations in building fences to disadvantage the workers of those nations beyond, and bemoans the false premise of international co-operation, when every state is pulling for itself in a loaded tug-of-war.

Trelawny, as though protecting me from having to carry a weight that Gramsci may wish us all to carry, interjects and says, 'Did you know that Antonio formed the Italian Communist Party, Finn, and was a very radical thinker back in his day? Although, as you can see, his politics are much more to the right these days.'

They all laugh at Trelawny's jest. Gramsci smiles his toothless smile, then laughs heartily. 'Have you met Sanchez?' he asks, as Shelley, floating feet pointed to the ceiling, dips his tongue into the wine glass of another guest, a fat, balding man who smells of cigars.

Sanchez again.

'Not yet.'

'Ask Sanchez about your generation, and the generations before yours.' Then, to lighten his somewhat accusatory delivery, he adds, with a sympathetic smile, 'And my generation too. He is an interesting fellow.'

I am suddenly keen to return to the cemetery to seek out Sanchez, and suggest a move to Keats, but he waves his hand towards Shelley, who is now balancing on his head on the bar counter. 'You have all the time in the world, Finn.'

I watch as people come and go, and make use of Gramsci, who, probably unaware of Lady M's evenings educating me, seems to find pleasure in acting as my interpreter, perhaps applying a little balm to a wound he may feel he has inflicted on me as he translates conversations not intended for our unseen audience. A stunning woman, immaculate in a short figure-hugging black dress, low-cut, which has Shelley's attention, and mine, arrives, orders *caffè macchiato* and sits opposite us, legs crossed, looking at her watch repeatedly in between running red-painted nails through her dark brown hair. Her eyes are deep green, which adds a further tick to her beauty. My eyes are drawn to her intermittently between other distractions as she waits. There is an air of expectation about her, like a child on Christmas Eve.

I guess that the man who just sat down with this woman, who I take to be half his age, is squeezing her leg below the table. He arrived in a Maserati, which he parked opposite the open doors. His suit is expensive, shiny grey, his white shirt immaculately ironed, and his black shoes hand-stitched. They scream wealth. Rita gives him a professional smile and greets them both expansively as she places the macchiato on the table. He orders champagne without reference to the stunning girl he now has his arm draped around.

Trelawny leans across Severn and tells me this man is the *paparino*. I ask what that means and Gramsci says in his wonderfully rich accent, '*Paparino* is the sugar daddy.'

Rita brings champagne and two glasses and I notice that she raises her eyebrows and shakes her head gently, smiling, at a woman who sits beyond them, texting. Rita is careful not to be seen by the couple, but we all see, invisible spectators that we are.

Gramsci says, 'The lady doesn't approve, but neither does she condemn. We all have to forge a role in life. Better though that this girl had her own means to stand proud, free from this man's money. This is age-old,' he says, with a shrug, 'and some day we will see a time when everyone will have a place of dignity.'

Shelley is now sitting on a chair opposite the couple. The man is whispering to the woman, so Shelley leans across and puts his ear beside their mouths. 'Ah, such poetry. Only John could make silken words more beautiful,' he says with an affected air of innocence.

Keats laughs, turning to me. 'Percy mocks me, Finn. You must take no notice, for he is only attempting to get me to respond that only he could write words so poetic and abandoned as to break the heart of every woman who ever lived.'

There is a pleasure in this occupation of time. I have a fondness for observing life passing, that thing of people-watching, but always in the context of a time-limited experience such as sitting on an underground train wondering about my fellow passengers between stations on a journey to or from somewhere, or outside a café for a break in an otherwise planned day, where I might shoot a few frames to capture a moment to save it from being lost, of an elderly couple hand in hand, or the antics of dog-walkers or eccentric bag ladies passing. But here we are, all of us, with nothing but everlasting time. I have no plans other than to seek out Sanchez, and Rubens.

The blonde girl I took for one fleeting second to be Hannah stands, swings her bag up on to her shoulder, leans to kiss an older woman who I take to be her mother, then swishes out into sunlight. Hannah flicks into my thoughts again, then out as quickly as she arrived, as I refocus on the now, and Trelawny's current tale about a robbery in Greece, with himself and Lord Byron as the victims. Keats is again smiling at me with amusement at the man's facility of imagination. *Pinch of salt* sings out loud about these tales, but he is without doubt a master storyteller, and our little group is enthralled. Trelawny, I am learning, weaves his tales with the skill of a silkworm, tailoring aspects of each yarn to include every one of his listeners. Romance, beauty, passion; equality or the desire for it to satisfy Gramsci – all listeners wooed by the suspense and breathless excitement of his craft. I know I will never tire of Trelawny.

I remark to Severn, who has moved to sit beside me, having wandered through to the kitchen the better to smell the scent of cooking, that I seem to have left my sadness at my loss of Hannah and my family behind. I ask if I should be troubled by this. Have I become a sociopath?

'The things we held so dear are still dear, my friend. It is the absence of worry, and the acceptance that we cannot change the past, in essence the removal of regret from our being, that makes you think this way. Your loves will always be loves, but a sense of loss fades into happy reflections on times gone by.' He pauses. 'What do you know of our young friend John?' He gestures towards Keats, who is now himself in the kitchen sitting on a worktop watching the chef as he grinds nutmeg into a pan.

'Only that he died young in a state of bitterness at being taken from life so cruelly, parted from his great love Fanny Brawne.'

My puerile thought suddenly has me smirking about that name, which has changed context from Severn's time, I suspect.

'Indeed. Love has rarely cast its light so brightly on two lovers who have been so cruelly parted. But do you hear Keats lamenting the loss of Fanny?' My juvenile humour causes me to smirk again as Severn continues. 'No. For she will remain his love, without lamentation, as you will continue to love without loss, for love is eternal.'

He places a warming hand on mine.

'Thank you,' I whisper.

I cannot think of anything more expressive to say to Severn. I think that says it all. He smiles, and pats my hand again. I want to ask Severn about Shelley, and Mary, and Edward Ellerker Williams, and Leigh Hunt and so many others, but decide that these things can wait. I have, as John observed, all the time in the world.

The *paparino* pays in cash, and waves a dismissive hand with a smile to Rita signifying that the tip is of no account as he stands and offers his hand to his companion, who takes it and rises, smoothing her rucked dress with her other hand as we all, with the exception of Gramsci, look on with faint amusement.

'*Bambola!*'

Shelley. I recognise this word. *Guapa* in Spanish. Doll in American. Stunner in English. An appreciation of beauty, and of the desirability of such a sexy woman.

'Beware the *femministe*!' I say, laughing.

'Oh, but there has always been hypocrisy, Finn. You think it is reserved to your generation? To now? No, no, no. There have always been those who wish to condemn man and woman for wishing to be free. Free of the servitude of society. African slaves. Romeo and Juliet. Socrates and his appetite for the *eromenos* against the comedic excoriation of Aristophanes about grown men loving men of equal age, The Ladies of Llangollen, with whom I am acquainted. So many free thinkers constrained by mores and false values taken from the scriptures or the laws and theoretical constructs of men, or their villainous subjugation by others for profit or power. When in fact all that has value, all that has meaning, is simply the purity of beauty, love and imagination.'

Keats applauds.

'There you have truth,' remarks Severn to me. 'There is a man who proves that every day in your new life here is a day to be savoured with the freedom of imagination previously denied you. Say what you believe, think what you will, admire whatever is admirable to you. You will begin to appreciate that, despite what you may have feared in your first few days here, your eternal life here is one of joy, not of purgatory.'

Shelley who took a rather theatrical bow in recognition of Keats's hand-clapping, wanders outside, reappearing again moments later. This is a man by whom life, even this life beyond life, is truly lived.

Something approaching relief filters through me at Severn's words. For, despite my recent lack of worry, the thought has been with me that if I did not suffer an eternal and unendurable loss for my love, my Hannah, then surely boredom must set in here in this never-ending life. I take a careful look around at my restaurant companions, and notice that the customers vary, some content in their moment, happy to be eating fine food and drinking sumptuous wines, but the lady texting, to whom Rita gave the knowing look, is clearly anxious, and, like the *paparino*'s *bambola*, constantly checks her watch. Uncertainty, concern, worry, insecurity. All exhausting traits of human frailty. Even Rita, with her passion and personality overflowing, has concerns. A sick or fractious chef. A power failure plunging everything to black. A delayed delivery. Frosts in Tuscany. What ifs. Life is full of them. My little clique on the other hand have been here, some of them, for two hundred years, and yet they behave as though each day is their first. They laugh, converse, and entertain one another. Sometimes with deep and meaningful conversation, and other times with humour so sharp that any stand-up comedian would be thrilled to deliver even half such wit to a howling audience. Contentment. The unknown answered. Knowledge that the light beyond the purple is pure, with colours vivid to behold, and an eternal life so rich that every day is a joy. A joy that stretches into the distance, at least to the borders of this spirit existence.

I glance out to the street as I did only a few weeks previously, before I kissed Hannah goodbye and waved ham at her. Two men dressed in togas and sandals pause to look in, then continue on their way. It is a beautiful day. I am amazed by what I see.

# brighter than in life

I was intending to seek out Sanchez, but thoughts of him drift away as Shelley, with a conspiratorial nod, urges me out on to the street. I excuse myself from the others and stroll out to Via Galvani. Even the sprayed graffiti on the building that houses Masto has a new radiance to it. I have moved on my view of that vandalism from vague annoyance to a desire to talk to the unknown painters, to seek out their reason. The meaning of the words is lost to me, so I resolve to ask Gramsci. Maybe their story is a treasure to be unearthed.

The light seems ever more beautiful. There is a quality to the sky which is breathtaking, almost edible. Its blue is rich beyond belief, like a sea I long to dive into from a towering clifftop. I am reminded of looking down on the bones of a ship, broken and wrecked way below the cliffs in Zante. Of the snow-white rock beach and blue sea, turquoise of immensity, a sea made from precious stones. A small dab of cloud is way off to the west, and birds fly across it, silhouetted. I am warm all over. I am always warm. Never hot. Never cold.

Shelley breaks my skyward fascination. I remark to him that everything I experience appears brighter than in life, with scents and colours so immense, distinct and vibrant.

'Imagination. You are free of doubt and worry, and your imagination is now free. Every day is brighter. You are here because your imagination allows it. Sanchez will tell you otherwise, affording your imagination to something of his own imagination.'

'What is it that he imagines?'

'God.' He leans towards me and gestures with a beckoning finger. 'Let me show you a sight of true interest.'

'Why me alone?' I ask. I am curious, as Shelley was at pains to lead me away without bringing the others.

'I doubt Gramsci would approve,' he says whispering, adding intrigue. 'Nor John.'

He points upwards then levitates to a balcony two floors above the restaurant. I follow. There, on the bed, half undressed, is the girl with the *paparino*. *La bambola*. She is simply beautiful. Her skin is radiant, and surprisingly milky against black lace. Her dress has been pulled loosely together as though modesty requires it. The *paparino* is smoking.

Shelley makes a tutting sound with his tongue against the roof of his mouth, and turns to me with a look of disapproval. I am expecting him to make a remark about the lewdness of an older man frolicking with such a beautiful young woman.

'Dear me,' he says, 'spent already? I should have provided this beauty with sparks flying into the night. I, my young friend, would, if opportunity still allowed in this afterlife, have given a far better account of myself when presented with such riches.'

There is a side to Shelley which at first appears to be a conceit, but which is more and more evident as probably the greatest sense of humour of anyone I ever met. I relax, moving from feeling slightly embarrassed at our current act of voyeurism to laughing aloud. The more I experience of Shelley, the more content I am with this new world. In a few short weeks I have gone from feeling immense loss at losing both my love and my life, to laughing out loud on a voyeuristic jaunt which relegates my swimming pool escapade to a far distant second. Shelley strolls into the room, places a gentle kiss on the *bambola*'s exposed nipple, breathes smoke from the *paparino*'s cigarette, then for good measure slides a spirit hand inside her dress.

# truly free

As we stroll back into the inviting interior of Masto, Gramsci is speaking Italian to the group. It hits me again that I am a stranger in a foreign land. I am not meant to be here. The others have chosen this as their place of destiny, but not me. I am here by a simple twist of fate. If I had hung on to my spirit for a while longer, instead of whatever it was that made me leap out – the Japanese ladies' distress or a desire to return to Hannah – whatever it was, I should have hung on; I could be in Highgate Cemetery now, chatting with Karl Marx, Christina Rossetti and Malcolm McLaren, maybe getting singing lessons from George Michael. I could be watching Hannah place flowers at my grave, and gaining insight from Alexander Litvinenko on the Kremlin, or discussing the finer points of literature with George Eliot. So many possibilities, but here I am, a stranger in a foreign land.

Keats looks my way, and raises a hand. Gramsci stops.

'Do you know Italian, Finn?"'

'Only a very little, I'm afraid,' I say, uncertain that my conversations with Lady M have furnished me with any level of fluency, and with that edge of embarrassment typical of my countrymen, add, 'Typically English.'

'Ah, well, you will learn. Gramsci will teach you, and I will assist if allowed.'

He looks towards Gramsci, who, earnest as always, nods his approval.

There is something truly touching about this moment. Here I am, an ordinary man, twenty-eight years old, never to become twenty-nine, with a literary icon and a world-renowned political philosopher promising to make my new existence better for no other reason than that their spirits, like their lives before them, are motivated by love and kindness, and passion. I have a sudden wish that by some means I could pass back through the purple tube to regain my life, so that I could announce to the world that we exist after death, all of us, everywhere, and tell Hannah and my family and friends just what fabulous people I have met.

I turn to my assembled entourage and tell them all how much I appreciate their kindness, and friendship. I tell them of my thought, and, somewhat surprisingly, it is Trelawny who answers, for once not looking to embellish or exaggerate, but simply to tell me that every one of my compatriots, and probably every spirit soul walking this unimaginable Earth, has thought that exact thought. He adds that, despite their actions and ills in the physical world, the creators of war, deceit and hatred, when passed to this life beyond, are as they were in terms of character but cannot act as they did; that they no longer have the power to hurt or enrage or terrify, and so are of no consequence to the good people this side of the mirror. As he puts it, they are mere immortals.

Keats leans forward towards me.

'This is true, Finn: even the rogues of history have no power here. Power to build, or to knock down, is gone. The power of words rests only in the listener's wish to hear and appreciate, or to ignore and let drift as pollen blows. The power to influence or dominate is gone. Much to Gramsci's delight, we, all of us here' – he sweeps his hand to encompass our gathering and Percy, who is again sitting on the bicycle – 'are equal. No leaders, no followers, no kings, no slaves. Women and men alike. No rich, no poor. All equal. All truly free. There are those who have thoughts impure as they had about their fellows in the physical world, and this is their purgatory, but the beauty of our afterlife is that such men and women are alone here, for they cannot harm. In this place, no man may be cut and made to bleed. The only power left to those beyond physical death is to enjoy this new world, or not. That is their choice, Finn. You will find that most choose to see beauty.'

Keats. I am past disbelieving in my spirit. If only I could find the purple light, the tale I could tell!

As though that speech closes our business, Shelley drops down from the bicycle and saunters to the door, pausing for a second to savour the exquisite scent of Rita's perfume as he passes.

Outside, the day is more beautiful than I remembered. Rainbows hanging from apartment balconies along Via Galvani that, when I walked along this very street a few weeks earlier, hand in hand with Hannah, had been merely the washing of ordinary people drying in the sun.

I ask Gramsci about the graffiti. He glances up and down the façade either side of Masto and simply shrugs. 'It is known only to the creator.'

'To God?'

'There is no God. The creator of the work. My generation used such paints to make a statement of resistance, to denounce the government of corrupt officials and Mussolini. Your generation make signs that are labels of them, their name or some twist on it that they think makes them unique. Always labels now. Slogans and tattoos. These people. Everyone occupied with self and celebrity, and trying so hard to be what they are not. We come into this world without asking, but we are defined, not by how wealthy or successful we are, not by the things we believe mark us out from others – we are defined by how we live, by how we move through the world and what we leave behind. We all leave something of us behind, whether that is a smile of remembrance or a sigh of relief from someone glad that we are gone. We all end up the same, Finn. Six feet under. Fashion-makers, moguls, tyrants, plumbers, doctors, teachers, thieves. All end up being the same in the ground. It is thought and words that make people unique, and deeds. It is not your fault that your generation thrives on creating something from nothing. On creating instant heroes, as though eating the things that an aboriginal people have eaten for thousands of years to stay alive as some sort of entertainment on a television show can make someone the kind of person you wish to spend time with or aspire to be. I ask you, what is celebrity? In prison I ate things those people would retch at, because I had to, to stay alive, to outlive Mussolini. He outlived me, but I suspect he hides below ground now, with his shame, alone. It is humanity that makes people worth aspiring to be, and deeds of kindness and generosity. When you meet him, ask Sanchez about deeds and the Church. Every person these days wearing a shirt with the names of élites. Millions wearing fashion designer shirts. I have a question for you Finn, about John Smith or his sister Jane.'

He pauses, so I say, 'Ask me, Antonio.'

'Does Calvin Klein wear a shirt with John Smith printed on it? Or Jane Smith? Or Finn Chambers?'

He then smiles, laughs wheezily, and walks ahead, a point well made. I look down at my prized Old Skool shoes, and instantly feel the need to laugh out loud.

Gramsci stops a short way along Galvani and stands looking through the shop window of D'Angelo Elettrodomestici where a huge television is showing a news feed, waiting for me to catch him up. I look at the screen. A missile is shown blasting off and heading out to sea, while Asian men in uniform smile and clap.

He shakes his head ruefully.

'Men of war,' he says, shaking his head again, adding, 'Seven years after the fascist dictator Mussolini came to power here in 1922, the Great Crash in America saw men of greed jumping to their death from skyscrapers for the loss of money, while poor people starved, desperate to live, and farmers destroyed food to keep prices high. When war erupted ten years later, the same starving poor of America, the white and black, fought side by side, as all-men-created-equal, but when the battle was over they were segregated again, and once more became "negroes", vilified and treated like disease by those who had encouraged them to lay down their lives for a country they had been begged to believe in, but which did not believe in them. And that, in truth, is a blight for which every generation since slavery carries a responsibility.'

I interject. 'But these things are way before my time, Antonio. How are we, my generation, to blame for what happened in the past?'

He looks me steadily in the eye before replying.

'We cannot undo the past – none of us has that gift – but every living person has a responsibility, whether they choose to acknowledge it or not, to learn from history, and to support the principle of equality, and accept that claim in others. Whatever our skin colour or experience, we all have the means to love others, to raise ourselves above the animals. Your generation cannot be absolved from guilt, Finn, for every generation carries shame. But there is always hope, for in every generation also there are so many good people who live life well, and so many more who will follow, and fight for others, for freedom, for justice, for equality. Eventually, who knows when, all people will be equal in life, as we now are in death. I do not, as you may have observed, believe in a god, but I do believe in the right of all to be equal.'

Gramsci pauses thoughtfully, adding idly, 'Do you think that if all the generals were women we would have this world?' He takes two steps then turns around to face me, as I unwrap the threads of my guilt from around me and stuff them into my pockets, like an unwanted tombola prize at some county fair. He smiles at my discomfort and says, more kindly, 'Indeed, you are right to be silent. We cannot put these labels on ourselves, for it is too easy for a lazy man to pin a badge to himself, or on to others, categorising everything as black or white when there is so much that is grey, so much that requires thought. A man like Sanchez is a man of thought. He is also a man who believes in God.'

He pauses. 'Each to his own, eh?' he adds in his heavy accent, smiling toothlessly as he turns away to follow the others along Via Galvani.

# changing times

Gramsci walks with ease for a man who, in life, was saddled with deformity and tragic ill health. His time as a political prisoner of Mussolini has left him toothless but nonetheless eloquent in speech, as interesting a character who ever spoke an original political thought, and a man held in great esteem by many as the founder of the Italian Communist Party. I am about to follow him when I decide to pause. I am in no hurry to rejoin the others, such is the beauty of everything around me. Keats was on the money: I have chosen beauty. It is everywhere. In the richness of colours. In the scent of flowers and aromas of cooking food drifting on the air. In the arcing flight of birds. In the shapes of clouds. In the goodness of heart of my new fellows. Beauty is everywhere. There is something ironic in the thought that I am becoming reconciled to my new-found lack of concern at a speed which would, in my former life, have been a serious cause for consternation, worry and self-examination.

I turn to look again into the window of D'Angelo Elettrodomestici, where the television is now showing a clay court tennis match. A taxi pulls to a sudden halt at the kerbside opposite Masto, and the driver, looking impatiently at his wristwatch, sounds the car horn. I think of Tariq, his calm demeanour, his hopes for his family, and his secret sex with his wife at the free drive-in. The same fat, balding cigar man into whose wine glass Percy had dipped his tongue earlier comes rolling out, dabbing at his sweating head, and climbs into the rear of the taxi with the grace of an elephant seal. He has barely pulled inside his briefcase and closed the door when it speeds off along Via Galvani. I wonder about Tariq. I hope he is safe.

I catch up to the group to hear Shelley and Keats talking about feelings. Shelley mentions Denis Diderot and Jean-Jacques Rousseau. Passion. He speaks with passion about these figures of the past whose names are unknown to me, and says, 'Would that they were here, gentlemen, for their vision would enliven our days.'

I take the opportunity, time now being what it is, a limitless commodity, to seat myself on the bonnet of a battered Renault and listen to Shelley and Keats entertain us, and find myself, someone who had never given too much thought to political ideas, fascinated by Gramsci's theories, so well explained that even I can understand. He does not lecture, but questions the structure of society, and asks how it is that the capitalist and political élites con us into the notion of *common sense*, to control us and maintain a status quo where the powerful remain at the head of the pyramid and the workers keep on working, increasing the wealth of the powerful; where *common sense* reassures us that this is the best we should aspire to. My new world. A world not of indefinite non-existence but of interest, of learning, of joy. A world which, despite my initial sense of hopelessness, loss and regret, is filled with promise, and the newness of difference in every coming day.

They are all seated or draped on the roofs and bonnets of parked cars. Trelawny is lying outstretched, propped on his elbow on top of an old Mercedes, listening intently. It strikes me that even among such illustrious company as Gramsci, who is a man of relatively recent times, Shelley and Keats, Trelawny and Severn, centuries after their deaths, seem like men of now. They are the diviners of beauty who search for the essence within everything that surrounds them. From nature and man. They are enquirers, and translators. Observing elements that few can see, they create vivid pictures for those such as me who cannot easily distil feelings, and paint scenes of beautiful and enthralling events, people and loves in poetry and prose for others to read.

Severn has ceased to surprise me with his youthfulness. There is an injustice in the living world that the elderly, having given so much during their lifetimes, and often having sacrificed their own enjoyment for the benefit of their children, should be rewarded with a creaking, resentful, arthritic body that pains them at every turn until they are gratefully set to rest below the soil. Yet here, in this glowing afterlife, they suffer no more, but regain the movement of the young, as though every joint has been greased and lubricated by an unseen mechanic, just as Claudio restores quiet ease to a grinding gearbox or worn linkage in a steering system.

A man dressed in office garb, shirt-sleeves rolled up and tie loosened, approaches the Renault, opens the driver's door and throws his linen suit jacket and a leather folder on to the passenger seat before sliding in. He starts the engine, winds down his window, lights a cigarette and, releasing the handbrake with an unconscious movement, selects first gear and with a swift backward glance drives off. I am still seated cross-legged on the bonnet in front of him. I am invisible. He watches the road ahead through me, taking a snatched look at his wristwatch. Time. Human living time. I wave at my friends, to their great amusement, as we head up Via Nicola Zabaglia. I jump off at Via Caio Cestio, and savour the aroma of gardenias drifting across the crumbling wall of a corner villa. The scent of flowers is everywhere. I drift up to the wall ridge and sit for a moment looking down on a most beautiful garden, laid out in ornate symmetry, of classical Italian form, where an elderly couple are engaged. The woman is on her knees, foam kneeler easing her aches, weeding between lavender bushes. The man is reading *Il Messaggero*, seated at a wrought-iron table, drinking what looks to be brandy, from the colour and shape of the glass. A bit early in the day, but who am I to judge? I died from such quality. I pass a pleasant hour simply sitting on their wall, watching them and listening to birdsong. I resolve to spend more time with them, but not now.

I drop down to the pavement, and walk through the leash connecting a mongrel dog to his mistress. I have often thought that funny. The concept of dog and master. Being realistic, who is served by whom? The dog-owner walks the dog, whether they want to or not, come rain or shine, because the dog needs a walk. The dog shits anywhere it decides, and the owner in the rain-soaked coat has to scoop up this reward in a bag and carry it to a bin to dispose of. The owner shops to buy food for the dog and feeds the dog when the dog demands, and the dog may turn up its nose if it perceives the wrong brand or is simply bored by the same old flavours. The dog takes the best seat in front of the winter fire, and frequently claims the softest side of the owner's bed. If the dog gets sick, the owner drives it to a veterinary surgeon, and parts with vast quantities of hard-earned cash to find a cure; but if the owner should fall ill they struggle on working to avoid paying a doctor's bill. So who is really master or mistress – dog, or owner? I shall ask Shelley, or Gramsci.

I stay on this side of the street and stroll into Claudio's workshop. Claudio has changed the month page along his entire collection of Pirellis. Every one changed from this morning's display. I am standing staring at Inés Sastre. April 1997.

'I thought I would find you here.'

Shelley. Grinning.

'Does he change them every day?' I ask.

'Mondays. He changes them every Monday lunchtime. Today is Monday. He is a man of ritual. He eats his lunch. He turns on the coffee machine. While the coffee brews, he changes the month along the row, each one, then he pours coffee and replies to his telephone messages. He writes with chalk on the board.'

Shelley nods his head towards a blackboard above a workbench beside the wash basin, which has various notes chalked, some with lines drawn through.

'Do you come here often?' I say, like a clichéd character in a bad film.

'Often. I like it here. Here resides a man of interesting hues. He is a man who loves cars as he loves women. He respects them, their beauty, their worth, their character and personality, and their challenges. He tends to these things with the care he gives to his life. You cannot ask more of anyone. You see his car there? When you see him working on that car, you see a man in love. That was his father's car. His father started this business, then retired, leaving the business to his son, and died I know not where but not here as he has never returned. I fancy the son does not really want to complete his task. Once completed, he will have to drive it, and then he will yearn for another to rebuild. He is like a medical man. He nurtures back to life, but, once the patient can breathe unaided, he must apply himself to saving another. His woman is loved. Truly loved. He says it with his eyes. Shakespeare knew. It is the eyes that are the windows to the soul.'

He moves along the Pirelli line, and pauses by Peter Lindbergh's shot of Navia Nguyen. April 1996. He saunters past me and Inés, along the line in rising date order, pauses by April 2005, Candice Huffine, and again by 2017, then turning towards me, eyebrows raised, says, 'Changing times, eh, Finn?' as he turns and walks off, passing straight through Claudio who is walking in from outside, wiping his hands on an oily rag.

# no greater weight

The gardener sits beside the toolshed eating cheese on bread. Simple food. Often the best. He pours coffee, black as ink, into a small clear glass, and savours its aroma before washing down his meal. I have spent uninterrupted time, contemplating this new life, watching the foxes, and marvelling at the changes through nights and days, which slide away unnoticed. I am now watching birds in the trees above me, and the to-ings and fro-ings of my fellow residents, the gardener, and a steady stream of visitors from my former world, as I lounge on the flat tomb-top of Devereux Plantagenet Cockburn, aged just twenty-one at his exit. I lie weightless beside the carved shape of that poor man, whose spirit must be elsewhere, as this tomb sees no spirit enter or leave.

A pair of parakeets whip past, flashing green, then gone. Shelley approaches from the visitor centre, and, to amuse himself, or me perhaps, he leapfrogs over a bored-looking boy of six or seven who trails his parents. I stand to greet Percy, and look from the gardener's boots, coated in fine dust, to Shelley's shoes, which are shiny bright with a silver buckle. I look then at my sneakers. We do not collect dust. We do not exist.

A week or more has passed since the last mention of Sanchez, and Shelley has finally again offered to introduce me to him, so we stroll along the flowery pathways towards the pyramid, passing various souls as we go, Shelley introducing me, as we pass, to anyone I haven't yet met, for there are many here who surface occasionally, as though to check their bearings, before resting again away from the eyes of others. I feel a faint glow of embarrassment as he introduces me to William Wetmore Story, and his charming wife, Emelyn. My cheeks feel as though a slight tinge colours them as I shake hands with the man I had silently censured for his irreverence on seeing him perched on one wing of the *Angel of Grief*, not knowing that he was both the creator of this beautiful sculpture and the rightful resident of the tomb, perfectly entitled to sit wherever the hell he chose.

Chagrined by my ill-informed judgement of before, I am pleased to move on along the path, leaving the Storys behind. As we pass Shelley's tomb, site of my demise, I ask Shelley about Edward Ellerker Williams, whose stone is laid beside his.

'There are those who, however fleeting their worldly life may be, touch us deep within our soul, and therein leave a mark that is forever. Such is the mark that Edward left with me. His spirit, however, does not reside here, but, from what little I know, dances on the sands of Livorno, or through the olive groves of Tuscany. Wherever it is, his dance is not here, although his stone bears witness to a friendship forever shared.'

I decide to ask no further, for fear that I have touched on something that I have neither the need nor the right to pry open. Not my business. I would have liked to make another enquiry, and ask of Mary and the tale of Frankenstein, but those questions can wait. We walk on, Shelley bouncing back from his moment of wistfulness, a sudden spring to his step as he points to a lone figure standing way down the gardens by the railings designed to save the unwary visitor from falling to the sunken ground below, where, unbeknown to them, Roman generals walk. His hands are clasped behind his back, his face raised towards the sun.

'Sanchez?'

'The very same,' answers Shelley. 'Take some time to know this man, Finn, for he has great wisdom about him and much of interest to speak about.' Then he adds with a smirk, 'Though you may find him a little on the religious side, somewhat devout in the theories of God and the heavens as he is.'

Shelley laughs out loud as though this is some side-splitting joke, then stifles his frivolity as Sanchez turns, suddenly aware of our approach, as though he has been rudely awoken from a dream. He is alone in this part of the cemetery with the exception of two women I have not seen before who are perched high on a granite tomb, the base of which is surrounded by small angels of green stone.

Sanchez has the air of a man torn. I do not know why that is my first impression, but it is. Something about him suggests the stern teacher who really wants to laugh with the misbehaving child, but dare not, in case all authority is then lost; or the policeman who, expected to arrest the teenage boy smoking cannabis behind the community centre, merely takes it from him, hits on the spliff, drops it to the ground and grinds it with his boot, before smiling and saying, *Don't let me catch you again, Bob Marley*, as he exhales smoke into the frosty night before walking on. There is a mix of authority and humanity, or maybe God and man, that is immediately both intriguing and appealing about him. I am grateful for Shelley's nudge. Sanchez is clearly a man to know. But who is he?

Shelley eyes Sanchez calmly, waiting for a move. Sanchez stands his ground, a look of expectation about him, eyeing us both, then moves slowly towards us. Shelley breaks the silence.

'Father Bernabe Sanchez of Mexico, man of the cloth, I present to you the English atheist Mr Finn Chambers.'

I extend my hand and splutter a response, saying, 'So delighted to finally meet you, Father,' adding, 'I'm not sure that the title bestowed by Percy is completely correct.'

Shelley laughs again. 'Just my little joke for Bernabe,' he says, 'for who am I to judge your belief?'

'I think you will find in time that Percy is both judge and jury when it suits him,' says Sanchez, accepting my hand. 'He tries to deny the existence of God, as he thrives on mischief, but I think below that cloak you will find great humanity, and a true man of God. For who, knowing what we all now know who are here with our forebears, and even with the people of ancient Rome, could deny the hand of God in this Heaven?'

Shelley, as if to reinforce his enigmatic status, or simply out of respect for Sanchez, bows to each of us in turn, makes his excuses, then drifts through the safety barrier and, turning slow aerial somersaults, glides down towards the Romans. I am left alone, in awe of a man I know nothing about, but who clearly is revered by some of the greatest men in history. Under normal life conditions I guess I would be shaking at the prospect of engaging with such a man. But normal life no longer exists.

Sanchez takes a seat on a large rectangular tomb, one of the plainest edifices in this quiet, less-festooned part of the gardens. My immediate thought is that of course a man who chose consciously to shun the glitter and pomp of life would settle on such a setting for quiet contemplation. A man of piety. Not necessarily a pious man, for that word, for me and I suspect for Shelley too, carries a note of sanctimonious arrogance about it. I sit on the adjacent tomb, even plainer than that which supports Sanchez's ethereal body, and feel strangely calm.

'I was sorry to learn of your demise here, Finn.'

His speech is tender, and honest. There is no coating to his words. They are what they are. His accent is South American Spanish, rich and melodic. Although I have plenty of time to get to know Sanchez, my inquisitive nature urges me on.

'How did you come to be here, Father? In Rome? In this cemetery?'

'Mine is a long story, Finn – and please, call me Bernabe. I am here because I ran away from God.'

There is solemnity and honesty to his words. I start to wish I had been less direct. This is still all too new, and makes me once again realise that I do not belong here with the great men of literature, history and principle. I belong with Hannah, drinking red wine, laughing and carousing, holding hands and kissing in the street. I am a superficial person whose days are measured by the number of kisses with a beautiful girl, drinks consumed, photographs taken, and minutes spent laughing. It is apparent in this moment that I am a man of simple enjoyments with few responsibilities, who has carried very little weight in life. Now that I am dead I have no responsibilities at all from my previous life, but face having to evaluate the stories of others. It feels as though I am entrusted with the scales of justice in some form.

'I am sorry to have intruded, Bernabe, I had no right.'

'Oh, but you have every right here, Finn. We discuss much, and we are finally free to be who we are. It is the strangest thing, is it not, that death has brought us all such freedom as we never could have felt while alive? For me personally, my belief in God, which was strong for the most part throughout my life, is now fully realised, and every day I rejoice in that. Regret is a thing we can ascribe to experience born from our worldly life and the follies of our humanity, but here? Here we can be our true selves. There are many things that with time – which no doubt you are now aware is infinite – will be answered for you.

'You may have noticed that there are not so many people here that they are living one on top of the other? By that I mean for example that you do not see our earliest ancestors, the men of flint and stone. The only explanation I can suggest for this is that they did not understand either God or the limitations on the spirit, so that they have passed into dissolution by following their nomadic instinct. There are also many who by choice rest within the ground where they were laid, content to lie undisturbed with their memories. The likes of you and me and Percy, however, are enquirers by nature, and I believe it is this that brings us out, to marvel at God's world. Percy will of course deny God, and this is his right, but I cannot do the same. Our friends in togas have their own beliefs, but those beliefs all come back to God. A rose by any other name is still a rose.'

I turn towards the pyramid and look down to the grass below at the Romans, a group of whom are laughing at some Latin joke being told by a woman who is stunningly beautiful. I wonder whether her joke is that funny, or her little group just want to please her. I am struck then by Bernabe's words: that here we can be our true selves. I guess that her joke *is* that funny. Shelley is sitting on a broken fluted column, eyeing her up and down.

'Belief is a strange thing, Finn,' continues Sanchez in his lilting, melodious tones. There is a hint of mariachi band to his speech that makes listening to him particularly pleasant: an unexpected treat, like hearing the distant strains of a Salvation Army band playing for Christmas shoppers in Bond Street. 'In this afterlife there is a certainty, a complete confirmation of the existence of God, that is undeniable. Yet, in my previous earthly life, I was tested and found wanting. My trust in my own Church became ripped and torn. You may not believe in the same things as me, Finn, and why should you? Many here profess belief in other things – in imagination and the spirit as an entity in itself, for instance – but none of these things takes away the existence of God for me. What took away my belief, and tested me before God, was man's inhumanity to his fellow man, and the artificial barriers and hypocrisies created by my very own Church. These are things which I now see are tests for those of us on Earth who aspire to be at one with God. Tests which men fail, and which I see now were never possible to pass perfectly, for perfection belongs only to God.'

I want to ask Sanchez about his references to his Church, decide to save that for another time, then think 'sod it' and ask anyway.

'How did your Church fail you? Surely a priest has prestige and a place of advantage within a Church?'

'Were you raised Catholic?' Sanchez has a slight smile lighting his lips as he asks.

'No, I was raised without any particular religion. Just prayers at bedtime as a child, and morning assembly at school.'

'I am Mexican. We are raised either with Catholic certainty or secular disbelief. All I ever wanted was to be a priest, living a simple life, trying to reach the people, and bring them to God. But in my time there was much to be ashamed of within my Church, and within my country. What do you know of the Cristero War?'

I confess I have never heard of it.

'Put simply, it was a war between the secular government of President Calles and the Catholic Church. It was much more complicated than that suggests, involving secular laws and the constitution, but beneath that simple view lay the deaths of many thousands of people in nineteen-twenties Mexico. Many were good people. Simple and devout. My Church, that most revered of institutions, never seems to recognise its own destructive path. Many times throughout its history it has failed to recognise that taking from the poor to build churches littered with gold and art and other symbols of wealth is not the way to celebrate the life of Jesus Christ. It is intended to intimidate its congregations. It represents power. It detracts from worship and the teachings of the Bible and of Jesus, and gives legitimacy to secularism, to those who will say that God is simply a construct by those in power to maintain that power over the peoples of the world. If you listen to Percy on that subject, you will hear a case well argued.

'In the midst of the crisis of violence and hatred that swamped Mexico, I ran. I had believed myself to be a man of God, Finn, a man of fortitude and belief, who would always be protected by God, because I was doing God's work. But when I received threats to my life I hid my clothes of office and abandoned my church in San Miguel de Allende. I put myself ahead of everything I had believed, and everything I had preached. I was a hypocrite.

'The peasants believed. They became organised, and so many fought with passion, losing their lives by proclaiming against the government, holding strong in their belief in God and their Church. They believed the Church would save them, but that very Church fuelled their plight by passing money to their organisers to buy arms to kill those who attacked the Catholic Church.

'They had more faith in God than me, their priest. I am relieved now to know that those who died were not cast into an empty void, that this Heaven in which we find ourselves was what awaited them, for I doubted the existence of God, and the possibility of eternal life after death in a Heaven as beautiful as this. I denied God, as Peter denied Jesus. I was mortal and weak. Despite my wishes, I found that I suffered the same fears as the next man. I was no different. In fact, I was much worse, as those who truly believed were willing to lay down their lives in the certain belief that they would ascend to Heaven. I did not. I changed my name, and stole the identity of a peasant I had buried. He had died fighting the army of President Calles, but his resemblance to me was sufficient that we could have been taken for brothers, twins perhaps. We were so alike. His wife had placed his identity card together with a photograph of herself in a glass shrine with a small statue of Our Lady beside his grave. I couldn't bring myself to look at Our Lady as I opened the box to steal, but, fearing abduction and torture more than the wrath of God, I took his card. I took the soul of Ignacio Pérez Hernández. I was so afraid. I betrayed my congregation, my beliefs and my God, to save my own skin. I sought only sanctuary, to escape the conflict around me. I was a coward.

'I sought the help of a priest I knew who had contacts with the Knights of Columbus in Aguascalientes, took money from him under the pretext that I wished to give it to the Cristeros in my diocese, and headed south, as far as I could go, slipping across the border into Guatemala. I had posted my vestments and passport ahead, to a priest I had studied with at the seminary, who had a congregation in San Mateo Ixtatán, and eventually, with his help, and the help of Catholic priests along the way who fed me and provided shelter, I ran as far as Panama.

'I carried guilt light as a pebble at first, Finn, then it became a stone, heavier with each day that passed, until I had the weight of the world on my shoulders. For there is no greater weight than that which a man creates for himself.'

I am enthralled. In my living days I think I would have been more inclined to judge Sanchez, but now I am willing to listen and not speak, for fear of breaking a spell and being denied what Sanchez has to reveal. I sit tight. Shelley has jumped up to the garden again, but makes no play of coming to interrupt.

I notice only that shadows are starting to lengthen, and that the green of the grass below my dangling feet is intensely radiant.

Sanchez takes my agreeable silence as a sign.

'That weight grew to become intolerable. Every day I sought forgiveness from God, and every night I slept the sleep of the wretched, until I was exhausted and desperate with guilt. I resolved to make my way to the Holy See. I planned to throw myself at the feet of Pope Pius XI and seek his mercy and forgiveness, believing that I would receive absolution from him, as God's representative on Earth. I found a freighter at Panama City bound for Bari and begged passage, once again wearing my clothes of office, for you see, my hypocrisy knew no limit. I had exchanged fear for my life for fear of excommunication. I had abandoned both my Church and my belief as easily as a warm man takes off an outer coat. There came a point when I, a man who only ever wanted to do good and to serve God, could no longer look in the mirror. That is a wretched place to be, Finn.'

He pauses, appears to listen to the sound of early evening birds chattering, then carries on.

'I begged money from churches in Bari, whose priests were sympathetic to my plight. I recounted my flight from Mexico and my wish to seek an audience in Rome. I had no money other than some Panamanian *balboas*, which were useless in Italy, but they were generous. Generous men who thought little of helping a fellow priest in distress. What would they have thought of me had they known that in my cowardice I had robbed a grieving widow of the only photograph she possessed of her brave and butchered husband? A man who would never see his own child born from his pregnant wife, until he released his spirit. I realise now of course that he probably witnessed my theft, and his wife's distress when she discovered his identity card gone.

'There are many here who have gone to their grave with guilt or regret, but it is the nature of God to forgive. I no longer feel that dreadful guilt, for, as you know, we are relieved of such burdens, but I sympathise with those here who had regrets at the end. Percy, for example, and John, of course. Fine men who died unfulfilled with much unsaid. And then there is Antonio, who suffered greatly for his beliefs, far more bravely than me.'

His candour is impressive. I find myself admiring this man, for death appears to have removed my judgemental inclination. In life I prided myself on being open-minded, a modern man, a man of reason; but in truth I had been inclined to label others, like so many of my peers. Labels. Slogans. Bald statements about matters I made subjective assumptions about. I was guilty of that arrogance, although I carried my own small shame within. Yet what was my source of guilt in life? The shoplifting theft, aged seven, of a chocolate bar, which preyed on my mind for years. Here was a man who did a very human thing in horrendous times, when priests were being tortured and thrown from cliffs like discarded dolls. I am starting to see my theft as of little consequence, and my subjectivity for what it was.

I make no effort to move away or excuse myself, and wait patiently for Sanchez to tell me more.

'There is a time in life that some men face and some are lucky to not have to face. It concerns the destruction of a man's belief in the very core of his being; the reason he gets up from his bed every morning with purpose in his mind. His reason for taking breath. I arrived in Rome with a preconceived notion, which I had played and replayed a thousand times on my journey across the Atlantic Ocean, as the ship rose and fell on that great expanse. That notion was that I would prostrate myself before Pope Pius, confess my sin, my failings, my dishonesty, and my betrayal both of the Catholic Church and of God. In my mind-play, Pope Pius offered me his hand, whereupon I kissed the Holy Ring of Office on his finger, as he pulled me gently to my feet and forgave me in softly spoken

Latin, making the sign of the cross on my forehead, to show me that God had forgiven me.'

He smiles wanly, and gives a slight shake of his head, which is almost imperceptible.

'I was overawed by the Vatican City. It is of a scale I had not imagined. Everywhere there is majesty. Wealth. Luxuries that I had never dreamed of. I entered the building through a huge oak doorway which led into a grand hallway sumptuous with fine leather sofas with red silk cushions, the most beautiful paintings of Biblical scenes adorning the walls, and everywhere, gold. The fitments and ornamentation were all of exquisite quality. In terms of the myths of the Americas, this was El Dorado. Riches beyond imagination.

'The official ushered me into a side room, which itself was magnificent with a huge oak desk and armchairs like the thrones of a king. He offered me refreshment, but I declined, so intimidated was I by the opulence and grandeur of that place. My clothes were shabby, and I smelled of stale sweat. The official, a priest just as I was, was immaculately dressed and smelled of perfume. I waited for what seemed an eternity, until I was joined by another official, who motioned me to sit as I stood from respect when he entered the room. He listened, expressionless, as I related my tale. I told him my name, my church's name, and that of the diocese in San Miguel de Allende. I told him only that I had received threats to my life, and that I had fled to escape torture and execution. I explained that I had come several thousand miles, halfway across the world, to seek an audience with Pope Pius, to seek forgiveness for my sins, in the hope of being reassigned as a missionary, or to some other post, whatever the Holy See saw fit for me, as my penance. I did not elaborate further.

'He made notes with a beautiful onyx pen. He then carefully blotted the notepaper, replaced the cap on the pen with a flourish, picked up the paper and excused himself, leaving me sitting in the smallest of the thrones, which I had selected as the most humble place within that room. I waited a considerable time, staring from one Biblical scene to another. I knew little of art, although I knew a great deal of the images in front of me. Scenes of John the Baptist, the sufferings of Jesus, Salome's dance to entice Herod to fulfil her demands, the conversion of Saint Paul on the road to Damascus. So many paintings of incredible beauty by Titian, Delacroix, Perugino, Raphael and Giotto. Unimagined riches. I felt privileged and overawed at the same time. But then, as I sat there gazing at my surroundings, a sense of offence started to flow through me at the vulgarity of such excess.'

He pauses, as though hesitant to say more, but continues. 'I started to wonder what God would make of this luxury in his name. I had served the poor and seen their wretchedness, and crossed through Guatemala, Honduras, Nicaragua, Costa Rica and Panama and seen poverty that brought shame on the riches of my Church. A sense of sudden anger rose within me that the Catholic Church and the Mexican government had both made use of others to further their aims, that even the Ku Klux Klan and the Knights of Columbus had had a hand in the mayhem that my country had endured. I wondered what God made of that.

'I was startled out of those thoughts by the entry into the room of a man in fabulous robes of rich scarlet. A cardinal. I stood up and held out my hand, which was ignored as he brushed past me, robes swinging as though a breeze had blown in. He sat in the large throne, and the priest who had made the notes about me took the seat next to him. I was given no indication to sit, so I remained standing. The cardinal sat stiffly, glancing through a file. It had never occurred to me that the Holy See had such immense bureaucracy. No thought that the vast distance from San Miguel de Allende to Rome was of little account, that an organisation as powerful and complex as the Catholic Church had cardinals, archbishops and bishops who charted and recorded the activities of their priests, as an army of generals, captains and sergeants keeps tabs on its foot soldiers.

'The cardinal glanced up occasionally from the papers within this file to eye me coldly. My indiscretions appeared to have been recorded, and my destiny already decided upon. He wrote briefly on the file, announced that I had betrayed both God and the Holy Catholic Church, informed me that I was now excommunicated, and stood to leave, with a parting wish that God would hold me to account in the next life. I begged for an audience with Pope Pius, but as he left he turned and barked that His Grace could not have his place next to God sullied by one such as me. He swirled out of the room with the air of effrontery he had brought with him, and the priest ushered me to the door without expression or comment. My rehearsed scene was over, with an ending I had not imagined.'

Sanchez has no air of bitterness about him. He has told a story which, I have to admit, if related to me in the bar at the Knickerbocker, I would probably have considered had a fitting ending for a priest who had abandoned his parishioners to save his own skin. Then again, perhaps I would have taken the counter-view, that priests are just mortal men, with fears and doubts to contend with like every other man and woman.

Sanchez continues. 'There is an irony to my story. Those fellow priests who stayed and were tortured and executed are saints now. I am glad for them, now that I know their souls are safe in this Heaven.'

I am curious to know how Sanchez coped with excommunication, so I ask.

'I was, as you may imagine, bereft. I simply could not believe that a religious man like the cardinal could deny me the forgiveness of God, and the possibility of redemption through service to the Church. I was willing to do anything to atone, and, on being denied that and cast aside, I confess, Finn, I felt great anger and bitterness towards my Church. That a man surrounded by luxuries and wealth, on a scale that neither I nor my congregation of peasant farmers and housemaids could ever have imagined, should cast me out without hearing my plea or understanding the brutality I had feared, was a hypocrisy. I resented his comforts, and the adornments of his office angered me to a point where I wished never to be readmitted to the Catholic Church, to ever break bread or hear confession again.' Sanchez smiles at me. 'However, I was not angry by nature, Finn. My father was a patient and quiet man, and my mother was kind and loving. I inherited much from them.'

It strikes me then that Sanchez is describing my parents, and Hannah's, and their qualities of love and kindness. I think of them all then with fondness, and I wish for happiness for them. My sense of loss has shifted from anguish to radiance, to an all-encompassing feeling of wishing everyone well, which I now recognise is what allows Sanchez his own inner peace. Shelley, Keats and me. Sanchez. Lady Mary von Haast. Severn. Gramsci. We all have a sense of peaceful radiance about us.

'So how did you come to be here?' I ask. 'This is the non-Catholic cemetery. Should you not be elsewhere?'

'My story has not reached its end, Finn. After my excommunication, my resentment was fevered. I swung between anger and dismay. What was I to do? How could I restore myself with God? I had little money, and no chance of readmission to the Church which had always put a roof over my head and food on my table. I approached several priests for help, and was rejected. The communication network of the Catholic Church in Rome was highly efficient, and although now, in this modern age, they can communicate with every priest on Earth within seconds, although this was long ago, in nineteen twenty-nine, their networks were highly organised. I found that my fame, or rather my infamy, had spread rapidly. I had many doors closed in my face, until the kindness of one elderly priest fell my way.

'I was sitting in the rear doorway of a church not far from here, sheltering from heavy rains. The door opened and a young priest came out, opening his umbrella to fend off the rain. He suggested I go inside and talk to God, and as a little joke he said maybe I should ask God to stop the rain for an hour so I could dry out, for I was clearly in need. I thanked him and took a seat at a pew and prayed to God. I was kneeling deep in prayer when I heard sounds of movement inside the empty church. Feeling like a trespasser caught, I stood to leave and saw an elderly priest watching me intently. He approached me, and I mumbled an apology to him and made for the rear door. He asked me to wait, but I was wretched with shame and anger, and carried on towards the doorway. He caught me by the arm, and asked me if I would like to make my confession. I still had my uniform of priesthood, for I had no other clothes to wear. I stated that I was a man who was no longer allowed in God's house, but he smiled at me then and said that he knew who I was, and that God welcomed every man and woman, no matter their sins, to pray in his house.

'To make my story short, he listened to my confession, and forgave my sins. He provided refuge in a robing room within the church, and fed me. He was a good man. He had much cynicism in relation to the wealth of the Church. He told me tales of times when he had been a missionary in Africa and said that the honest smile of one poor child on being given a bowl of food and a prayer book meant more to him than all the gold of Rome. Father Gianni Falcone was his name. As good a man as any I ever met. He hid me in that room, allowing me to pray whenever the church was empty, and he made me believe again in the goodness of men. I had suffered some signs of illness during my sea crossing to Italy, and my health had deteriorated, but he nursed me as best he could, and his young priest, Aldo, ran errands for medicine and he, too, never showed me anything but kindness and understanding. It was pneumonia, although I had not suspected anything so severe. I died peacefully enough, sitting at a pew, praying to God.'

This was an incredible story. I could not have imagined such hardships, or such belief through adversity. Contrasted with my First World concerns about how my hair looked, and whether I had the latest version of iPad, Sanchez's tribulations put my past life in a file marked 'meaningless'.

'What happened then, Bernabe? I mean, how did you come to be buried here?'

'The Catholic Church arranged for me to be disposed of quietly. Buried in an unmarked grave here in this cemetery, created for those who cannot be close to God. Heretics who do not believe in the sacraments or teachings of the Catholic Church. Those who have no right to the inner enclosure; to be with the Catholic God, who' – he smiles widely – 'is different from, and better, obviously, than anyone else's God. It is a hypocrisy, like so many others, that the only God belongs to them. So here I am, and now I occupy that tomb that you sit on, so, if you seek me out and cannot see me, you know where to call my name.'

Sanchez's story takes some beating. Turmoil, terror, trial, tribulation and, ultimately, salvation. A happy ending even. I am keen to find Shelley, to seek out that famous atheist's justification for the non-existence of God, for Sanchez's belief is hard to ignore.

As a parting shot I ask Sanchez his age at death. Thirty-four. Just six years older than me, and my life experience so inconsequential in comparison. For a fleeting moment I wish

I had stolen a whole box of chocolate bars, but what would that prove? What weight would that amount to? Aged seven? Perhaps no weight at all. Or perhaps a weight I would have been unable to carry. Maybe we all carry weights of differing values, some light and easy, and some, like Sanchez's, so crushing that no man should have to bear it.

# a puddle of melting green

I leave Sanchez, my mind full of thoughts racing, a kaleidoscope of past events crashing up against my present. I am reminded of Gramsci's words that Sanchez has much to say about my generation and the intervening years from his time as a priest in San Miguel de Allende to now, and I am intrigued to hear Sanchez's opinion, just not today.

I think about seeking out Rubens, then decide that one interesting person of passion may be enough for one day, and flip a mental coin which falls in favour of a visit to the old couple in their villa garden, as the day still has some of the brightness of early evening. The simple lines of their beautiful garden have an immediate appeal in this moment of contemplation.

I turn cartwheels up Via Caio Cestio because I can. I haven't done that since I was maybe nine or ten years old, but something about my time with Sanchez makes me seek a little levity. I straighten up and leap over a passing child and his mother walking hand in hand, try a couple of handsprings for the hell of it, then jump up on to the wall at the villa, above the engraved brass nameplate: Casa di Pace. The child has an ice cream in his free hand, which looks like tutti-frutti, and I would have loved to either take a lick of it or knock the top off. The thought of knocking the top off is spurred by a memory of the loneliest day I can recall, when I was a student in London and all my friends were missing, visiting families for the weekend, or occupied with girlfriends or boyfriends at events I wasn't invited to.

It had been a beautiful early June day. Sunday. Hot and still – unseasonably hot. Finding myself at a loose end, and having no one to call on, I'd decided to walk along the towpath of the Regent's Canal from the Angel up towards Camden. I passed once-derelict warehouses which cute property developers had bought for a song and converted to canal-side apartments and loft spaces, now crammed with bankers and tech start-up gurus and trendy journalists who espoused the claims of the proletariat but sipped champagne at Islington garden parties and poured scorn on the likes of the bankers whose bonuses they despised in print, but in truth envied. The politics of envy. Gramsci might have something enlightening to say about that. The metropolitan élite with their superiority and arrogance in knowing what's best for everyone are no more a unique feature of my day than they were of Gramsci's, or of any other epoch. It is simply the power of those with power: power to push their agenda for their own ends over the powerless. I mean, what power does a teacher, or car mechanic, or bus driver, or doctor, or restaurant manager, or nurse, or salesperson, or farmer have? The only people who have a voice are people who have acquired power through their wealth or privilege, or those who have gained the opportunity to espouse their views through access to media, like the newscasters wearing hideous designer ties, for all the world like the kid's tutti-frutti ice cream, and the third-rate somebodies on television game shows and reality this and celebrity that who think that they have a God-given right to shape the news. What next? Celebrity skating on junk food wrappers? Rock and roll stars who think, as they shift millions of records, that that gives them legitimacy as the voice of their generation? That they can cajole ordinary people who earn fuck all into giving up their hard-earned cash to 'heal the world'? As Bob Dylan said, 'Money doesn't talk, it swears,' but who knows how much stinking money Bob has made from singing protest songs about the poor and dispossessed? And then there are the producers and directors and actors in films that rail against the oppression of men and women, who earn fortunes from depicting heroic, broken, ordinary or evil characters, but who never wait in line at fashionable restaurants or clubs? And the judges who sit in judgement of people they can never understand.

The simple fact is that the living world is not equal. The US Declaration of Independence says *all men are created equal*. Really? I make a mental note to ask Gramsci his view, and recall my loneliest day again, glancing at the sun lowering but still beating the air. I had no money. Leastways not enough for a cooling beer at a trendy canal-side bar, where beautiful young women sat at aluminium and fake-wood tables, half naked, laughing at unheard jokes, checking their nails and glancing up slyly to catch an admiring look. I recall wanting to pass through that day as quickly as possible. Beautiful people hand in hand, smiling and loving. Sun shining and glinting off water, tin chimney cowls, chromed narrowboat cleats, diamond rings and metal bird mobiles hanging from warehouse balconies. Mallards and swans drifting and preening and fishing. Everywhere people in love. Young couples, girls and boys, boys and boys, girls and girls, and pensioners, hands locked as though afraid that if they let go the other would be gone forever and their love affair of decades reduced to only memory, not the physical and tangible joy of the now. And me. Me the observer. The voyeur. The resentful and jealous watcher loaded down with a loneliness so deep that my trouble seemed real and unending.

I had fought the urge to spend my remaining few pence on an ice cream treat, until a point was reached where my limit for suffering was almost breached. My bucket about to overflow. The meniscus bowed across the very top of the pail, fearful of one more solitary drop. One millilitre more might have broken that uneasy strain, leading to an outpouring and gushing of sentiment. Of bitter tears. Of broken, selfish sobs. Unable to delay the moment further, heading back towards my flat, coming up towards Camden Passage, I stood in line at the ice cream parlour that had been Baskin-Robbins but was then some name I forget. I drooled as I stood, waiting impatiently under the glowering sun. Then I was in through the open door to the relative cool, and a pretty blonde girl, tired as she approached the end of her shift, smiling against the heat, red-faced, pushed her hair from her face with the back of her hand as I requested a single scoop of pistachio in a cone. All I had money for. Pistachio. My favourite flavour. Exotic promise of the East. I paid and thanked the girl, and took my delight outside to savour. I stood, back to a wall at the side of a converted warehouse, one leg bent, knee raised, foot flat against the wall behind me, like a flamingo. I closed my eyes against the straining sun and extended my tongue slowly to touch the round green scoop. Bliss. The taste of such cold sweetness melting fast in the scorching heat was a half-second of pure pleasure, so I pushed my tongue harder against it, to gather in that wonderful flavour and forget my loneliness for an instant. The ball toppled faster than I could react to save it, and landed on the dusty concrete by my flamingo foot. Boom! I stared at it in disbelief, then made a desperate attempt to scoop the ball back into the end of the cone. Futile; the ice cream melting into a mush of green, speckled with dust from the ground. I was distraught.

I laugh out loud now, as I recall my rashness, and the pathetic sense of loss at a puddle of melting green and my First World trauma. I am dead now. I now know what real loss feels like. That day was one of the hottest of a beautiful summer and what did I, a nineteen-year-old student from a good family with the promise of a world-is-your-oyster future ahead of me, have to feel lonely about? I laugh again at the thought that what I had perceived as my 'loneliest ever day' had so easily been righted and erased from memory by Ravenscroft knocking on my door armed with a fistful of cash, taking me off to the Camden Head to meet up with Clerkin and McKay before heading across to the Fox then up to the Albion and a night of hedonistic celebration. Loneliness was forgotten in a wealth of camaraderie, bad jokes and wreathed smiles. That day had stayed with me not as a memory of loneliness but as a stark reminder, writ in letters of flashing neon ten feet high, that I never knew loneliness, that loneliness is the preserve of others, of those whose thoughts cannot be shared, who crave the conversation or touch or smile or simple proximity of others, but whose days are a void, of emptiness, where there is no respite from aching lonely tedium, where there is no Ravenscroft waving cash, and no McKay or Clerkin shouting up the next round, beaming and swearing and jesting.

The garden is as I remember it. Orderly, and beautiful. Clipped boxwood hedges define the lawns, and gravel paths run parallel, edged by lavender with squares of peace lilies radiant at the corners. Umbrella pines provide shade along the borders, where carefully placed seating offers respite at differing times of day. These are separated at precise intervals by cypress trees which are neatly trimmed into tubes of green, flat-topped to echo the umbrella pines. Two long rectangular ponds with identical small stone fountains at their centre are a perfect element within the design. Two high-tailed fish, which drop a constant stream of water from open mouths, provide a lyrical aural backdrop which plays quietly on the still of evening. The water is green-blue, the colour of early-morning dreams, with goldfish swimming lazily like orange segments scattered for effect, a deliberately random infringement on the designer's sense of order. The ends of the ponds furthest from the house are framed by arches of wrought iron through which grows overflowing bougainvillea as red as a cardinal's robes, which casts my thoughts briefly to Sanchez and his lesson in unforgiving punishment. On the wall beside the steps which lead up from the garden to the terrace there is a trug half filled with weeds, beside which are a pair of gloves and a wood-handled weeding knife. The trug is made from woven wood slats, cracked and broken in places. It is a thing well-used, and well-cared-for, its breakages simply the effects of sun and frost and time, which mirror the creaks and groans of its owner, who, like all men and women of her age, has knots of veins and arthritic bumps about her hands. No matter how skilful the surgeon's careful cuts to the actor's or actress's face, the hands are always the hands of time.

The lady, having finished weeding, is sitting at the table with the man. She is wearing sunglasses right out of the Fifties, and has a bright silk scarf around her shoulders. She must be in her seventies but carries herself like a woman half her age. Two manicured lemon trees heavy with bright fruit sit in large stone cubes. She reads something out loud from a magazine she is holding, and the old man laughs, his face creasing, showing teeth betraying signs of a past spent smoking and drinking and living life. There is something about their ease that says love. That makes me love them too. I think then of Hannah, and for a fleeting moment imagine us as a couple of age, still in love after half a century of life passed. I hold that thought with a smile as I wave unseen to the old folks, then drop down into the garden, and walk up to sit on the wall beside them, to share their evening.

I pause briefly to look into the water at the fish, and wonder what they think of their home here in this magical garden. I smile to myself; I suspect fish do not think, other than about how to feed and avoid becoming food. The fact that there are no spirit fish fits with Sanchez's observation about there being no men of flint and stone. No dinosaurs or wolves or mammoths here. I sit beside the old man, and, as I look back along the garden towards the wall where I had perched, I appreciate the lady's need of sunglasses. The sun, low in the sky, spills across the garden to spread a shimmer as rich as liquid amber over the grass and plants and the gravel pathways, turning the pond-water's surface into two long bars of gold.

This is, I think, the most beautiful garden on Earth. A Garden of Eden. A garden which is nurtured and loved by its creator, and very much appreciated by her husband, and, I imagine, their children, grandchildren, friends, the postman, the telephone engineer, the repairman, and anyone lucky enough to have cause to visit. There are black patterns cut by shadows of trees over bright violet lavender, flowers which throw nectar to bees who flit about their purpose, making lavender honey, and I fancy it is perhaps for the murderess Rita of Masto.

## two people in harmony

This garden is another world. A treasure I am allowed to enter without invitation or a pass code, or the implicit acceptance of a guest list. I am not their son, or grandson, or neighbour, or postman, or housekeeper, or maintenance man, or delivery driver. I am an interloper, the kind of uninvited guest who in life might be unwelcome, meriting despairing looks exchanged between the old couple and sly glances at wristwatches wondering how long I will intrude upon them, when I will leave. I'm thankful they are oblivious to me. I am simply an observer unobserved. I am dead. A spirit. I hold none of their time. None of their attention.

I sit a while, watching the ease with which they occupy the garden. The ease of their life together. Two people in harmony. There is something intangible coating them, as though an aura tells their story of lives lived fully and that their love remains; that neither have suffered the slow rejection of a gradual flatlining death of relationship, the kind of endgame that reduces a man or woman to 'spent' status – to worthlessness – to a misery which then mutates to become a parasite, eating away at their core, until all that remains is a husk which exists, but does not truly live.

The man stands, pushing himself upright from the arms of his wrought-iron chair in a motion I imagine to be automatic from years of similar effort. He takes his wife's glass without comment and disappears through open French windows into the house. I watch her as she reads. Every few seconds she pauses to look at the garden, admiring her work, and checking for weeds she might have missed. There are none. The man returns with the glass, sparkling clear liquid with ice which tinkles melodiously, and a crescent of lemon bobbing as he sets it down. He places an arthritic hand on her shoulder as gently as he placed her drink, and, without looking up from her magazine, she puts a slimmer veined hand on his. There is something wonderful in this simple intertwining of affection which makes me think of Hannah, and the ease I felt with her in Masto, and that moment at airport departures when it dawned that I was truly in love.

I imagine if Shelley were here he would stick his tongue in her gin.

I walk in through the open French windows, and am amazed by what I see. I am in a living room which doubles as a library. The far wall is remarkably plain, painted with light green paint which has been left untouched for decades and is flaked in places and tells of the age of this beautiful house. The three remaining walls are panelled to above head height, shelved in dark oak, each wall with two tall but narrow windows designed to allow limited sunlight through. The room is huge and is the entire width of what I take to be the back of the house. There are books to stretch-height on the three panelled walls, thousands of them, and above them paintings suggesting various influences, Picasso, Gauguin and Matisse, but clearly of another hand, although their style suggests the same artist's work. A crystal chandelier hangs from the high ceiling, with a million cut-glass droplets slicing light into shards as I move my eyes. There is a round table of rosewood in the centre of the room, on which stands a sculpture of a naked man. The sculpture is cast in bronze and stands half life-size. I go across to look, as something draws me. It is the old man. Naked, with his left arm across his waist, hand meeting the elbow of the right, which leads up to his chin where his folded fist sits against his lips. His expression is one of amused thought, not anger, as the viewer might think from a distance. He is middle-aged. Lines in his face and around his eyes tell of a man happy with life. There is complicity with the sculptor in his look.

Wood-panelled doors are the central feature of the far wall, directly opposite the French windows. A single shelf runs the length of the wall. The shelf is broken only by the doors and two carved stone fireplaces, and displays a number of smaller bronzes, figures and abstract casts. They are by the same hand as the table statue. There are velour sofas and a chaise-longue in a three-sided arrangement which makes the left fireplace a focal point, and a writing table with two chairs to the right, set back from the right-side fireplace, creating two distinct areas suggesting work and play. Two smaller tables in the work side of the room bear magazines and vases of flowers. White lilies and yellow irises. They are set in such a way as to receive little sunlight in this most beautiful room, and it strikes me that there are no paintings on the green-painted wall, as the sun would strike them directly from early afternoon until evening, since the right-side windows face south, and the French windows west.

I cross the room and pass through the closed double doors. I find myself in a grand hallway with a curving staircase leading to the upper floors. The staircase is panelled and carved with the same grape and vine leaf design as the skirting in the living room library. Another chandelier hangs from the ceiling way above me. Several doors lead off the hallway, which I imagine doubles as a ballroom. There is a long dining table here, with seating for many guests, and a grand piano sits at the far end. Opposite me, beyond a large glass doorway, are huge grey-painted double doors, which appear to be the main entrance to the house. I walk through the glass, and stroll across the marble flags and oriental rug to a table set in the vestibule which leads to the grand front doors. Windows either side of the doors, set with stained glass images of Lady Godiva on a white horse to the left of the door, and Charlemagne in purple robes on a white horse to the right, allow light into the spacious entrance hall, where umbrella and coat stands vie with boot racks set back from a series of busts of Roman gods on marble pillars. On the long table sits an old Bakelite telephone, and a small pile of post. I look at the post for clues to the owners. An unopened letter on top has a plastic transparent window. The envelope has a printed clue. Accademia Nazionale di San Luca. The names of my unwitting hosts are there. Al Signor Vito Mazzi e Signora Alessandra Mazzi. Vito and Alessandra. I am delighted with my new-found familiarity. The society of artists of Italy. I know now who the artist and sculptor are.

# the spirit of someone unseen

I walk through the locked doors out on to the gravel driveway which leads to the entrance gates of Casa di Pace from Via Caio Cestio. The driveway is constructed in an L-shape, designed to hide the villa entrance from the roadway. The large wrought-iron gates give little away to the passer-by as to the house beyond. There are lawns visible, towered over by flat-topped pines, with the boundary wall to a neighbouring property beyond, and a high stone wall bordering the driveway along its right margin, and a similar wall, trellised with showering bougainvillea, to its left, where the driveway turns sharply out of view. Away from prying eyes.

I wander around the side of the house to take a last look at the main garden in the fading light. I take leave of my hosts by jumping up on the high wall to perch momentarily and wave goodbye. They make a fine couple, sitting talking, smiling at each other in the rich evening light, drinks in hand. I back-flip from the top of the wall, and leave them in unobserved privacy.

Shadows cast purple across the gravestones as I enter Cimitero Acattolico. Gramsci is lying on the roof of the gardener's shed again, as he was when I first saw him, when Shelley had called him to accompany us to Masto. His hands are clasped behind his head, and he is slightly turned to one side owing to his deformity. I'm minded to ask him about the Accademia Nazionale di San Luca, then decide against it, as he looks peaceful and absorbed in thought. No rush. I hear the Subdudes and Louis Armstrong singing different tunes of similar title in my head, and I know I have all the time in the world.

I walk slowly to my space around the shrubs and fox hole. There is something there that draws me as evening approaches. I feel affinity with the fox and her cubs. We had a dog briefly when I was a child, plus a tortoise named Peter, rabbits galore, and pigeons that my brother and I bought every Saturday for months until we were broke, which was a form of recycling of birds. We bought them, fed them and let them go, assuming ownership. They would then fly twice and sometimes three times around the house roof, then head straight back to the pet store where we had bought them. The following Saturday we would go back to the shop and buy identical-looking birds, much to the patient amusement of my mother and father. Years later they delighted in telling my brother and me that the pet shop owner must have loved us as their best customers. We were nine or ten then, I guess.

Rubens is nowhere to be seen. The Kraafts are out for a stroll, aged son chatting amiably to his youthful parents, and a passing Roman in toga has one hand on the butt of his companion, her arm around his waist. They are the first Romans I have seen in the *cimitero*. Maybe they need time away from prying eyes. My glance is drawn to the presence of a man of incredibly erect stature standing alone, grey cloth suit glowing silver in the sharp beams of setting light. His head is turned upwards to the sky. I find his composure, his stillness, somewhat unsettling. He is statuesque but he moves slightly, giving away the truth of his spiritual being.

Settling by the shrubbery, I await night falling and the foxes, who I am sure sense me there. There is immense beauty in the fall of evening here. The fade of colour of the sky through the slowly evolving hues of rainbow to darkness is a joy. From midday blue through a slow-fade of yellow, orange, green, indigo, and vermilion and finally to black. It is wondrous. Living, we never allow time to observe the world. The evolution of a single day is seldom met. How many of us, other than an injured climber or prisoner, have time to simply observe night pushing into day and falling through the hours, minute by minute, and second by second, until the dark night falls again and cloaks the hours of day passed? We are missing out. If I could have my time again, I would go up to Hampstead Heath to Keats's home, or the Brontës' Haworth in Yorkshire, and sit there through twenty-four hours, awake and sober, and observe.

Night falls slow and conniving in simmering shades of plum as it does each autumn evening until colour gives way to dark. I am sitting awaiting the foxes. My patience is rewarded when the lower branches of a shrub part and the vixen pushes her face cautiously into the night. She looks me in the eye. I marvel at the inbuilt sense of plus versus minus that two or three seconds reveals to a wild animal, and she moves fractionally, swaying her flank, signalling safety to her cubs. They spring around her and out into the garden. Full of life, frivolity and curiosity. I watch as they fall about, play-fighting and rolling over each other under the watchful and cautious eye of their mother.

Rubens drops from a tree limb, and the vixen stiffens. He looks around casually then jumps back up into the tree and out of sight, as though he has seen nothing to draw his interest. I realise at that moment that what I have seen in my living days, when I was watching a dog stand still in its tracks for no apparent reason, or a deer skit as I sat unobserved in Richmond Park reading on a summer's day, was the presence of the spirit of man or woman, sensed by an animal, whose awareness of these things was way beyond mine. The spirit of someone unseen.

## art made simple

I sit through the night, pale moon frizzing with clouds. The speed of their movement high in the sky amazes me. Whenever I flew, I had a habit of checking flight progress on the video screen. It would impress me to see a tail wind of one hundred and twenty miles an hour, to realise that this was normality in the upper atmosphere. As normal as daffodils in spring, and snow in winter.

The foxes have retired at the approach of day, cubs seemingly oblivious to me, but the vixen eyeing me momentarily, as though I am no great threat but put on notice. I wonder what she senses of me. I wonder how I appear to her. I wonder if she can see me.

I am toying with the thought of going back to Casa di Pace to see whether Vito and Alessandra are up and having breakfast, or going to seek Sanchez or Shelley, but it is still early, and light is pulsing in the stillness of air. The promise of day. My indecision is ended by the sudden appearance of Rubens, who drops down in front of me.

'August,' he says.

I am no longer sure of days or months, but I know I arrived here in September.

He says something in German, and extends his hand. I take it without verbal response. He says something further in French. I don't belong here. I don't understand him. I start to feel a sense of isolation. I am a foreigner in a foreign land.

He grins. 'August. That is my name. August Riedel,' he adds in mildly accented English.

'Finn Chambers,' I say, relieved, still holding his extended hand.

'I know,' he says. 'I was just having fun with you, Finn Chambers.'

He laughs to himself, and the creases in his face are exaggerated. His is a face rich with character. It is a face well-lived. He reminds me of Vito.

'What is it you like so much about the foxes, Finn?' he asks, letting go of my hand, steadying his shoulder against the tree trunk like some nineteenth-century rake in a satiric sketch, arms folded. 'You seem drawn to them, as though they hold some special meaning for you.'

'They remind me of England,' I say, realising as I say it that the foxes are my only real connection to my past, when I could walk up to Turnham Green station following a fox at six in the morning, on my way to the airport or to catch a train to Newcastle or Torbay. City foxes are unlike their country cousins, who shy away from humans. In the countryside, human beings are predators. City foxes swagger and roll, like rock stars, pausing to pose for photographs before vanishing over a six-foot fence as easily as I now flip up to the cemetery wall. Always as though they are expecting the whirr of a Nikon motor, or the artificial clunk of a digital shutter, with a faint air of *get a move on* in their stance. Rock star foxes of London Town.

'So you're a country boy, then, Finn?' Riedel lays his head to the side to emphasise his quizzical look.

'No, a city boy through and through,' I reply with a grin, feeling suddenly at ease with this stranger who, although he must be in his eighties, is youthful and welcoming. I throw my hands wide as though I am confessing something grand. 'My sympathy is with the city. The guarantee of early-morning coffee and late-night bars. I guess those things bring the foxes too. The city creates waste. One man's meat and all that. It's an infrequent sight, a wild fox in the English countryside, but in English cities they thrive. In the city they have no predators, they're just curious observers, and the excess of city life is theirs for the taking. Their table is filled by cast-off food from the likes of me, the gluttonous consumer. The humans who shoot them in the countryside feed them in the city. It is an oddity, but that is how it is.'

I have talked as though I know something. I doubt I do. Riedel looks amused.

'Finn Chambers, photographer. What made that your path? A search for truth perhaps? The instant capture of a moment in time? Art made simple?' He chuckles as though he knows some secret.

Feeling slightly defensive, I think before I answer. *Art made simple*. My pause causes him to chuckle more.

'I just like capturing images,' I reply. 'I always have.'

'Me too!' he says, booming and beaming. 'It is a thing of beauty, isn't it? Recording something that remains forever in that moment. In my day it was the brush and in yours the camera. Both capture beauty and truth.'

He looks at me straight in the eye, and continues more softly.

'Or maybe they capture a flattery, and disguise the truth; or, with the collusion of the artist, misrepresent a truth to inflate the ego of a willing client, or, worse still, deceive an ignorant public.'

He bows with affected grace, then jumps back up to his favourite tree limb, pulls his old cloth cap over his eyes and adopts a position of repose which is effective in ending our conversation.

I am somewhat stunned. I don't know whether to feel offended or amused. I choose amusement, laugh out loud, and wander off to find Shelley and Keats.

As I stroll towards the old part of the cemetery Lady Mary is standing by the tomb of Karl Pavlovich Bryullov, talking to the grey-suited man I saw yesterday evening.

'Oh, Finn, darling!' she says, taking me by the arm, waving her free hand towards grey suit. 'Reverend John Barrington, please allow me the pleasure of introducing my newest friend, Mister Finn Chambers. Finn is a photographer, you know.'

Barrington holds out his hand with a stiff formality which indicates neither welcome nor rejection. Despite Lady Mary's enthusiasm for me as her *newest friend*, I have an immediate sense that the Reverend John Barrington is a man for whom material life and the arts were never a honeypot into which he wished to dip his tongue.

Something about Barrington does not excite me. He regards me with a calculated aloofness that is the greeting equivalent of beige. His demeanour is that of my old headmaster. There is an expectation of respect without cause. I suspect he will forget my name. I suspect he already has.

Without wishing to pre-judge him, however, priding myself as I do on my openness and generosity towards my fellow man and woman, I decide to give Barrington a mental two-fingered sign, smile benevolently at Lady Mary von Haast, invent an appointment with Shelley – which gains a face-twist of disapproval from Barrington, confirming my suspicion that here is a man I can do without – and I skip quickly along the pathway and leave them behind. I make a mental note to ask the joker Riedel about Bryullov, whose painting of Pompeii I know.

Shelley is nowhere to be seen. Keats, Severn, Trelawny and the children are lying on the grass. Arthur is waving his legs in the air, giggling, while William tickles his chin with a daisy flower. The men are all flat on their backs staring up into the sky, which is radiant blue with dotted lumps of white cloud. They are engrossed in identifying country maps, or ships, or Michelangelo's *David*, or whatever it is they believe they can see. I decide to leave them at play.

It is still early, but the gates are open and a group of German tourists are following a guide to Keats's tomb. I cross out through the gates as Claudio arrives on the red Vespa. He parks it on its stand, and takes a bunch of keys from his pocket as he approaches the workshop door. I carry on up the street, admiring the shafts of sunlight that catch tiny flecks of flint in the paving stones, flashing messages in Morse code as I stroll along. Winter is late arriving. Autumn has held summer in her arms longer than is decent, but the flavour on the air is of rain, and a cooling. I imagine that the messages are signals from Hannah, saying, 'I love you', or from Rita saying, 'I am sorry for killing you.' My thoughts of Hannah are intermittent, shaved away by time and my realisation that I can never go back, that my eternity is here, until I decide maybe that nothingness is preferable to eternity and stride purposefully towards my other love, the sea.

Vito and Alessandra are on the terrace, drinking coffee. He is smoking a fat cigar. A *cohiba*. Castro's favourite. I make a further mental note to ask Gramsci his view of Castro. He probably loves him. One communist to another. Alessandra has on a quilted jacket, as though she might go horse-riding. Vito's heavy woollen jumper is a sign that mornings are cooling. I look forward to snow. I may have a while to wait.

I sit beside Alessandra. She takes delicate bites from a croissant, interspersed with sips from a coffee cup. She is ladylike and slow-paced. I envy her. I, at least when I was alive, always seemed to be rushing. One hand through my coat sleeve, grabbing a last mouthful of coffee then sliding my other arm in before dashing out of the door. That kind of frenetic racing about which creates urgency and stress in modern life but which is easily reduced by the simple act of rising earlier. Or by just not giving a fuck. I think we actually – twenty-first-century people, that is – like to create stress to make our lives seem more important, more vital. Vito is a man whose air suggests devil-may-care. His espresso and cigar and smiley disposition combine to enrich this scene. People who live life. I start to wish I were alive again, so that I could change my outlook, live a life more bohemian and adopt Vito's hedonistic character. Except we are who we are, for good or bad, and despite my sudden longing to live life without limit, to swish Hannah off her feet and dance with her every day, there is no going back. I am dead.

Being dead is something I am getting used to, but I occasionally wonder if one morning I am going to wake up next to Hannah and jump out of bed panicking that I will miss a shoot in Helsinki or Madras because I had too much Rioja the previous evening and forgot to set the alarm. In my 'I am definitely dead' moments there is a joyful element. I know something that none of my living contemporaries, friends, family and Hannah knows: that there is a world beyond; that we do not simply lie in earth, still and gone. Then there is the balance. The counterweight. The element of disappointment. Of feeling cheated out of the right to become old, to hold Hannah's veined and wrinkled hands, to smile into her still sparkling crow's-feet eyes and revel in the fact that we had made it that far. Three kids, four grandchildren, no mortgage, one dog, and a cottage in Robin Hood's Bay. To be able to stroll below the cliffs at low tide on a perfect winter's day, and watch a crazy dog fascinated by its own reflection in rock pools, suddenly startled by the sideways movement below the mirror top of a crab scrabbling. To cast eyes up to a clear blue sky, dotted with wheeling gulls, and the sun, low in winter, throwing shards of glitter across the rare calm sea to cast the cliff face in purple and mauve slashed shadows. To walk slowly back up the boat ramp arm in arm, creaking with arthritic resentful joints of age, to a seat by the window in the Bay Hotel, a crackling log fire with the hiss of green wood newly added, and hot tasty food and red wine relished before finishing our walk, and the end of another weekend retreat before we head back to the city.

I click back, breaking through thoughts to the day around me, and the crisp air. Scents start to gather from flowers awoken by the strengthening light, and a lone bee, early-risen, hesitates over yellow heads. Vito blows a cloud of smoke as he turns to his wife, smiling and chuckling at something he is reading in his magazine.

'*Sandra, è divertente!*' he says, shaking with laughter at what he has read, but I only catch the fact that whatever it is is funny. He lifts the magazine to show Alessandra. The article has a photograph of Silvio Berlusconi with his jet-black hair and turtle's face, a young woman on his arm who is fifty years his junior, so I make the assumption that the former leader of Italy is the source of Vito's amusement.

'*Solo quell'uomo!*' says Alessandra, laughing and shaking her head as though she is exasperated. Only that man! I get that much. I'm picking things up.

There is a delicacy to this morning that belies the approach of winter. Irises, purple-hued and vibrant, stand guard in a weathered stone trough between the ponds. Sentinels of green with yellow-flashed helmets as though cast from a scene at Waterloo. Alert, and anticipatory, and not yet ready to die. A bird, small and brown and indefinable, flits from the trough to a low branch of a nearby cedar, swallowed by shade and disappearing as if by magic, only to reappear two seconds later, back at the trough. A crow perched on a television aerial set against one of four chimneys hacks out its harsh call and draws my eye upwards. I am immediately struck by the image of a lone figure looking down from a top floor window. A woman who is staring straight at me.

I look away briefly, as though embarrassed. A voyeur. I look back and she has gone.

# refusing to admit defeat

I realise that my essential nature, my character, which I had always regarded as being stamped out by the genes and DNA that I no longer possess, is actually part of my soul. My spirit. My politeness is no doubt learned from my mother and father, but there is something deeper that surpasses that biology. I have no blood. No beating heart. My spirit is what makes me visible to other spirits. We appear normal to one another. The lady at the window has set a realisation within me that challenges my status. Without my beating heart, why should I care about who or what I am? But I do. I care as much about who I am as ever.

Disturbed somewhat by my feelings of intrusion, and concerned that I am no longer welcome at Casa di Pace, I take my leave of Vito and Alessandra. A sudden pull of winds heralds the changes coming. Leaves rustle and the irises bob in salute. I take this as my sign for exit, and, after a half-expectant glance up to the empty window, vault the wall into the street. The sun has risen higher in a cloudless sky and the pavement no longer spits messages at me. I wander along Via Caio Cestio without a plan other than to seek out the wisdom of Shelley and Keats.

As I approach the *cimitero* my thoughts are interrupted by banging. Claudio is hammering at a wheel assembly on an old Fiat which is supported on a trolley jack, the removed wheel on the ground serving as a rest for Claudio to kneel on. There is rust the colour of tobacco all around the brake drum. This is a car which has seen better days but is refusing to admit defeat. The breaker's yard can wait. She is not done yet. The wheel arch above the drum has sympathetic rust, holes eaten through the pearl-grey paint.

A postman arrives with a bundle of mail wrapped in a rubber band. He wanders inside, returns empty-handed and stands looking at the car.

'*Consegnalo a Dio*,' he says grinning and shaking his head. Deliver it to God.

'*Eretico! Questo è il bambino di qualcuno. Çinquant'anni, ma ancora un bambino!*' responds Claudio, laughing. Heretic! This is someone's baby. Fifty years old, but still a baby! There is a beauty about his face which matches him well with Claudia, whom I long to see.

My eyes follow the postman as he crosses the street, bag bouncing against his hip as he goes. He takes a letter from his bag, posts it into a wall box, presses twice on a bell-push beside the box, then wanders up to a yellow Vespa, which he starts and rides slowly further along Via Paolo Caselli before stopping and dismounting again.

I stroll to stand beside Claudio, who is still hammering gently at the casing, trying to unsettle years of settled rust. He mutters something I cannot make out, pushes himself upright, and walks inside the workshop, where his shape becomes amorphous in the gloom. He returns with a spray can and readopts his position on the tyre. With a practised motion he sprays behind the drum casing, making use of a plastic straw connected to the nozzle. A sweet smell hits the air, attracting a wasp, which Claudio bats away with his free hand. The wasp persists, so Claudio sprays it from the can. It flies off to an unknown fate, which I suspect is death.

Inside the workshop the Pirelli ladies have changed. I wander along freely admiring as there is no one to witness my voyeurism. No one to disapprove. Navia has been replaced in 1996 by Eva Herzigová. Naked but with arms folded. Nothing revealed. Beautiful. Inés Sastre has disappeared. There is also a new addition on the opposite wall. Signed photographs of Totti, Gattuso, Andrea Pirlo and Gigi Buffon. All beautifully framed in shiny gilt, as though gold is the only colour worthy of these footballing gods. Never having had much interest in cars or football, this information is a surprising addition to my existence, which holds the promise of newness, of each day bringing more to me after death than it seemed to bring prior to my unexpected descent.

Outside, Claudio is sitting in a plastic seat, smoking, waiting for the lubricating agent to do its job. A pot of nasturtiums is on fire in sunlight. This is new. The footballers are new. I suspect Claudio has Claudia to thank for these changes. Subtle. The marks of change. Of a woman making her mark quietly, like a doe rabbit which digs a burrow to show the male she is a homemaker. Nature. We may define it as other things, as Gramsci so directly pointed out about modern man and woman's need to label, dissect and account for every single thing, and to attach meaning to everything. Something about us, about modern people, means we need to be identified as fashionistas or geeks or movers and shakers or kings of cool or something we can hang our hat on to say, *this is me!* How about just being ourselves, for better or worse? I look down at my Old Skools. I think of Gramsci's question to me: *Does Calvin Klein wear a shirt with John Smith printed on it? Or Jane Smith? Or Finn Chambers?*

I sit in the chair beside Claudio. The day is warming judging by the attire of passers-by, causing me to wonder whether winter will ever come. I do not crave it, but I have an expectation of seasons. An Englishman's pleasure. The smell of cigarette smoke does not faze me as it did when I stood in bus queues with the acrid tang rolling around me from some kid or king of cool or inconsiderate old dear puffing and wheezing. Conversely, I always loved the smell of pipe tobacco and cigar smoke. My uncle had a scent of pipe smoke around him and through his house. Something wondrous about that scent. Something wondrous about that man, too. Gone too soon, but a gentler man would be hard to imagine.

Claudio is about to rise, his hands on the chair arms, when Claudia pulls on to the forecourt in a smart Mercedes. I guess it is a company car, but I may be wrong. She has on a business suit, and looks so beautiful it is hard to suppress whistling like some builder annoying a passing girl. She strides across to Claudio, every inch the catwalk model. She bends to kiss him, then sits on me. I want to remain where I am, but chivalry overcomes me and I float out through her to sit up on the apex above. The view from here gives me sight of the treetops in the cemetery, and the pyramid beyond. Some view. I can also see part-way down Claudia's blouse, which I find pleasing, although my instinct not to be voyeuristic overcomes me and I look back at the umbrella pines. Shelley would no doubt ogle Claudia's breasts openly if he were here.

Speak of the devil. Percy is standing in the *cimitero* gateway, looking around. He spies me on the apex and strolls across Via Caio Cestia. The postman, having finished his round and come full circle, cuts through Shelley on the yellow Vespa heading to his depot. There is a confidence to Shelley's swagger I envy. Even through the centuries a man can be sure of himself, assuming, that is, that he has something to be sure of. I am minded to press Shelley about his views on God's existence again, but I do not get the chance, as he jumps up beside me and immediately peers down Claudia's top. He grins at me, and sighs.

'The only thing I miss Finn,' he says brightly, 'is the feel of a woman's warmth around me.' He grins again, and winks an eye at me before adding, 'Around my cock.'

There is something so lewd about both his words and his manner that it makes me want to do two things. I want to laugh, and at the same time I want to show my disapproval, as though somehow this would be polite to Claudia, who is blissfully unaware of either of us peering down her blouse.

There is a saying that we have two sides. What if it's much more complicated than that? Maybe we are circular and we start at good, and roll through one hundred and eighty degrees to bad and back again through another one-eighty to become good once more? More likely we are spherical, and each tiny point on our entire surface is fractionally more of one thing and less of another as we move the pointer. Even the simplest of us is complex. We build around ourselves the mores of convention, and rules of behaviour and laws to judge by. Every society has them, from the chivalric tradition of the monarchs of Denmark to the Amazonian peoples who run naked in the jungle. All with some sense of organisation and etiquette. Belief. Western secular societies mock the idea of any god, as Sanchez so eloquently identifies, but for the rainforest peoples there are spirits and gods so powerful that the existence of them is without doubt. I have wondered what a group of babies without parents, growing into completely feral children, totally alone without human contact, would become. Is restraint the construction of man through evolution, or would a feral child simply exist for the consumption of food until death? How many of us really would love to throw off the expectations of others? To live life without so much as a passing thought for those around us? To live a truly hedonistic life where boundaries are unseen or unknown?

I look at Shelley, but hesitate to ask for fear of appearing naïve or uneducated, or in some way accusatory, as though I am applying a label to him.

He looks into my face. 'Ask.' He says this as though reading my mind.

'Do you believe a man can be truly hedonistic? Truly self-loving, without care for anyone or anything. Truly free, Percy?'

As he starts to drop to the floor, he pauses.

'The prisons of the world are full of such men.'

# benefit of the doubt

We wander inside the workshop for a last look at Pirelli's delights through the years. This week it is the month of August on display.

'Rubens is a funny guy,' I say absently, reminded of him by the month.

"Rubens?"

'I mean August Riedel. I named him Rubens before I knew his name.'

'None finer,' says Shelley. 'And interesting. A man who has tales to tell. A man for whom imagination is king.' He looks pleased with himself at making his case for imagination before adding, 'A man who sees dreams and paints them.' He turns on his heel. 'Let's go for a walk.'

We stroll outside as Claudia slides into the driving seat, showing an expanse of leg, much to Percy's satisfaction. Claudio shuts the door, claims a kiss, and the Mercedes flows quietly into Caio Cestio as the window rises silently to close out the world. We turn the opposite way. Some schoolchildren pass by. Maybe seven or eight years old. Walking, not being driven. Animated, as though constant motion is necessary in every waking moment. They should make the most of it. Soon enough they'll be glued to computer screens, gaming their lives away. I am having a nostalgic moment, questioning just how little I actually did in my brief time in that world. I could have done more. There again, I could have done less. I decide to give myself the benefit of the doubt.

We are walking and talking about Claudio and cars. For a man born before the age of mechanisation, Shelley has extensive knowledge on every subject, or at least that is how he appears. A man with limitless thirst for life, even after death. We pass the 1930s couple, her beach pyjamas defining a shapeliness that draws Percy's roving eye. He makes a remark about the joy she could bring him, and bows slightly towards her as they say, 'Good morning,' in unison again. Two spirits joined in synchronicity. Forever.

He stops suddenly, then floats up to the crest of a high wall and motions me to join him. I am looking into a garden with beautiful flowers crammed into raised walled borders, and a blue-tiled swimming pool. The walls are tiled and the feel is of the Orient. Tangier. Algiers. Tripoli. Marrakesh. Between the pool and the terrace of an imposing house lies a sunken garden with a central fountain spouting water, which fills a wide shallow bowl before spilling into an eight-pointed mosaic gully, to be recycled over and over. Tiled pathways of zigzag grey and white create symmetry to connect areas of seating, and a further two lion-head fountains are set into the garden walls to east and west, facing towards the sunken garden like guardians, watching. These fountains are bordered with ancient gold and green tiles of Moorish design, bringing to my mind the summer palaces of Spain, of Granada and Córdoba. There are rainbow roses, birds of paradise, clematis rich in ivory, leafy banana trees, double-headed pomegranate flowers the colour of neon sunset, and palms large and dwarf, creating an exotic motif so unexpected and dazzling to my eye. I whistle in appreciation. I could be in the Alhambra. This captures my eye the way that Claudia's legs caught Shelley's.

Shelley waves to a man in a long green robe, his head covered in a twisted gold scarf. He is seated in a corner of the garden, enjoying the scene before him.

'Suliman. Prince of Nubia. He, like you, has no tomb here, but finds, in this garden, unending joy. You see, Finn? Every day has surprises. It is the beauty brought about by imagination. If someone has true imagination, they can create anything they choose. Riedel will tell you so from his passion, in his own time. You may have learned that he is a man for whom time is to be savoured, not devoured.'

I offer no reply, but smile in recognition, a vague feeling of relief filtering through me that August did not dismiss me as a person of no future interest. His manner was simply his way.

We sit motionless for a while as I take in the quiet beauty. Shelley seems happy to sit beside me, silent and contemplative. I wonder where his thoughts are.

I am content to remain here, taking in this new surprise, but Shelley waves again to Suliman, then takes a sudden lead by back-flipping to the pavement, taking a bow as he lands, exaggerating the decadence of his act with a swirling flourish of his leading hand as befits the principal dancer receiving a standing ovation on opening night. Suliman grins and waves as I applaud. I wave back as I drift downwards, taking the moment for all its worth. It is a moment that feels rewarding to my soul. Here I am, Finn Chambers, grammar school boy, being entertained by one of the most famous men to ever walk this world, surrounded by colour, beauty, princes and poets.

# the simple things in life

Entering Masto always feels like coming home. This is the closest I will ever again be to my own home. To my family. To Hannah and my memory of love. Keats, Severn, Trelawny, Gramsci and Lady Mary are gathered in conversation around two tables. It is still early and the locals are few. Rita is busily whirring coffee beans in an electric grinder. She tips a quantity of ground powder into an aluminium box, then sets about preparing coffee for herself and her chef. The air is thick with the aroma of arabica beans freshly ground.

I sniff this scent and feel joy. The simple things in life. After life.

Gramsci beckons me to sit between him and Lady Mary. I lean forward to take Lady Mary's proffered hand, and kiss it lightly, with a smile on my face. I find this level of old-world courtesy both amusing and satisfying in a way I find hard to rationalise given my previous concerns in life about being fashionable. About being a king of cool. About building mystique.

I take my seat and Gramsci says, '*Hai un modo affascinante, Finn. Avresti fatto un grande italiano!*' He laughs across the table as Trelawny translates.

'You have a charming way about you, Finn. You would have made a great Italian!'

They all laugh, and then I say, '*Antonio, ho imparato maniere eccellenti dai migliori insegnanti!*' I tell Gramsci I have learned excellent manners from the best teachers.

'Bravo! Bravo, Finn!' Keats leans across the table to shake my hand. 'You are learning. Soon Antonio will have no secrets to tell himself about you.'

They all laugh at this, which causes me slight suspicion that Gramsci has been mocking my fashion or views. Probably with good reason. I glance down at my guitar shop T-shirt. He smiles, eyes creasing, and says, 'John is a mischief-maker, Finn. In his own quiet way.' He guffaws at his own words and raises an imaginary glass to Keats. Lady M claps her hands with delight, reminding me of a young girl – since it is she who is my secret teacher, who, for twenty-eight evenings, and every time that we have strolled in the garden and talked, has gifted a slice of Italian to me, as a grandmother would spoil a grandchild with pizza. I don't now count the days that pass, whether in days or weeks, but the more time passes, the more I am beginning to love these people.

Two old men shuffle in. I cannot guess their ages, but their slowness and stiffness of gait puts them close to the end of their lives, maybe eighties or nineties. They take a seat inside the window, as though the distance to the far wall under the bicycle is an unnecessary effort. Rita beams at them, takes their order for coffee and bread, and touches each gently on the shoulder before saying, '*Sto arrivando! Qualsiasi cosa per i miei uomini preferiti!*'

I translate for the amusement of my fellow spirits. 'Coming right up! Anything for my favourite men!'

I surprise myself. I have only been learning for a matter of weeks. There is something about my dead state, peculiarly, which is allowing me to absorb knowledge, and language, like a sponge. If I had possessed this during my time at grammar school, I would surely have merited the label of genius. This time it is Gramsci who leans across to shake my hand. Everyone is beaming at me. I feel suddenly at peace with myself.

I look across at the two old men. Slowed by age, but expressive. Hands are an artist's brush. Waving. Underlining. Outlining the background, then bringing attention abruptly to the fore. Flicks of wrists scatter words across the room, adding to this rich display to emphasise a point well made. I am trying to guess their former professions. The elder of the two has on a busy checked jacket. The checks are small: brown, red and black overlapping squares which stand out fairly garishly from the tan-coloured wool. When they came in from the street he had a pale tan gabardine raincoat draped across his shoulders in a way only an ordinary Italian man or a movie star could carry off. He sports a checked trilby that matches his jacket. Effortless to the casual eye, but this man does not simply wear clothes. He *dresses*. Below the jacket he is wearing a grey jumper, a pale blue shirt the colour of thick ice, and a tie striped with brown, pale blue and grey. Every inch thought about, down to the dark chestnut trousers with their razor crease and honeyed claret shoes which are long-owned, but polished to meet the approval of any *maître d'*. He is slight and keen-eyed, reminding me of the brown bird that had once captured my notice with its magic disappearing act in the garden at Casa di Pace.

Rita brings espresso, warm bread that sends a spell into the air, and a bowl of olive oil of golden green that is surely the promise of perfection itself. Shelley nods approval. She returns a few seconds later with two small glasses of grappa. She places them on the table to mild protestation, says nothing, smiles and skips away. It is early, but the hint of winter is strong in the air.

I think of naming the two old men, but find my attention drawn more to their story than their names. The younger man, probably still in his eighties, has rheumy eyes, and carries more weight. Although moderately built, he has jowls hanging slightly towards his neck, and a protrusion of stomach. He is casually dressed, but his combination of burgundy wool jacket, dark trousers and dark striped scarf, worn tie-like and contained within a navy cashmere sweater, gives him the air of an academic. He has on half-lens glasses, over which he peers as he converses with his older friend.

I excuse myself from Lady M and move to sit by them, to eavesdrop. Their conversation is of politics, films and art. My kind of guys. Interesting men. The elder passes a comment about Rita's shapely bottom as she bends to clear a table. Life. It does not really change with age. Lady Mary and Trelawny are proof of that.

Style and money. In any other country the two are inseparable. In Italy nobody needs money to carry style. It is inbred. Like a bloodline in racehorses. *You've either got it, honey, or you ain't.*

Keats comes to sit beside me. 'They are interesting fellows, are they not, Finn?'

'They have so much to say,' I answer. 'Men of limitless thought and conversation. Lives well led, I guess.'

'They were both rascals in their day.' He smiles, glancing across at them, before continuing, 'And soon they will join us, and be as shocked as you to discover that life does not end, if one has the imagination to continue it. Finn, you had no expectation of an end to your life, whereas I did. Despite my belief in the true beauty and power of imagination, I faltered.

I could imagine nothing other than an endless darkness, a lost eternity of blackness, and the loss of my spirit, of my soul. Despite my belief in romantic ideals, I became embittered against my illness. Do not forget, I was a young man, and my impending loss was a torture to me: that I would never cast my adoring and, as Percy will remind me, lustful eyes on Fanny Brawne again. Such cruel fate should never visit the young, for those left behind are saddled with loss and grief so vast, with little hope that there is truly a heaven, a world beyond, as you now know, Finn, but you had no such expectation. You expected to be back in Masto, drinking wine, eating *jamón* and loving your beautiful woman. Yet here we are, in this most wonderful of all worlds, truly blessed, despite our loss of others. The people you see here, all of us, had the imagination to believe in something beyond their own existence. Whether that was a belief in God, in heaven, or simply that there must be something more, that, in my view, is why there are relatively few spirits here, that we are not cheek by jowl.'

It suddenly hits me that Shelley, Keats, Trelawny, Lady Mary, Gramsci, Sanchez, Riedel, Barrington and everyone I now know, particularly the Romans, have seen stunned spirits emerge from thin air for decades or even centuries past, and will do so for all time to come. And I am now one of those who will see the living become dead. To see them rise again, like Jesus. To know their secrets. If the *bambola* stays here long enough, or meets her demise too soon and joins us here, will Shelley confess to placing a hand inside her dress and laying his lips on her breast? Probably.

I am about to ask Keats whether he knows who the window-watcher is at Casa di Pace, when I decide against it. I decide that knowing robs me of enquiry, opportunities to question, to guess, all of which are part of my journey now. If we knew everything, what would be the point in living on, simply passing through the centuries without investigating or assessing? We might as well be dust.

I return John's infectious smile, whisper, '*Grazie mille*,' into Lady Mary's ear, and stroll outside to look again at the graffiti on Masto's walls. This is a city where graffiti offends tourists, as though their brief presence here in the Eternal City is somehow special, worthy of pristine walls and demanding the deference accorded to heads of state. A modern conceit the inhabitants care to ignore, immersed as they are in celebrating the living of life.

I blame the cavemen. They started it. Shame there are none here to ask what it meant, whether it was to do with seasons, calendars or mystic spirit gods. Probably just for art's sake. Now that would be a laugh. Centuries of academic inquiry reduced to *I just did it because I felt like it! It didn't mean anything, it's just a doodle. It was raining outside and I was bored. No, it's not a seal, that was my mother-in-law. Those lines and crosses? A calendar? What need did we ever have for time? Day and night. Warm day, cold day. Arguments. The number of arguments I had with my mother-in-law. My wife was great, but her mother was a bitch. Even her father, who was short-tempered and in truth a rather unpleasant self-opinionated man with a tendency to club his neighbours, thought she was a nasty piece of work. Vindictive. It was her nature. She wasn't happy unless she was arguing. Even the sabre-toothed tigers steered clear of a tongue that sharp*. So much for centuries of academic debate and books written, archaeological sites scraped away, documentaries filmed, X-rays and carbon-dating. Just life. Life being lived. I am hoping that there are caveman spirits somewhere, who now tell it like it was.

I am trying to decipher the spray paint when my attention is caught by a familiar figure crossing the end of Via Galvani. Sanchez. I drift along the street towards him, but he is unaware of me as I wave to catch his eye. As I turn the corner into

Nicola Zabaglia to catch him, he turns into Via Giovanni Battista Bodoni. I follow just in time to see him as he walks straight through the closed doors of the church of Santa Maria del Rosario.

# colours of your choosing

I am a voyeur by nature. An intruder. The worst kind of Peeping Tom. In my life I would look side-on, or from under sunglasses that shaded my intention. Shifty. I lacked the courage to stare. To confront. A couple arguing in the street. A strange man carrying a backpack on an Underground train. A suspicious fashionable ladies' handbag hanging by both handles from the back of an unoccupied chair at the Red Lion in Whitehall. A fellow shopper slipping an expensive watch up his sleeve. A pretty girl walking by, figure swaying. Shelley, on the other hand, seems not to give a damn for the mores of his time or mine. Fearless or simply sociopathic. Shifting times mean shifting labels. I find him to be a braver man than I ever was, and now ever will be.

I move towards the door, then pause. I have nothing, in truth, to fear. What would I fear? I am dead. There is nothing more to fear. I pause to think, and again I am surprised by my lack of trepidation, about being scolded or embarrassed. I have, without doing so knowingly, acclimatised myself to the fact that worry is a state for the living. I smile and shrug to myself. I am free of that. Nothing can now harm me. I cannot lose my self-respect by throwing up in someone else's home and sit stinking and vomit-stained on a crowded Tube train. I cannot scold myself and feel the harsh glow of failure for forgetting a dinner date with Hannah's friends to which I have dashed thirty minutes late with false excuses about having to develop proofs for a client who is a complete bastard but pays well. I cannot be made to feel *beneath contempt* for my late arrival for a shoot, even though the cause of my lateness is nature itself, the herald of winter bringing chaos to transport systems designed only for spring. I cannot be prosecuted for submitting a false tax return where dinner receipts with Hannah are muddled in with camera lens purchases and photographic paper costs to make up the gap for genuine receipts I have carelessly mislaid. I cannot even be arrested for an act of indecency such as I witnessed Shelley commit. We are immune from laws, prosecution, imprisonment, torture. If only those falsely incarcerated by oppressors knew what I now know, they would have little to fear in telling their tormentors to go to hell. Hit the road, Jack. But they dare not because they are unaware that there is freedom awaiting them. Freedom. Who would have thought that death brought that? Not me. I suspect that Shelley was always that way, from his substitutions of woman for woman or man for woman, and his refusal to kowtow to the board at Oxford, and, highest of all, his belief in his beliefs. Imagine that in the living world? Being so passionate about beliefs held as to never hide them, or deny or disguise them? Me? I would sit at a dinner party and spout forth on a subject I believed in, only to reshape it and make it fit snugly into the contrary view expressed by a woman I wished to impress. Shelley, on the other hand, would have impressed her ten-fold more by arguing his corner, with intelligence, wit and passion, and looking her directly and unwaveringly in the eye, with a gaze that said *meet me later, and I'll show you passion.* As the evening progressed she would no doubt lower her eyes with a blush of cheek and make an excuse to her beau, apologising for leaving early due to an invented malaise, having taken Shelley's note hand-slipped with an address and time for rendezvous later that evening. Scoundrel? Chancer? Depends how you look at it I guess. Lover? Romantic? Depends how you see it. Man of his time? Man of any time probably. For good or bad, human nature is what it is, and who am I to draw a line of acceptability? Or you, for that matter. Who are you to lay down a code for others to follow, when you yourself have aching chasms of hypocrisy to fill with good deeds and repentance? There again, why should you? Put simply, why should any one of us fit a suit of clothes designed by someone else? My view now, post death? Wear only the clothes that you yourself design. Stitch your cloth in colours of your choosing, in a style that is yours.

I pause before the doors and look down at my Old Skools, I move across to see my reflection in a glass pane to view my Haight Ashbury T-shirt, and I laugh out loud at my former stake in life. My desire to be a trendsetter, which I now see as blind obedience to fashions dictated by business moguls, designers and media sycophants pandering to a financially rich but emotionally bereft clientele. Those whose parties would be so blandly dull without champagne and cocaine that even a simpleton like me would not wish to be invited. The consequential link? The decline of individuality brought about by the incestuous clamour for recognition from those who wear that art and design, and who fête life in a brew that is initially satisfying but ultimately noxious. I am relieved of the embarrassment of the living world. A chained slave continues to row the boat towards a future filled with misery and hopelessness, in the faint hope that ahead may lie the promised land, or more likely because the crack of a whip or the fear of being thrown to sharks is stronger than the will to resist.

I shake my head and wonder what Hannah ever saw in me. Then, as quickly as that thought arrived, I scatter it to the winds, reasoning easily that that was then, and this is now. That is life. Or the lack of it.

I am content in my new-found knowledge that we – my fellow spirits, that is – are immune from laws, prosecution, imprisonment, torture and all the things that created pressures and boundaries in the living world; we are now only subject to the censure of our peers. I have to question whether this, ultimately, may be a far harder thing. We are immune from laws and taxes, and free of illness, frailty, incest, philandering, deceit, ageism, sexism, racism, bigotry, homophobia, nationalism, imperialism, and every other thing which had turned my living world into a maelstrom of hypocrisy: the coded fascism, hidden agendas and thought-police rules and ties that bound us, and allowed those who had the rudder of the media to steer us, as we desperately tried to view ourselves as right-thinking people. We were not right-thinking; we were in truth swallowed up and mired in endless conceit and self-perpetuating snobbery. A society where people with little talent, no skills, knowledge, insight or vision can be fêted by an adoring population of followers on social media, or television viewers who somehow ascribe success to meaningless consumption, where gambling is promoted as cool, and everyone has to understand everyone else's failings, as though no one can be a loser; where children all get stars for just turning up at school and every poor person is a victim of a society built on a satanic conspiracy; where success in business is something to require apology or self-effacement, unless the successful are film stars or rock stars, who have *carte blanche* to tell the rest of us how to live when they are sitting in soft-leather smugness, telling the ordinary working people how they should go without and dig ever deeper to save the world. Hypocrites and parasites.

I had carried a degree of cynicism, as human nature imbues us with, but had never really seen this all so clearly in life. Gramsci's words have set my mind to examination, and in my present existence I hear Calvin Klein laugh fit to bust at the thought of a Finn Chambers T-shirt. I was – I have to face facts – a consumer of bullshit. Of the *design, create, market, sell, purchase, repeat* hamster wheel of commerce driven by the modern human desire to be recognised, to be an individual. Christ! Individual? Self-assured in my Haight Ashbury T-shirt, designer jeans and Old Skools. Perhaps I am now a harsh judge of my living self, or maybe it is just a truth long overdue.

In this limitless afterlife, free of so many things, I am beginning to understand that we are never truly free of one another, even after death, unless we choose the existence of the hermit, or find that we no longer desire this endless future, and determine to walk to powder or nothingness or whatever it is that we disappear into.

I pause again, smile to myself, and wave an arm in the direction of the houses on the other side of Via Giovanni Battista Bodoni. I want to laugh at myself as I consider that I am immune even from my own past. I walk up to the oak doors of the church, and glide straight through them.

# hail, Caesar

Sanchez is on his knees at the altar. I suspect this is the church where humanity and compassion was shown to him. A place of refuge and his restoration to belief in his God. The place he died.

Despite my recently acquired immunity from worry, I am aware that my presence here is an intrusion. Even spirits should be allowed solitude. Privacy. I drift silently upwards to sit on the ornate gilt fascia of a gallery set above the main doors. Angels and *putti* float below me. Once again I am a voyeur. A spy.

Sanchez is muttering. I suspect it is prayer, but he could be making a mental shopping list, or calling down fire and brimstone upon the Holy See. His body, crouched low as it is, suggests the former. His hands, palms pressed together, appear to be on the floor in front of his knees, and his forehead is pressed down on his thumbs. He looks for all the world to have adopted an advanced yoga position, from whatever level exists in yoga hierarchy that is equivalent to black belt in judo.

I ponder the thought that even after death, and his rough treatment at the hands of his church, Sanchez is still seeking the redemption of forgiveness. He need not, obviously. Nothing can hurt him here. His sole fellow worshippers are two old ladies clothed in black, bent forward like a pair of roosting crows.

He remains in this position, mumbling words I cannot hear and can only guess at, until my sense of myself as intruder overcomes me and I float out through the wall and drop to the street. A dog sniffing at a lamp post stiffens slightly as I descend. Can he see me or does he just sense me? He barks once and skips away along the street, sniffing as he goes. A pair of men in business suits walk past me, oblivious to my presence. They turn into the Ancona café and I follow. Let's face it, I have time.

There is no beguiling element here. No *these guys look interesting*. Nothing at all, just maybe some light release from my intrusion on my unwitting prey. Sanchez the rabbit? Far from it. Sanchez, despite his worldly failings and frailty, is a principled man. A strong man. A man whose raised arms carried a weight that few could endure. Sanchez carried a cross of stone. A cross of stone bored out and stuffed with lead.

I sit across from the taller man, next to his associate, who is a good foot shorter. David and Goliath. He smells nice. Chanel Pour Monsieur, my favourite. If there are two things that Chanel got right, it was scent and the little black dress. Longevity. Like Rolls-Royce and the Ritz hotel. Some things just deserve to continue. The mojito, for example, and the tango. The twist on the other hand deserves to be exactly where it is: rolled out on some crap Christmas show with Chubby Checker grinning like the proverbial Cheshire cat. Spare me. At least I won't have to put up with any more Christmases surrounded by bad jumpers and cheap cards that don't stand up as they weigh less than dust, and recycled television shows from decades gone by which are packaged as great memories of Christmases past, but in reality are just the result of penny-pinching by broadcasters getting away with boosting their revenue figures by banging out historic rubbish which was hardly funny the first time around. Times change. Move on! No more pains over what to buy, no more wandering into department stores to be met by a waving plastic Santa, a leaning fake tree, and a beautiful cosmetics sales assistant selling a brand I've never heard of, of which I find myself buying vast quantities, to be told on Christmas morning, *That is so beautiful of you. Do you still have the receipt? It's not really my skin tone, but it was a lovely thought. I only use Bobbi Brown. I thought you would have noticed.* Or to receive a set of *Hits of the Eighties* from a maiden aunt who remembers those days in a 'Save the World' way, not knowing that I a) know nothing of the Eighties and have no desire to, and b) the music is, to my ears, dross. At least I will not have the usual issue that Christmas has to be spent with Hannah's parents as opposed to mine, for reasons of mystery. Hannah wanted everything equal, right down to me buying my own toothpaste, except that we had to spend our Christmases with her family for eternity as she *hardly gets time to see them throughout the year*. Her family home is in Sussex. She sees them twice a month. My family home is in Yorkshire. I saw them twice a year.

I laugh to myself momentarily, and feel a sense bordering on relief that at least Hannah has her family close by to help her through my unfortunate exit from the stage. It is a relief of sorts, my sense of worry, concern and regret being what it now is. I only want good things for Hannah. I only ever wanted good things for everyone.

I laugh again, thankful that Hannah cannot see me doing a Shelley, sniffing at my companion while he takes a sip of his espresso. Oh, that combination: Chanel Pour Monsieur and espresso. Sublime. I chuckle to myself again. The easy delights of being a spirit. I can recommend it.

The men are discussing a contract to provide bottled water. Water with a slight natural fizz. Saints' water. The taller man has a laptop open opposite me, and the shorter man a receipt book with duplicating lower sheets. They discuss various orders from restaurants, bars and clubs. The national museum is mentioned, and given a discount. Twenty per cent. Generous. The owner of the café, a fat man, sweating and wiping his brow with a cloth with which he will no doubt then wipe glasses, brings a Cognac each. On the house. Obsequiousness flows from him. Something greasy and shifty about him. He makes great play of letting the other customers know this is on the house, waving his arms as he bows his head towards the two men, who nod towards him without smiles or recognition by words. I assume they are *mafiosi*. He backs away with a flourish. Despite my newfound state of affability, I instinctively do not like this man. Smarmy. They discuss him, and add five per cent.

'*Quel bastardo picchia sua moglie. Sua moglie è mia cugina Chiari. Ragazza adorabile. No, no. Dieci percento. Secondo pensiero, venti, il bastardo.*'

I am becoming good at this. That bastard beats his wife. His wife is my cousin Chiara. Lovely girl. No, no. Ten per cent. Second thoughts, twenty, the bastard.

My instincts are good. I would like them to add fifty and be done. They cannot be *mafiosi* or they would have sorted him. Put a horse's head in his bed or a bullet in his mailbox.

They move on to their accounts. The arbitrary nature of their business is something of a shock. Tall guy reads out the name of the venue, and Chanel states the rate. They run through a series of names which I suspect, since they are not alphabetical, are part of a route whereby the two deliver invoices.

The Vatican is mentioned. The shorter man, playing with rosary beads as he speaks immediately smacks on fifty per cent.

*'Quel covo di fottuti ladri. Afferrare da ogni uomo e donna buoni. Agglungi il solito si? Cinquanta percento.'*

Tall boy nods in conformation and grins. That den of thieves. Grabbing from every good man and woman. Add the usual? Fifty per cent.

I am laughing to myself when it strikes me that these men are ripping off their customers. They are biting the hand that feeds them. Distaste overrules my sense of justice for Sanchez against his punishers, who I believe deserve the judgement of a fair but equitable God, capable of condemning them to eternal repentance for the torment wreaked on him.

As they are about to leave, tall boy closes his laptop and throws a question at small man. *'Chi ricevera il regalo questa settimana? L'ospizio o il club giovanile?'* Who will receive the gift this week? The hospice or the youth club?

*'Entrambi, eh?'* Small man smiling. Tall man nods. Both, eh?

I feel pleasantly surprised, at the realisation that even after becoming a spirit I can make judgements which are as flawed as in life. There is something comfortingly human still about placing mistaken labels on others, and being able to rub out the label and reattach it. Labels. Even in the afterlife. Coco Chanel would be proud. I glance down at my Old Skools. Satisfied that my coffee companions are Robin Hood and Little John, I make my way out into the daylight.

Winter is making its mark on each day now. More people wearing overcoats and scarves and hats. Everywhere there are signs of Christmas coming. I remain as always neither hot nor cold in my Music Center T-shirt. Plastic Santas and reindeer multiply in shop windows, and children, hands held by parents and elder siblings, point excitedly at the latest games and gadgets displayed. Sprayed snow borders glass frontages, and holly, red berries glowing, is lit up by light-emitting diodes.

Frenzy. Not yet, but it is coming. The final few days before the holidays marked by panic-buying parents and partners and husbands and wives, and children making paper cards at primary school showing snowmen with carrot noses and reindeer with stick legs and cigar bodies, and the note *Buon natale Mamma e Papa di* written by a trainee teacher in a grown-up hand, followed by the scrawl of the kid's name. Happy days. To be stored in a heart-shaped box at the bottom of a wardrobe or placed with other boxes marked with labels or permanent pen in a house attic, to be added to other simple treasures, to be seen only by chance when looking for something else, or never again until bereavement brings cause for a trip along Memory Lane. Such is the nature of people, and the passage of time. Universal.

Instead of making my way to Masto today, I decide to walk streets I have yet to discover. I come across a square edged with lavender which is cut across by harsh shadow from a tall building defying the watery sun. Winter. Sun failing to rise high. Portent of darkness and silver skies. The occasional burst of skies as blue as the Caribbean and glinting windows, when sunglasses suddenly have a use once more against the copper orange of the low setting sun, beautiful but blinding. The sharp days of crisp air, and early-morning frosts which sparkle and cast a billion fragments of diamond light from a frozen metal gate, or the links of chain preserving the parking spaces of city dwellers, until the first person out or in disturbs that beauty with a key in the padlock, dropping ice dust to the concrete floor, destroying nature's art. Such beauty August Riedel will admire but never better.

A line of parked scooters sits within a painted yellow box; order in this disorderly city, in this disordered world. A group of toga-clad Romans, men and women, variously sit or lie across the scooters, listening to a man who is perched on a parking payment machine. I am stunned. Julius Caesar. Am I mistaken? I've seen various busts of Caesar in museums and I'm sure it's him. He has the rapt attention of the group, and makes expansive gestures as he speaks. He has a laurel wreath about his head. I have no idea what he is saying. Latin. One year of Latin does not a scholar make, I think to myself. I am reminded of a line of graffiti I wrote inside my Latin textbook. *Latin is a language as dead as dead can be. It killed the ancient Romans, and now it's killing me.* I thought I was a real comedian back then, aged eleven. I clearly still think of myself as hilarious when, passing them at my closest point, I call out, 'Hail, Caesar!'

There is a brief silence, with the exception of a stooped old man passing who laughs into his hand. The man I address my flippancy towards gives an offhand wave of his arm which is suspiciously like flipping the finger and carries on talking to those who matter. I am not included in this group, and feel a shred of relief that he only flipped a digit at me and did not award me the gladiators' feared thumbs-down. I am momentarily relieved there are no spirit lions chained in this otherworld. I wave back, letting my index and middle fingers extend marginally to give my sense of humour full play. The classic response of the English archer. Hail, Caesar? I wonder where Marcus Brutus is now. *Et tu, Brute.* Presumably not draped across a Lambretta.

I make a mental note to myself to find out if this really is Caesar or just some Roman senator. I know a man who will know.

# a simple ceremony

Claudio is under the hood of another 500. This one is cream, with parallel green and red stripes crossing from front to rear on the driver's side. Class. It brings to mind Hannah's handbag. If I were still alive I would buy a 500, in these classic colours. Claudio has a heavy jumper below his overalls, suggesting the change to cold. The postman slips in and out of the workshop, taking his time. I watch him through the open doors as he drops post on the desk, then slowly peruses Pirelli's finest. He crosses the street to the houses without saying anything other than *ciao*, which goes unanswered by Claudio who is unaware. I carry on past Claudio's and acknowledge a wave from the Kraafts' elderly son, who is perched on the cemetery wall. He is a cheery chap. I resolve to get to know him better. I wonder what story he has to tell away from his young parents. Must be weird to be older than your parents.

It strikes me that the *cimitero* is populated mainly by foreigners, of which I am one. The Italians, with a few exceptions like Gramsci, who denies God, are buried elsewhere, the

Cimitero Acattolico being a refuge for those deemed unclean or unworthy by the Catholic church. It seems that times have moved little from the origins of this place as the burial ground for those the Roman church rejected: Protestants, Muslims, Jews, and those with no religion. We send men to the moon, and cameras to Mars, but religious hatred, as it did in history, still powers societies and even nations. What world is this? The creation of a loving God, or gods, or, as the poets would have it, just an imagined world, or some strange film being made by an invisible director?

I carry on up towards Casa di Pace, and as I pass along the footpath I give an unexplained little skip, a celebration of whatever. Christmas is approaching; maybe that is why. Every year while alive I looked forward to Christmas. Although the sun in Rome is bright and some trees still have leaves, the presence everywhere of jackets and scarves signals a change. In London now I imagine there will be sleet and grey skies.

Thinking of Christmas, I skip again, and, as I do so, a long black limousine slows beside me, indicating to pull across to the *cimitero* gates, waiting for a car and a van to pass. I am stunned to see Hannah, her mother, and my mother and father inside the car. All thoughts of Vito and Alessandra fall from me. The car pulls across into the bay by the entrance gates, and the smart lady from the *cimitero*, whose shapely form I have increasingly admired on the many occasions I have seen her, approaches the car. Hannah, Claire and my parents appear from the car, together with the young girl from the embassy. The facilitator. She greets the *cimitero* doll in Italian and announces her party in English. *Cimitero* lady shakes hands with Hannah, Claire and my mother and father before extending a hand to Miss Embassy, and acts with great grace by expressing her sadness for the loss of me in attractively accented English, and thanks them all for coming so far. She invites them to attend her office. They troop across to the office and I walk beside them, putting an arm around Hannah for a few brief seconds, then hugging my mother and father, though my arm simply slides through them all. My father has on his best navy suit and his old university tie. I smile to myself about his love of formality and my lack of affection for it. They enter the office together; the door closes before me.

Capable though I am of walking through the closed door, I decide that I have done sufficient spying for one day, and leave them to their business. After a few minutes the gardener arrives at the office, knocks, then enters. A minute later he leaves carrying a slim cardboard box, which is dark red, and tied with a black satin bow. He disappears towards his shed. A short while later a power tool bursts briefly into life, with a few staccato bursts, then silence. Birds have flown in profusion, scattered like confetti thrown to winds. There was something of the firing squad about the sudden sharp reports. Gramsci is lying on the gardener's hut, and raises a hand in greeting to me.

A minute or two passes before the gardener emerges from the far side of the garden, smoking a cigarette. I watch him as he leans against the edge of the Duke of Leeds's tomb, deep in thought, blowing smoke into the cold, still air. He takes a last draw, inhales then exhales before dropping the cigarette and marching purposefully towards his shed, where he deposits a toolbox before walking to the office. He knocks again and enters after a muffled call from within. The door remains open, and after a few seconds he leaves and heads down to the old part of the garden. *Cimitero* doll holds the door while Hannah, followed by my mother, father and Claire, pass slowly out from the office. Embassy girl brings up the rear. Doll lady closes the door and moves to head up the procession, smilingly wanly as she points the way to a branching path. Hannah, who is now holding Claire's hand with her left,  takes my mother's hand in her right, which gives me a sudden longing to hold both their hands; to hold them both tight to me, to bury my head in their coats, and feel loved again. I am tempted to do just that, but something holds me where I am, following. An unobserved observer. They turn around the slight bend on which an acacia tree hides view of Shelley's tomb. They stop together in a line, facing the wall behind Percy's stone, like a firing squad. There, on the wall, is a small brass plate. It carries a simple sentiment in few words. *In loving memory of Finn Chambers.*

That is it. Nothing else need be said. Nothing funny like *Shelley 1 – Chambers 0*, or overly elaborate, such as *International photographer Finn Chambers snapped his last here*. Plain words, well chosen and used for centuries to convey a sentiment, so fitting for so many. Hannah, standing still, looking straight at the plaque, starts to sob quietly, gathers herself, then takes two red roses from her Italian flag handbag and hands one to my mother. They both then lay their flowers by the wall below the plaque. I am touched. A simple sentiment, with a simple ceremony. Just how I would have liked it, assuming that an untimely demise had ever featured in my thoughts, which it had not. They are both silently tearful, as are Claire and my father, and *cimitero* lady too. Embassy girl is stoic. Stiff upper lip with no sign of a tremble. Professionally detached. British to the core.

I do not belong here. I belong with Hannah and my folks, roasting chestnuts, and drinking mulled wine and opening thoughtful gifts I will never use. Except I shall never have use for gifts any more. Not ever. The thought then occurs to me that perhaps I do belong here. That just maybe, in some preordained plan, I was destined from birth to be here, to walk and talk with great women and men.

Everyone, except embassy girl, stands head bowed looking towards the roses on the ground. Embassy girl glances at her wristwatch. She clearly has better places to be. I'm not sure what I feel now. A sense that I should not be viewing this. Finn the spy again. I am peculiarly devoid of the heart-wrenching emotion I imagine I should feel, watching my parents and Hannah broken, and even *cimitero* lady shedding a tear for me, a man she never met alive but only saw lying dead above Shelley, a shock she might well never have had to experience had I been a little more careful and less of a devil-may-care-must-rush-back-to-my-love kind of guy. I feel a slight sense of mock guilt, not at being the cause of this demonstration of love and loss, but at taking a longing look at *cimitero* lady and wondering what she looks like naked. I am imagining her in black lace underwear when something causes me to turn away momentarily to see my friends, Shelley, Keats, Lady Mary von Haast, Trelawny, Severn, Gramsci and Sanchez, arranged in a loose group watching us. Suliman, the Nubian prince I have yet to converse with, the Reverend John Barrington and John Kraaft stand a distance back. All have the look of sympathy about them. Solemnity. A respectful group, and behind them August Riedel stands, holding his cap in clasped hands, for once looking respectful, and without his habitual amused expression. I turn to my family gathering and call, 'Hannah!' There is no response. No twitch suggesting she is hearing my call. I call again. No reaction. My father holds my mother, a tender arm around her waist as he pulls her gently into him. I hear him speaking quietly. 'Finn's here with us. I feel him here. He's with the angels now.' I would like to correct him on that score, and tell my father that angels are a figment of the imaginations of biblical scholars and artists paid to create beautiful images to support a doctrine based on idealism and power, but I cannot. I just think it, and leave them with his words, hoping that he, my mother, Hannah and Claire, and Miss Italy, take some comfort from that sentiment. I have caused enough suffering.

Hannah steps over the flowers and reaches up to the plaque on the wall. She touches it with her hand, then places a kiss on the brass, which I imagine now feels cold to her soft lips in the chill winter air. It is a touching scene, and as I glance behind me I see Lady Mary, head bowed, her hands in prayer mode, and Sanchez crossing himself and placing his hands together in supplication. I notice his lips moving. He is praying too. Hopefully their prayers will bring some relief for Hannah and my folks, and I wish at that moment, more strongly than for some time, to be alive again, within the bubble that is my family's and Hannah's love.

# no going back

The last thing I hear as they head back to their waiting car is a few more words from my father. After the others climb inside the car, he turns towards the cemetery gates, and whispers, 'Merry Christmas, son.'

I whisper back, 'Merry Christmas, Dad.'

Once again I watch the car move slowly down Via Caio Cestio, indicate, and turn out of sight.

I walk slowly up towards Shelley's tomb and Hannah's brass plaque. I am curiously unsure of how I feel. I decide that space in Vito and Alessandra's garden will allow me freedom to think through my feelings.

I have just vaulted the cemetery wall out to the street when I am arrested momentarily by the harsh call and sudden flash of green as three parakeets shoot by, and then by a sudden bang as a scooter turns from Via Nicola Zabaglia, slides on ice, and hits the side of a parked car. It is Claudia. I rush across the street to her. Powerless. I cannot assist her. She is fortunate: she has on a thick woollen coat and appears to be shocked but uninjured.

She stands up, takes off her helmet and calls someone. Claudio. The Vespa lies on its side; the smell of petrol floods the air as the engine stalls. Seconds later he rushes into view, driving the striped Fiat. His concern is evident. Only a man truly in love can laugh so loud when he holds his lover in his arms, finding that despite his worst fears she is safe. She kisses him full on the mouth.

Passion. It is the best feature of human life. In that moment, I realise that it is the only feature that truly matters; that of all the characteristics of human personality, of all the traits valued by people – sympathy, compassion, kindness, generosity, empathy – of all these worthy things, the greatest of these is love. True love. Not lip-service love, but the passionate love that makes life exhilarating – that is what rises above all others. Passion for art, music, drama, medicine, charity, all of these make life worth living, but surely, the greatest of all is the passion of love for another human being. A dented car or a torn painting or a scratched record or a musical instrument with broken keys or strings, these can be repaired, like a broken window; but a broken heart may be beyond repair. A physical heart can have stents inserted, be transplanted and fixed in various ways by dedicated surgeons, but the emotional heart? What price that? Who fixes the broken hearts of my mother and father? Of my brother? Of Hannah?

I am reminded of some words of wisdom my father imparted to me on occasion. Simple but truthful honesty. *Life isn't complicated, son. People make life complicated.* And then I think of my own view of life, that mantra I carried about being the kind of man I would be happy to call my friend.

I had good teachers.

After writing a brief note on his business card, and glancing with a professional eye at the dented door of the rusty Lancia, Claudio slides the card beneath the windscreen wiper blade and hands the keys of the Fiat to Claudia. He restarts the scooter, then follows her back down Caio Cestia towards his workshop, her helmet slipped through the crook of his arm as though he, Claudio, is protected by the gods.

I am relieved Claudia is safe and uninjured. I turn a cartwheel and float up to the coping tiles on top of the garden wall. It occurs to me that I have all but forgotten the touching scene of minutes ago. Am I becoming someone I should loathe?

The French windows to the terrace are closed. Vito and Alessandra are not on the terrace as I anticipated. The chill air may have forced them indoors. I look up towards the top-floor windows, but they are blank and speak of nothing. There is no sign of window lady. The small brown bird flits from shadow to the urn by the pond. I am convinced this bird knows me. Perhaps even sees me for who I am. A spirit lacking conviction. A spirit unreconciled to fate and destiny. As much a dichotomy as I was as a living being. A contradiction. A loser, perhaps.

I sit on the terrace for a while, watching the small brown bird flit back and forth on the lower branches of the cedar. As if to break the monotony, or simply for a change of scene, brown bird whips across the width of the garden to be lost in the shade of another tree. I get up to make my way into the house and back she comes. She flies straight at me and then, just as I expect her to pass through me, she swerves around me, and lands on the urn. She can see me, I am sure. Aloud, I ask her name. She ignores me. I ask again in Italian: *'Come ti chiami?'* She ignores me again, and flies across to the lower branches of the cedar to end our conversation. I am thinking she, but maybe she's a he. I can only tell robins apart; small brown birds all look the same.

I pass through the French windows into the huge living room. I love this room. It is as though there is a story about it, hidden tales. The striking art, the paintings and sculptures, the books and the arrangement of furniture, all suggest a place where magic has happened; where dinner guests have spoken great words, and left the essence of conversation still floating in the air; where the aroma of fine wine and brandy lingers entwined with the scent of oregano and rosemary and cigar smoke. I would dearly love to have been a guest in this house. To listen to the thoughts of fine minds, and the irreverent humour of guests high on Chianti, cigars and Cognac; bohemian souls with a lust for life and the telling of tales, both tall and true.

I stroll through the door into the hallway. There is something about passing through walls with which, unlike Shelley, I am not yet completely comfortable. Time will probably bring that ease, but it doesn't feel natural to me, just more of a dare. The old couple are nowhere to be seen. I had anticipated that Alessandra and Vito would be sitting at their kitchen table, drinking coffee, reading the daily papers, laughing at Berlusconi and his orange face and jet-black hair. Maybe they are shopping, or out at a lunch engagement with friends.

I decide that their absence gives me licence to explore this house. I feel less like an intruder and more like a weekend guest whose hosts have gone to a prearranged function saying *make yourself at home* before dashing out of the door. We are practically family.

I look into all the ground floor rooms. I marvel again at the lavish dining room with its wonderful central chandelier and long yew table that could seat half the population of Rome but probably only sees use on birthdays and Christmas. There is a striking portrait dominating the far wall. It is the woman in the window. She is younger, but it is her. There is another painting of her in the drawing room, dressed in a wedding gown. She is beautiful. This room is smaller but purposely furnished to provide a calm and intimate space looking out on to a quiet area of garden which is simply composed: a gravelled square with a central fountain, bordered by ferns and broadleaf and evergreen shrubs to provide interest on the harshest of winter days, which in truth are rare in Rome.

A study. Books everywhere. A desktop computer, a couple of laptops, a desk littered with papers, and every wall covered by framed paintings. The work of my new family is clearly evident, along with occasional contributions from Old Masters, and new ones. Richard Hamilton, Warhol, and what appears to be Yoko Ono. Yoko Ono? Surely not? I feel the recent familial bonds beginning to stretch, and contemplate the probability that I have brought my artistic prejudices, and quite possibly my political, religious and social ones too, with me into this otherworld. I stand in this room, looking from painting to painting, scores of them, wishing I could see them without prejudice. I am somewhat at a loss. It is a question I must pose to Keats and Shelley, and Sanchez. How can a man who passes through the veil of life to this afterlife bring with him his prejudices? Surely this transition carries some form of absolution where the ills of the past are filtered in the purple tube that carries us from that state to this? I am baffled to find my strongly held views on art still with me, and no doubt also my views on literature and music. Perhaps I have been too bound up with analysing my reaction to the loss of Hannah, my family and friends and my former life, to honestly assess the aspects that made me who I was in my past life and whether they remain? Woe is me. Am I simply Finn Chambers, photographer, follower of anticipated and expected fashion in a clichéd T-shirt and Old Skool shoes? A worthless caricature of my former self? Stuck forever within a defined radius from a moment of carelessness? I want to shout *Fucking hell! Somebody save me!* So I do. I shout it loud, from a point above my diaphragm, so that my words bellow and recoil around this room. I feel the force of my words, my yell, as though it rattles the paintings on the walls, and imagine that Warhol and Hamilton, dead somewhere else, will prick their ears and hear my call.

I stray into a studio. A room full of canvases, some nearing completion, some sketched and part-formed. This appears to be Vito's private studio. I am a voyeur again, looking on things the artist may well wish to keep private from prying eyes. I decide to leave, and wander through to an adjacent room where again various studies have been sketched out, and small clay models, sculptures in differing stages, announce Sandra's works in progress. I leave here too. I want to return when they are here, to see them work, and, if they discuss their projects, to hear their thoughts on what they are creating. I think there is something marvellous about their art, and their age, that they are as full of creativity, inspiration and passion as they most probably were as art students way back in the past millennium.

I stroll to the magnificent central staircase, and pause again to admire the chandelier hanging from on high into the lower hallway. I wish I could have lived in a house this grand in my worldly life. *C'est la vie. Asi es la vida. So ist das Leben. E la vita. That's life.* Or, as I am tempted to think, the lack of it. Such is life. Such is what it is. The irony is that there truly is no going back. No undoing of wrong turns. No making amends. If only I had known then what I know now.

## he loved art more

I stroll upstairs. I could levitate but I wish to maintain my theme of house-guest, rather than snooper. All doors on the first landing are closed. This is such a grand house, a quiet statement of wealth. Doors are ornately carved, large and solid, and occasional sofas are placed around what is a minstrels' gallery overlooking a central ballroom, which has the chandelier over it, as though a hovering angel guards the dancers. Exotic vases sit on carved Chinese tables, flowers filling their centres, cultivated in glasshouses as the sudden cold of winter has denied cut flowers from Alessandra's garden.

There are a series of single doors, but in the centre of the galleried landing are double doors, imposing and inviting. I stroll towards them.

'I wouldn't. Don't you hear that noise? They are having sex. He is just like his father.'

I spin around to see window lady. She laughs into the air.

'I should know,' she continues, holding out her hand. 'I'm his mother. Daniela Mazzi.'

I take her outstretched hand, looking into her eyes as I do so. They sparkle and dance just like Vito's. I see now the resemblance between them. She is younger than Vito, but only by a few years. Another anomaly, as with the Kraaft family, where the son is older than the mother.

There must be something in my stare that offers my thoughts to her.

'Pneumonia,' she says simply.

'My name is Finn,' I say. 'I am recently arrived. Killed by quality.'

She smiles, as though being killed by quality is normal in Rome, and lets go of my hand, then motions for me to follow her. She levitates up through the ceiling to the next floor landing. We are standing on what is in essence an identical landing with an equal number of rooms. Only the differing sofas and vases on tables signify change. She walks through a closed door and I follow.

This is a room filled with paintings. There are so many that the faded terracotta walls are mostly obscured. A beautiful woman features heavily. She is nude in various poses. Her eyes sparkle and her mouth is mischievous. The woman is Daniela. It must be some male instinct that made me see only nudes on passing through the door, because there are many others. Portraits, charcoal sketches of her in clothes that reflect the passing decades of her adult life, and a beautiful oil painting, life-size and almost photographic, of Daniela as she appears to me now but a few years younger as she has fewer lines to her face. She is staring at the painter with a hand under her chin and her index finger flat against her cheek; it's a pose which could suggest annoyance, or deep thought, but the turn of her mouth says amusement and love.

I cross to peer at it. I whistle to signify my admiration. The hand is deft. An artist of immense talent.

'Did Vito paint this?' I ask.

'His father.'

I am open-mouthed, but perfectly at ease looking at her naked throughout time. The changes in her from a young woman through to her current age, that locked-forever state, are beautiful to behold. Even as she aged into her late sixties, around the time she passed through purple, she was, and still is, forever, incredibly beautiful.

'I know a man who would love to see these,' I say, as though I am alone. I turn to look at Daniela, who smiles.

'I was thinking out loud,' I say, apologising, and add, 'Just a painter I know.'

'Bring your friend along.' Her honeyed accent is musical, and sexy. 'A lady still finds attention from an admirer thrilling, even in this afterlife.' Her eyes sparkle. 'And Inni, my husband, would approve of another artist admiring his work. He was vain that way.' Her eyes still sparkle, but her words have the slightest edge to them.

'Where is he now, Vito's father?'

'His body lies in the Verano Cemetery. Do you know it?'

I shake my head.

'The noble people of Rome are buried there. Innocenzo was from a notable family, with a long history in Rome. They claimed they could trace their lineage back to ancient Rome, but he was never interested in that. He was a man of the moment. He loved life and art, but most of all he loved women. His name means *innocent* but that was his parents' little joke, I think.'

I love the way she pronounces *art*. She adds a sound which is faintly sexual to the end which gives the word definition and stature. She gives it passion.

I ask her where his spirit resides, as I look around expectantly, hoping he will appear through the walls.

'With his mistress,' she answers simply.

'Oh,' I say, feeling once again like an intruder, or the unknowing person who assumes all to be well but causes an embarrassed silence at a dinner party by asking an innocent question about the whereabouts of a missing guest. Innocent. There have been popes named Innocent. Innocent the Third? Far from innocent. As well as inciting the slaughter of the Muslim occupiers of the Holy Land, he excommunicated King John of England and declared the greatest social advance in English history, the Magna Carta, null and void. Maniac. Tyrant. He regarded himself as landlord of all England and like all his kind thirsted for money and power. Money and power. More money and greater power. Ask Sanchez about his Church and money, power, and God, and which of these comes last. Innocent was a pope with no qualms about riding over everything and anyone in his way, claiming authority as the will of God. Putting heretics to the sword, or fire. *Heretic*: a convenient label to dispose of opponents. Labels. So easily attached. Gregorovius said of him, *Thy words are the words of God; thy deeds are the deeds of the devil*. A canon created by Innocent for the papal lands decreed Jews wear insignia so that they could be identified and vilified by the badge. Innocent III, precursor to the Nazi SS by over seven hundred years. Labels. Everyone loves labels. A black deed which lasted long past his time, and on to now. Good old Innocent. Divide and conquer. Reunite under the papal banner. Even the least scrupulous of modern politicians are better than that. Or are they? There are so many still creating conflict, miring their people in poverty and fear in this modern world, who give the lie to the thought that we have civilised ourselves and are way better than the tyrants of history, than men such as Pope Innocent. Most of us try to be civilised, or in my case were, which also belies the saying that people get the society they deserve. Not if they live in war-torn and famine-ridden countries, or in the cartel-dominated countrysides of nations rich with resources whose police and armies are so hideously corrupt from the top down that they roll in a mire of filth which knows no end in its depravity. Ask the hill farmers of Columbia or Mexico if they prefer to harvest poppies and coca leaves and have food on the family table, or to lie dust-covered, bloody and butchered, in a ditch, their throats cut and their hands and feet chopped off, or shot in the head. Ask Sanchez. He knows. He knows only too well on all those counts.

I wonder if I should make some form of apology for prying into Daniela's personal life, but she heads me off.

'Inni was always mine, but always his own man too.'

I feel a faint sense of relief that she is relating her story easily, and in her best English for my benefit. She has a quality to her voice which is Sophia Loren and Silvia Colloca rolled into one. I could listen to her forever.

'He had a lover at the studio he shared with his artist friends. Painters and sculptors who loved him as he loved them. They were such great company for him. They stimulated his sense of freedom, of his art. He was an intellectual, with a great mind. He saw things in art I could never see. He loved me, but he loved art more. There were many models, many lovers. I didn't mind. He brought me love and light and enchantment. Our son took much from his nature, but much more from me than Inni took from his own mother. She was a narrow-minded woman, very much a woman of high but staid society. Inni's father married her in an arrangement between both families designed to keep their bloodlines pure. To keep the walls from cracking. That is how it was in those days: noble families interbreeding to maintain their dominance. Inni pushed against his upbringing. He viewed his heritage as belonging to the past, which is why he fought to be an artist, not a man of status in society. He was embarrassed by his lineage, and railed against it. He was very taken with a friend of yours, and his view of the nobility of Italy, which they shared, although from vastly different experiences. Although he would laugh about much that your friend said, he had an affinity for his views and thought well of him as a man of humanity.'

'A friend of mine?' I am puzzled. I have only ever seen Daniela once before at the window, and then I saw her alone. Both of us apparently alone.

'Antonio Gramsci.' She smiles, and continues. 'I passed you walking with him one day, and you were clearly taken with him. Your attention was with him only. You have an interesting collection of friends from the cemetery. You will make more. There are many you have yet to meet. You are welcome to bring them here. I know how much you like to sit in the garden. Alessandra has maintained these gardens with love and added to them well, which I approve of. She is a woman of great heart and passion. She has made my son a happy man for all his life. No mother can hope for more. I shall be glad when they join me here in time, although if you were to call upon them now you would see that they still enjoy the life of the living.'

She laughs loudly at her own joke, and turns to leave me there.

'I hope to see you soon, Finn. You are welcome here whenever you choose. *La mia casa è la tua casa.* Bring Antonio and your artist friend. And Percy. He always amuses me. I would like that. I continue with my habits from life. I like to lie quietly and listen to the birds and the breeze through the trees, and to music when Vito and Sandra put on the radio or play the piano and cello. That is a pleasure to me. I shall say farewell, but promise you will come to see me soon.'

I nod. She smiles and blows me a kiss before adopting the exact pose she holds in the large painting, then floats backwards through that very painting so that she merges into her own image as she disappears, leaving only Inni's masterpiece to remind me of her beauty.

# brighter than average

I decide to make my exit. I shake my head as I think of the over-seventies banging, and float down into the hallway and out to the garden. Brown bird watches me from a bough. It is as if she senses my amusement. She opens then flaps her wings without flying and sings out lustily. Sweet melodious song. Daniela's music.

I drift up to the coping stones and perch briefly, looking up towards the upper windows in case Daniela is watching me go. The windows are empty. I flip backwards as Shelley so often does, and walk back to the cemetery, casting a glance towards the dented Lancia and thinking momentarily of Claudia and Claudio and what they have. I gain pleasure now in this other world from the happiness of others. I feel no envy, nor wish to be Claudio as living human me might well have done. Even with Hannah to hold and love, I would occasionally cast a lustful eye towards a beautiful girl, which filled me with guilt. Now I have the thoughts of Picasso, who denied guilt. I think back to my school and university days and my envy of the year's star: the guy who stood out as every girl's dream date. I was never that, and lucky as all hell to have Hannah agree to date me, become my girlfriend, and love me. I was one lucky man, until Shelley got the better of me. Lucius Annaeus Seneca said, *Every guilty person is his own hangman.* He was a smart guy. That was back in the first century after Christ. A man ahead of his time. We all have guilt. No matter how pious, or how good, we believe we are. I mean, who does not really think they are better than most? Everybody's child is *brighter than average*. Every school report pretty much says, *Has above-average ability*. Really? So where are all the *average* people, then? I have news for you. That is you and me. Average. If you want above average, try Einstein, or Catherine the Great, or Andy Warhol, or Beethoven or Vermeer or Gandhi or Chairman Mao or Tim Berners-Lee or Prince or Marie Curie or Adolf Hitler or Ted Bundy or Percy Bysshe Shelley or John Keats. Somebody who, for good or evil, had the imagination, the drive and the ability to do something you or I could not have done in a million years. For the betterment, or to the detriment, of mankind. Poachers and gamekeepers. Light and dark. Yin and yang.

I roll back along Caio Cestio. My recent encounter with Hannah seems long ago. Strange that time should seem to pass that way. I would have suspected that time in an everlasting world would drag, but it does not. It is just as vibrant as ever, but without the fear that the candle is burning down, which sets in motion the drive to do more before you die, so that at the end you can look back and think, *I gave it a good shot*. No regrets. No *torschlusspanik* here. There is a reassurance that runs through me and causes me to skip over a parked car in exultation. The car is a Maserati. My dream car. I realise that I am free. Even within the confines of the invisible circle, beyond which there are dragons or another world or nothing, I am free of envy, of materialism, of worry, of illness. Of the fear of death.

The Kraafts' son is sitting perched high on the cemetery wall. I am reminded of Vito's mother Daniela's observation that there are many I have yet to know, so I cartwheel across the road to amuse him, then flip upwards and come to rest beside him. I ask him how he is doing and he replies that he is fine. He is a softly spoken man. I ask a lot more questions, and he answers in a small voice which, despite his size, for he is a big man for his generation, suits him. He has a gentleness of disposition that matches his voice. He tells me, without regret, that his time alive was an uneasy mix of difficulties which he now cares to forget, or at least to view as a past gone and no longer of consequence. I am beginning to find 'Finn the Inquisitor' an easier role with every day that passes. Matching Kraaft's calmness, I speak quietly of my own life, my experiences, limited though they were, and my sense that I had not achieved greatness, but that I could have achieved less. I mean, I could have spent my time sitting on my arse swigging cheap wine, playing pointless computer games or watching daytime television, easily amused by nothing of consequence, never having to think beyond cheap takeaway pizza and tinned beer. Easy. In response to my disclosures, Kraaft loosens his grip on his past. His parents, first his mother from typhus, then his father from influenza, died in their prime while he was a boy. His family fortune evaporated on boarding school fees and maintenance to his family home, which was administered by his father's executors, his godparents: his father's brother and sister, who cared much for the high life and entertained lavishly on his trust fund reserves, outwardly presenting this as a means to bring him to note in society as a young man of future prospects. In truth they arranged parties with potential brides and their mothers where the good and great of Rome society were fêted, not for the benefit of young John Kraaft, but to enhance the prospects of his uncle to marry a widowed lady of wealth and bring the soft life of moneyed leisure to both him and his sister, who was very much his driving force. The female Machiavelli.

'Where are they now?' I ask, referring to the Machiavellis. 'Are they here?'

'I am thankful that they are not here. I do not know where they are, and I care not. Probably Sorano. My uncle married the Contessa di Sorano. He courted her with luxuries from my inheritance, creating an image as a wealthy Roman investor, filled with lust as he was to join the aristocracy by any means. There is a mirage in Italian life. Status is deemed synonymous with success, prosperity, and of course wealth. He gave her trinkets, a diamond ring and the Grand Tour. After their marriage the countess had little to give him but a society status thin as gossamer, and syphilis.'

The corners of his mouth twitch with mirth, and he starts to rock slightly. I am warming to him. Here is a man with a subtle sense of humour, which suits him.

'As soon as I was of age, I sold my family home to be rid of my aunt and uncle, bought a small house by the sea in Livorno, and sailed to England to study medicine while I still had the funds to do so. My parents' family were German, but my English was sufficiently good to study medicine, and an English-speaking doctor could find work anywhere. I was loath to leave Italy as I love this land, but sometimes a man has to make sacrifices to escape his family. I hoped my godparents would remove themselves to Germany, but they chose to stay where my father had built his wealth, here in Rome.'

He turns to me and, looking slightly downwards, expresses that his circumstances were different from mine.

'I have seen the anguish you have suffered,' he murmurs, adding, 'We have both suffered.'

Livorno. I start to ask him if he is aware that Shelley drowned off the coast near Livorno, and think better of it. Of course he knows. There is little unknown to the souls here. Daniela Mazzi had proved that to me.

He carries on, as though lightened by his reference to our suffering, which he recognises as something, in his case at least, long since passed.

'I took to life as a ship's doctor, and found myself very much consoled by time at sea. The oceans have beauty and space, sometimes fierce and at other times serene. I signed up for long voyages to the Americas and the South Seas, to places where I could escape my past, and place distance between me and my former guardians. The pox the *contessa* gave my uncle did for him in the end, and my aunt, like my father, passed from influenza. By the time they both removed themselves from my life I was very much wedded to the sea, and remained so occupied until I retired to Livorno. I chose to move to Rome again later in years, to be able to visit my parents here. It was, as you will imagine, a great surprise to find myself reunited with them.'

As though reading my thoughts he pauses, adding, 'It was the strangest experience, to find myself older than them both. Some may think that a cruel trick of God's humour.'

He looks down as the Reverend John Barrington strolls out of the gates and crosses towards Via Paolo Caselli, and nods in his direction.

'There is a man for whom God has no faults, despite these tricks of eternity. Oh to have had his faith in life, eh, Finn? Surely a man with complete belief was a happier man than you or me?'

I find it strange that a man of John Kraaft's generation should have some doubt in God, but there again, why not? Shelley did. Shelley does.

Then, the oddest thing. As we watch, the reverend walks across the junction, passing through one side of a parked van delivering bearings to Claudio, and out the other side. He strolls past the forecourt and the workshop entrance, then, after a quick look around, passes through the roadside wall and into the interior. I am filled with thoughts of Barrington the hypocrite. Barrington has Pirelli on his mind.

I ask John Kraaft if he is coming to find Keats and Shelley, and, just as I do, the reverend reappears through the side of Claudio's workshop and stands looking at us, as we stare straight at him. He turns abruptly, and walks away from us along Paolo Caselli.

Kraaft smiles again with that slight twitching of mouth barely concealing his mirth.

'Not today, thank you, Finn. I think I shall deliver a slice of amusement to my parents. Well, I never. I've known that man for many a year and never have I seen him enter those premises. Shall I tell you what is of interest there, Finn?"

'Oh, I already know, John. Some of the finest photography of the twentieth century.'

He nods his head and says, 'Fit for a king. Or even a man of the cloth, for men are men, whether kings or clergy.' Then he adds with a grin, 'Or ship's doctors, or photographers.'

We both laugh as I float down into the cemetery and walk off to find the poets.

I am deep in thought as I pass by the gardener's hut. Gramsci calls to me from the roof and I ask if he has seen Shelley or Keats. He replies that they went to Masto with Lady Mary. He says he will be along later. I carry on up past his tomb and head for the fox lair. As expected, Riedel is napping on the tree limb, hat pulled down over his eyes. I call up to him. He waves a hand in acknowledgement but does not move otherwise, speak or remove his cap.

'August, will you accompany me later? I want to show you something.'

He gives a thumbs-up signal with the same hand but does not speak. I find this strangely modern for a man born in the final year of the eighteenth century.

I move on, pausing only to look down the length of the cemetery, and to take Daniela's cue and listen to birdsong. A robin, breast as red as new rust, stands on a bare twig staring at me. I touch my brow in acknowledgement. I believe he sees me. Continuing around the loop, I pause by the tomb of Karl Bryullov, who, if here in spirit, I have not so far seen, then stroll across to Shelley's stone, glance at Edward Ellerker Williams's heart entwined, and resolve to ask more questions, to seek answers, and to make the acquaintance of those I have not yet made. The living have the excuse that life is short to miss out those who may pass by, but here, I have all the time in the world, and little excuse for neglecting to learn something of those fascinating souls around me.

# one hell of a painter

I have started as usual to walk in the direction of Masto, towards familiarity, when a rebel kick stirs me. I turn around, and walk away from the restaurant, up past the Piramide di Caio Cestio which has lost none of its power to awe, along past Piramide metro station, people emerging and entering, a constant sign of modern rush, and up Via Marco Polo. I throw a right and eventually hit Porto Fluviale, where I am astounded to see a building painted with faces the size of houses, and on I march until I reach water. Like John Kraaft, there is something in me that loves the sea. Perhaps my hell is never seeing the sea again, or feeling spray upon my face from waves split into dust by the prow of a racing boat. I stare down at the Tiber from the bridge. Ponte dell'Industria. The bridge is girder-built. Tank-grey. It could be across any river or rail track in any state in America. Built for strength and economy. No-frills bridges. Ponte dell'Industria reminds me of so many bridges I will never see again.

I will never travel again. Never board an aeroplane and pull my seatbelt tight, fearing the worst I know will not happen, then tighten it again, just a notch. Just in case.

Graffiti softens the bridge in one way, adding colour and sentiment, but to the trained observer of places to avoid it suggests beyond this water may lie dragons. A few hundred yards upriver lies Ponte Testaccio, a far classier bridge. I cross the roadway to lean on the great flat plates above the low guard rail and look towards the rail bridge. Nothing elaborate there either. I look down to my feet and up and around me. Huge plates of steel bolted together. Tons of quiet giant. Bolted and welded. Grey-painted with spots of rust threatening its future. Even the footpath is metal, punched with upraised lozenge studs to aid the trudging pedestrian in rain and ice. Angled vertical girders, grey as leaping dolphins, are slashed with bleed-lines of rust streaking down which give away the hiding places of rusting bolts beyond the painter's reach. Like arthritis in an old man. Unseen but betrayed, nonetheless. Worsening with weather and age until the limb no longer has the strength to support the uprights and needs replacement, before the weight causes the body to collapse. I look again towards the rail bridge, an uninspiring work of utilitarian engineering taking the strain of hundreds of tons as trains cross back and forth between Roma Ostiense and Trastevere stations. I am tempted to take a ride on a train for the hell of it, but have a sudden and overwhelming desire to follow in the footsteps of Jesus.

I flip over the parapet and drop to the Tiber. I walk on the water towards the rail bridge, laughing to myself. I fancy the reverend would find this sacrilegious and an affront to God. I find it mildly amusing, and I think that God would too, if there is a God. If she were here to see me. For, let's face it, if there is a just and forgiving God, with unconditional love for all children, God must be a woman.

I wish Hannah could see me now. She would laugh like hell. But there is no Hannah.

I levitate up from the Tiber after one last skip along the brown water, churned as it is from recent rain. The air is crisp with cold, judging by the look of the people, collars pulled high with wool scarves and hats to keep them warm. Two Romans, togas bright as new snow, sit talking as I rise up to Lungotevere Testaccio. They nod towards me but do not speak. Courteous. They obviously were not in the audience for my *Hail, Caesar* stunt.

I walk along past Mattatoio, with its mass of symmetrical arches, which stands guard above the Tiber. Once the grand complex of animal slaughter for Rome, its presence now offers graffiti artists and morons alike the opportunity to make their mark. Being objective, they are not all Banksy. Gioacchino Ersoch did not plan his masterpiece over ten hectares in 1890 to be the site of spray-painted insults from Gino to his former lover Carla who, quite rightly I suspect, ditched him for Nico. Some of the art is inspiring, most forgettable, but, whatever it represents to its creator, it all adds colour to what would be a site of decay. These are the modern cavemen. Not a calendar in sight.

I pass by the Gay Village. It is closed. Too early for dancing and cavorting. I wonder what Barrington would make of it. Rainbows sprayed around the entrance. Who knows? He clearly likes the ladies undressed – maybe the gentlemen too? Who am I to judge? He can feel what he wants. Percy does, so why not another Oxford man? In the shadows I notice small pools frozen over. Winter. I hope it snows.

Standing high on the bank above the water, I look down through a gap between naked trees. A log drifts by. A bird lands and perches there. Free-riding. Water holds something indefinable for me. I could admire a heather-filled moor, purple and green, lush peat bogs with bracken yellowing in late summer where a stream below sparkled sunlit, but the wonder of coming to the crest of a rise to see blue sea before me was like no other feeling for me as a boy. Now, I can see blue sea and catch the scent of beached kelp and the suddenness of salt spray only in my imagination. Imagination. Shelley and Keats would approve.

Everywhere along Lungotevere Testaccio there is a sense of rebirth. Ambition and bright ideas poorly funded. The towns of England are the same. The Global Village. The world in one tent? Concepts are the lifeblood of regeneration, and investment is the lifeblood of success or failure. I admire various ventures as I stroll along. Doomed to failure because the controllers, the make-happen people, the councillors and decision-makers and investors, want more than artistic or cultural vision. They want profit and benefit. Money and power. More money and greater power. Like Innocent III and the Catholic Church. Ask Gramsci. Ask Sanchez.

I pass an old man who stands, eyes lost. Ragged and torn. Guarded from the chill of the swirling breeze, his back to the brick in a recess where the wall steps back a little way, to re-emerge again in its relentless line. Bearded, unkempt, vacant. His mouth twitches, but his words, if any, remain unheard. A silent witness to the passage of time. His coat, filthy from rough sleeping, has torn cardboard stuffed inside. A bungee cord around his cardboard corset holds San Pellegrino and Lavazza coffee to his coat, the zip fastener of which, like his mind, failed long ago. He bears the scars from battles lost, or psychotic episodes or drink-fuelled stumbles. Dried blood mats his hair. He reminds me of the Chelsea world of rock stars and actors who pay a working man's wage for the unkempt, tousled look that this refugee from life makes his own. He is not saving the world, though; he himself needed saving, but now it is all too late. My only wish for him is a swift death, without pain, and the release that will bring. The other side of purple. I fancy that, should he release his spirit on the other side of the tube, he will simply shuffle along a road to oblivion and dissipate. To dragons or monsters or demons or Valhalla or sunlit clouds or vestal virgins or whatever lies beyond the circle. To a place no one knows.

I stand to observe him. He is muttering and wringing his hands. At first I assume he is wringing the cold from them in his fingerless gloves, snot-wiped filthy grey, streaked with brown like the bridge. I see no maintenance planned here, though. No nuts and bolts replaced or rejuvenation. I see only confusion and disarray and decay. Emptiness. The fragile nature of modern man stripped bare. Cavemen surely had it better. The wringing of hands is simply a repetition of something half-remembered from his past. Wringing out his soul. Over and over and over again until his hands are raw and chafed. A man for whom time has no meaning. Dark is sleep. Light is hopefully food or drink. Pleasure is a discarded cigarette butt. Half-eaten food from street bins or the hoppers at the back of restaurants, vying with rats for a share. Day or night. Hot or cold. No calendars here. No lines with a diagonal bar.

I can do nothing. I walk on, following the river. Then, seeing a green, white and red furled umbrella raised high, with a line of Chinese tourists following, I pause. The umbrella calls to mind Hannah's Italian flag handbag, and the sight of her running, panicking. I decide to add myself to the rear. I am intrigued. Never having travelled in organised company, I find this straggling line of nervy people makes me want to laugh. But who am I to laugh? What do I know of their culture, or of them? Following umbrellas may be a national sport.

I follow along behind a man who has a taste for garlic. His shoes squeak as he walks. He is trying to read something on his mobile phone as he shuffles along. The tour guide is babbling in Mandarin. I am guessing Mandarin because these people look like mainland Chinese. Recently rich, but without style or distinction. First trip outside China. Hong Kong Chinese are discernible, confident. They dress classic stylish Western and carry themselves with entitlement. They know the difference between espresso and macchiato. They do not need to ask.

I could float through them all, and pass through the ticket hall without lining up. I could just as easily walk in through the side wall. But something amuses me about standing in line. A Chinese couple anxious to keep up with their companions walk through me to stand closer to them. Their guide stands smiling and bowing, umbrella pinched between his knees, and hands out tickets to each, sending them across to the far wall by the bag drop. Those with bags hand them across in exchange for a numbered token. I hold my hand out for a ticket but the guide ignores me and follows the last of his sheep to the wall. He starts to babble in Chinese so I drift through glass into the exhibition which is entitled *Russian Art: The Classical Age to Agit-Prop.* I am intrigued. What I know about art is pretty much limited to A–Z. That being Andy Warhol to Tony Zemaitis, and Tony made guitars. In most things, though, I know what I like, and I like a lot of things. Diverse. Eclectic. A lot of things I like a lot.

The entrance is crowded with people. All nations. All ages. Crammed together. Sardines. That is a feature of exhibitions. People take the start seriously, as though they have to suck every pulse of light and shade and colour and expression and meaning from every painting or pot or sculpture or construction the very second they are in through the door. As though, since they have paid to see it, they are going to get their money's worth. In truth it is because they are afraid, in their limited knowledge, or their limited freedom, to say, *This stuff bores me,* or *I only came to see the surrealists,* or *I only came because you wanted to come but I really want to go to the cinema and eat popcorn and fudge and ice cream, or sit in a bar and drink beer*. People. So unwilling to be themselves, and so resentful that they do not have the guts.

I find new-found guts. Having decided that Soviet women striding forward with red cheeks and glittering eyes, arms raised and pointing, are becoming predictable, I stroll through the throng, invisible as ozone. Except I am not. I turn a corner to see a huge painting. *The Appearance of Christ Before the People.* It is stunning, and after a series of world-dominating women, and men wielding hammers stark against furnace light, it pulls me into its impression of openness and distance. I wander across towards it, and notice as I do so two bizarre figures sitting unseen by mortals astride a tall sculpture by Vladimir Tatlin. They are staring at the painting as though it holds some secret. One of the observers is August Riedel, and the other I have not seen before. August waves. I wave back then stroll closer, and see in it something the *femministe* would rub the artist's face with nettles over. There are, I count them, thirty-five people, of whom only two are women. One of the thirty-three men is Jesus Christ. Two of the men bring to mind Tom Jones and Izzy Stradlin. I hum 'Shuffle It All' to myself and move to read the information card beside the frame. I pause to look up again, to take in the immense beauty of it, and to admire the painter's skill. I read a bit of blurb about the artist, Alexander Andreyevich Ivanov. Reading on, I am staggered. This guy did six hundred oil sketches, drawings and smaller paintings of this one work. Six hundred! What a goof. He started it in 1837 and completed it in 1858. Twenty-one years. He got a rather unpleasant verdict, rather like an emperor's thumbs-down, from his contemporaries. Jealous bastards. He must have been choking, wanting to throttle every artist, critic and detractor from Rome to St Petersburg for that. I stand back again and marvel at his talent. He may have been a goof, and, reading into the blurb further, a religious maniac too, but it has to be said that he was one hell of a painter. Critics. Shelley will have something to say about that I imagine.

I wander on, looking back at this staggering work for one last appreciation. Then on through the gallery. Marc Chagall dissolves through Natalia Goncharova to Wassily Kandinsky and on into Karl Bryullov. Bryullov. Another name from a tomb. I wonder if the stranger with August Riedel was him.

I am done for the time being. It occurs to me once again, ruefully, that my likes and dislikes are as they ever were. Living, I would visit art galleries or museums but forty-five minutes did it for me, so I would leave when I started to check the time on my watch, or glance at my phone, hoping for a message inviting me to lunch or simply requesting my attention elsewhere. The very act of checking time signifies one of several things. An appointment – having to be somewhere at a certain time, whether that place is school, work, dentist, funeral, romantic date, event, even bed. Or stress. *How long have I been in this meeting? I have more important things to do. How much longer must I listen to this shit?* Impatience. *How long until we get to where we are going? How long have we been in the air?* Despair. *How long until they give me these results? How long have I left to live?*

Time. Invented by cavemen with their calendars marked in deer blood and charcoal. Or by a god who wanted human beings to calculate their lives on Earth? To need a god to pray to. Who knows? Not me. Not even Shelley.

I make like Superman and dive forward, arm outstretched rather like the earnest but subtly sexual women of the Soviet dream, straight through the east wall and out into Via Beniamino Franklin. Feeling moderately amused, I regain my state of mind, and stand on hard ground, normal man again.

Well, dead normal man. I stroll around the corner into Via Galvani as autumn leaves, trapped for weeks behind a street bin, ochre and rust, spin up in a sudden gust of winter breeze.

# he was a liar too

A kid on a skateboard scoots past me, wrapped in a down coat with the hood string-tight over his baseball cap, half-smoked unlit cigarette dangling from his lips. He is around eleven years old. He is unaware of me, but I see him. He stops briefly, lights his cigarette, spits like an old man, then pushes his way along towards Masto, drawing red fire, sending clouds of white smoke into the freezing air. Announcing a new pope. He reminds me of me. He does not have Old Skools, but what does that matter? He is eleven. He has all his life in front of him.

He cuts off left at Via Ginori, flicking his cigarette into the road as he leans. It spins glowing red. My guess is he lives here. A final act of juvenile rebellion before home, reality, a return to childhood.

A young couple walking towards me on the opposite pavement show body language that tells its own story. She is upright, stony-faced, lips tight. Marching. Eyes fixed on the distance. One hand clamped over the zip fastening on her tan shoulder bag, the other hand thrust deep into a coat pocket. He is turning in towards her as they walk, hands waving, opening and half-closing like some mechanical toy. He is beseeching one second and cursing the next. I do not know his transgression, but I guess at the involvement of another woman. I think I am on the money. He reminds me, in his features, of Pinocchio. He was a liar too.

I reflect on Hannah as I look at them. We never fought. A sudden quiet pang rises somewhere deep within me, as though whispered from far away. I hear Hannah calling to me. My gaze is drawn to the still burning end of the boy's discarded cigarette. Sleet has started blowing in on the breeze, and an icy drop falls on to the tip, extinguishing its glow.

The 971 bus, diverted from Via Marmorata due to roadworks, passes, interior lights on. I scan the faces, but none is Hannah. Sleet is collecting in icy clumps on the restaurant sign. I turn into the doorway of Masto to see, to my surprise, among my merry troop, the Reverend John Barrington, and Prince Suliman.

Lady M eyes me with a twinkle. She is a minx. Amusing and amused. Loving and loved. Smart and appreciated. Thoughtful and revered. No party in this new existence would be complete without her. I cast eyes from hers to the reverend and back again. She raises her eyebrows slightly to acknowledge my unspoken question: *What's going on?* Her raised eyebrows suggest the answer: *I'm not sure.*

Gramsci, sitting opposite Barrington, Keats to his left and Shelley to his right, is listening earnestly to the reverend, who then points a hand in my direction. Suliman smiles at me and pushes out a hand, palm stretched up to face me, which I take as a sign of welcome rather than rejection. Under normal conditions, say, for example, being alive, I would probably feel troubled at being the object of discussion by such a group, as though I were responsible for something of enormity. But in my new untroubled state I do not care, and enjoy the prospect of listening to the views of my fellows, whatever they may be. I decide to leave them to it, knowing as I do that I have endless time to hear their views. I decide to head up to the *cimitero*, to keep an appointment. I do not have a watch to look at.

# the nature of people

Snow, fine and slow-falling. I am elated. Winter appeared as suddenly as a set change at a theatre. Autumn here one minute, one swift curtain fall, then curtain up and a whole new world. I am outside Masto and, for the hell of it, drift up to the *bambola*'s apartment to see if she is naked. Her apartment is empty. I drift down through the snowflakes, keeping pace with them to the ground. As I walk up Galvani I pass Sanchez, who appears to be heading to Masto. He calls out to me about the beauty of snow, and adds that this is another creation of God's perfection. I smile and wave without comment and head on. Christmas is approaching fast, and I for one long for that rarest of events, a snowy Christmas in Rome.

Snowflakes increase in size, falling in slow motion towards me. Day is fading fast. This reminds me of being a kid, when darkness fell early and I would stand under the streetlight opposite my home and poke out my tongue waiting to catch snowflakes, to feel them melt cold and hot at the same time, and the frustration I felt that I could not prevent my eyes from blinking as flakes landed on my eyelashes, causing them to flutter as I fought to keep them open to guide my outstretched tongue.

I am willing the snow to thicken, to coat the world in white. Maybe there is a God who listens, for the flakes multiply to fill the air and blanket the rooftops and street and cars. I stand staring for a time, then flip up to the top of the wall to look into Suliman's Moroccan garden. The tiles are covered now by snow, and the fountains, water turned off by timer or human hand, are filling with flakes. There is something exotic about desert plants under falling snow, a kind of dreamscape, as though this combination should only exist in sleep.

I mimic sliding as I did as a child, running forward then stamping both feet down, one ahead and one behind my centre of gravity, and slide along, much further than I ever managed as a child, although of course I am not really sliding on snow, just skating on air. I leave no tracks of disturbed snow. I disturb nothing. I vault the cemetery wall and land by Keats's tomb. The children are chasing snowflakes, and Joseph Severn and Trelawny are sitting watching on, chatting about who knows what. Maybe about their own childhood memories of winter snow. The Pyramid of Caius Cestius resembles my favourite cake, and calls to mind memories of visits to Fortnum & Mason in Piccadilly to sample a Mont Blanc cake and a cup of steaming java. Simple pleasures. We all have them. Or we should.

I pass the Kraafts, deep in conversation. August is lying on his tree branch, snow falling around him. I call up to him. As though he has been waiting for this moment he drops down without a word and, taking a bow, extends a hand towards the cemetery wall, indicating me to lead. His face is creased in a grin that is mischievous but knowing. As we start to walk, he stops and turns to face me.

'What was your feeling for Ivanov's grand work, Finn?'

I reply that it is one of the finest paintings I have ever seen.

'It ought to be, given how many goes he had at it.' Riedel laughs to himself, then adds, 'Genius. You people of now marvel at music made by electricity. At computers that allow mathematics in zeros and ones to create art. This is how it is for you. I make no judgement on that, for it is progress, is it not?'

Involuntarily I look down at my sneakers as August continues.

'It is the nature of people to create and appreciate, and to criticise and reject. That is the same in every moment in every century. The benefit of each generation is that they have more to take from life. They have their own time, but they also have the past, and each generation has more past than the previous generation to enjoy. And now you people of today have the ability to talk to and see people on a mountaintop on the far side of the world, and to send monkeys and dogs and women and men into space, defying everything that would, in times past, have been called heresy. Your doctors can save those who in Ivanov's day and mine would have joined us here for the want of a simple cure. I sometimes see you looking at your shoes, and I ask myself what you are doing, but in truth I know the answer. You are questioning your time alive, your values, and your purpose. Your very essence, if you will. There were many who criticised Ivanov's work. How could they believe they had the right to do so? you may ask. Well, I think we all have our likes and loves and even things that we fear or reject or that disgust us. I for one dislike unripened plums. A rich, ripe, sweet plum is a delight almost as good as sex, is it not? But a sour, unripened plum is something to be spat out. And therein, my fine young friend, is life itself.'

This is a lot to take in, so I open my arms, palms upwards, my invitation for us to walk together, as if to say, *I have no answer to this.* He is still smiling as we walk to the wall and vault it together, landing silently on the far side. A delivery van, tyres slipping on compacted snow, slides gently against a line of parked cars, causing little more than scratches, and in true Italian style the driver gives a *nothing to worry about* shrug of his shoulders behind the steering wheel and drives on without stopping to assess the damage. He probably figures that the next van coming along will do worse.

August laughs and says, 'Italians – you have to love them, do you not? They only care about food, wine, their dress, art and love. The rest is just so much stuff unworthy of worry. For me that was at first a challenge, and later a release. We Germans are like you English. Too concerned with ethics and status and reputation. And what joy does that bring?'

He laughs again to make his point, and, without asking where we are headed, passes through the gates of Casa di Pace. My mind is whizzing with thoughts in response to his observations, so much so that I forget to ask him if his companion at the gallery was Bryullov.

# if walls could talk

Boot-prints in the snow along the driveway. Fresh. We pass through the closed doors to see Vito stamping off his boots in the hallway. We watch as he pulls them off, pulls on soft house shoes, then picks up a bag from the floor and walks into the kitchen. We follow as he passes Alessandra, who is taking a coffee pot from the stove top, and with his free hand pinches her bottom through heavy wool. He pecks her cheek and she pulls away with mock shock and comments on how cold he is. She takes him black coffee as he sits at the table and fishes magazines from his bag. We sit too.

Alessandra disappears and returns moments later with two crystal glasses. She places one beside Vito's coffee, bends gently to kiss his head, then sets her glass beside me before pouring herself coffee. I sniff the aroma of coffee and brandy combined. Heaven. August nods his approval.

'These people. Their love. Their lives. This, Finn, is what makes Italians the finest people on earth.'

Alessandra sits down through me on to my seat, so I move to a seat opposite. August smirks. His point well-made about the English and Germans. She picks up a magazine and turns to the contents page. *Noi Donne.* The feminist magazine. I look from Alessandra to the doorway where her dead mother-in-law has appeared. Daniela Mazzi floats across the table horizontally, looks at Sandra's magazine, raises her eyebrows in mock boredom as she passes, and, hovering above Vito's brandy, kisses August on his lips, which I know will simply feel like warmth, but I am somewhere between shocked and amused. She drifts back across the table and through the wall to the vestibule and, as she starts to disappear feet first, flicks back her hair and says, '*Femminista*,' tipping her head towards Alessandra. Then she disappears, which we take as a cue to follow. August floats through the wall as I walk through the open door into the hallway, pausing to marvel again at the beauty of it all and the chandelier, lit now with a million cut diamonds. I pass through the closed door into the garden room, where a table lamp lights up the bronze of Vito, as darkness descends across the garden, making mirrors of the window glass.

Daniela is draped across a sofa back, and below her, lying on his back just as he does on his tree trunk, is August. They both look towards me as I appear in the room. There is a familiarity about them that suggests this is something that has been repeated many times past. And to think that I thought I would be introducing August Riedel to Daniela Mazzi. I am naïve still, despite growing into my time dead.

I ask Daniela why she disapproves of Alessandra's feminist magazine. She looks at me in the same mocking way she had about her when she raised her eyebrows on glancing at it, but her lips twitch into a smile.

'Oh, but I don't disapprove at all, Finn.' Her accent is honey. 'I was a *femminista* in the days before Sandra was born and grew and married my son, as was my mother before me, before your generation gave such strength of womanhood a name to market. Do you think there is too much labelling and not enough doing in this age?'

Labels again.

She smiles ruefully, and says, 'Everything is a movement these days, and everyone must have a label. Everyone *wants* to have a label, to identify who they want others to perceive them to be, holding up a banner to declare themselves this or that, wanting to bear a label as though that somehow makes them unique, when all it really does is strip them of independent thought, of being able to stand alone.' She adds, 'People should take care to remember labels from the past. Everyone I see now decorates their skin, as though that fashion gives them individuality, when it just blends them into an increasingly sterile picture, until they all look the same, all bit-players in a modern mime. Those of us from the past have seen a time when to be tattooed was the worst dehumanising thing, when a person with a name simply became a tattooed number on their wrist, a record in a ledger, before they were gassed and burned.'

I look down at my Old Skools and decide to shake my own tree. 'Isn't it the case that conformity is just human nature, and that we label things for understanding? We can't all be leaders. Some will lead, surely, and the many will follow. Isn't that the way of things both now and in your times?'

I feel I have made a well-thought-out point.

'Labels can be useful,' says Riedel playfully. 'Butcher, baker, candlestick maker.'

'Street names. Numbers on buses. Jars of jam,' I say, feeling justified that labels are needed just as much as anything else, and that my shoes are simply my choice, something that gave me pleasure to wear, that expressed something to the casual observer that said something about me.

Daniela has watched me look down at my feet.

'Tell me, Finn, has fashion now not become an order of labelling? I look out at this designer-conscious society, where aspiration is not about how well something looks on a man or woman, not about choosing a style that suits their shape or features, but all about how much it cost, and how current it is and who is wearing it in a magazine. And your cult of celebrity? Your obsession with the minutiae of the artificial and trivial lives of others. You people of today, you have created a world based on vacuousness, where everything is image, labels and false status. Where cakes look beautiful but taste of nothing.'

I reflect momentarily on my brief time as a living man. Perhaps I lived for pleasure that was meaningless? I am starting to feel slightly uncomfortable, in an unthreatened way. My accepted norms are being challenged by people who have seen a hell of a lot more than me. In my previous life I might have raised my hackles and sought to defend my generation, my values and my Old Skools. But I have an odd sense of defencelessness. I have that feeling again: maybe I do not belong here after all.

'Butcher. Baker. Candlestick maker. Witch. Heretic. Pederast. Fornicator. Sodomite. Jew.' Riedel lists these words evenly, then adds, 'So many of these labels I have seen used as a means to single out people for persecution, through my time both alive and dead. Even now, in every country, you have a nation divided by labels. For and against. And within that labelling your society will argue and justify on both sides, and, regrettably, miss the point. The point of life, as Goethe summed it up, is life. Of living. Of recognising that we are born free-thinking. Individual. With differing capacity of thought, imagination, skills, desires. People who have influence – and that includes politicians, writers, artists, musicians, journalists, kings and generals – should beware of the labels they apply to others, for, like the labels on streets or buses or jars of jam or the finest wines, they are easy to attach, but far more difficult to remove.'

I feel relief. This is observation. They are observers, not persecutors nor prosecutors. I look down at my shoes, which will never wear out. Everlasting shoes.

Daniela slips down from the sofa ridge, and lays on August. They look into each other's eyes. I slide backwards out into the hallway, and on through the grand doorway out to the snow. August was right. I am still very English.

Light bursts all around me. Snow has fallen and the streetlights are lit. The sky is overwhelming. Black clouds pile high into the dark night, but in huge gaps stars sparkle. They eclipse the hallway chandeliers. My senses are filled in a way they seldom were in the world B.F. Before Falling. I recall the wonderment I felt the first time I stood on the eighty-sixth-floor observation deck of the Empire State Building in Manhattan, as though I were king for a day. A crisp late autumn afternoon, so clear and mesmerising as I'd watched daylight fade and the lights come on all over New York City. Breathtaking. Tens of thousands of skyscraper lights and car lights in rivers of white and red. I recommend that experience to everyone. At least once before they fall.

I roll into Masto, expecting to see the others and Barrington and Suliman, but only Lady Mary remains, in conversation with two women who have acknowledged me only with a slight nod of the head from a distance. They are usually perched on the corner wall high above the drop to the pyramid base, or astride the tall granite tomb with green stone angels where I first saw them when Shelley introduced me to Sanchez.

Lady Mary beams at me, and asks in perfect Italian if I have had the honour. I reply that I have not. She has been a great teacher. Even I am impressed by my fluency now. I kiss the hand of each woman in turn, to Lady Mary's obvious delight. First eighty-six-year-old Malwida von Meysenbug, then fifty-three-year-old Constance Fenimore Woolson. They both smile as though they are genuinely delighted to meet me, and Constance pats the seat beside her, inviting me to sit. I know nothing of these ladies, but their demeanour sparks interest in me. I am keen to learn. It seems that everyone I meet here has a story which is rich, as though they are the covers of countless books with endless tales of limitless chapters.

Rita bustles past, arms full of fine-looking bottles of wine, which she places on a shelf. She orders them neatly and stands back a foot or so to assess her work. She cocks her head slightly, then gives a twitch of a smile denoting satisfaction as she heads back towards the kitchen for more. That's right, Rita, load up the attraction so some other unwitting fool buys into the quality trap. I still harbour the thought that I may be the only person ever who could justly claim to have been killed by quality.

I must have been staring at Rita, because Lady Mary's polite cough draws my attention back. I apologise, then, seeing the quizzical looks on the faces of my new-found friends, explain my theory about quality having led to my demise. They appear highly entertained by my account, and Malwida claps her hands in approval.

'Oh, but that my passing had been such an adventure, Finn,' she says laughing. 'With me it was simply the case that I had outstayed my welcome.'

All the ladies laugh. I join them. Why not? I am finding lots to laugh about.

Constance is lucky to be here. She died in Venice. Beautiful city. I would be happy with being there for eternity. But maybe some day it will submerge. Here, where she chose to release, though – here she has some of the greatest minds and surely the most entertaining people who ever graced the earthly world. I have no idea who may be buried in cemeteries in Venice, but I shall take a big bet that they do not match up to Cimitero Acattolico's members' club.

The sugar daddy appears, crossing the road from his car, stamping snow from his shining shoes as he enters, letting the door swing shut on an elderly couple. He suddenly senses them behind him, and makes a grab for the handle. Apologising profusely, he holds the door for them. In his other hand he has a shopping bag marked La Perla which is beautifully presented and tied with red silk ribbon. He seems distracted and sits without ordering, glancing repeatedly at his mobile phone, as though expecting it to burst into life. Rita greets him and wishes him a festive Christmas. He smiles an empty smile and wishes her the same. He orders an espresso, and requests brandies for the elderly couple with his apologies. Rita smiles at him. A genuine smile. Despite her internal disdain for the *paparino* she is forgiving. We unseen observers are privileged to see the gestures and sidelong looks hidden from the living. It is that old thing of *if walls could talk, the tales they could tell*. My companions have tales to tell forever.

We talk of many things, as I learn their stories of lives well lived. Alive for almost fifty-four years of joint time, there are similarities of view and spirit that bind Constance and Malwida. They both remind me of Daniela. Malwida recounts her life. Radical writer and thinker whose feminist ideals broke her bond to family, her passion shining, without regret; and Constance, writer, free spirit and friend of Henry James, whose life story is another joy to hear. I ask about her sister and niece, whose tombstones I have seen beside hers on my inquisitive strolls around the little avenues of stones.

'They rest elsewhere, Finn. My only wish would be to have their company here forever, but we all have that small cross to bear, do we not? Those missing whom we held dear? But we always have our fondest memories, and, strangely, they are enough.'

I find myself agreeing. Lady Mary places her hand on mine, reminding me as she does so of her kindness and pity for me when she cautioned me gently that Hannah and my family could neither hear me nor see me. For a moment Hannah, my mother, father, and brother fall into my thoughts, then as swiftly fall away again as I become distracted by the *paparino* dialling on his phone, leaving a beseeching message ending with '*Per favore richiamami.*' Please call me back.

He rises from his seat, approaches Rita, and gestures for them to move across towards us, to be out of earshot of others. He asks quietly after the *bambola* and Rita shrugs and replies that she gave notice on her apartment, paid her rent to date, and left with two suitcases by taxi a few days earlier.

There is pain in his eyes as he takes this in.

'She said she would leave if I didn't leave my wife,' he says in almost a whisper. 'I can't leave my wife. She is a sick woman, and I will always love her. God can be cruel, can he not? Five years ago my Isabella suffered a stroke that robbed her of movement and speech. Before, she could dance gliding on air, and sing like a bird, but now she cannot properly stand or say what she is thinking. Out of nowhere came hell. What kind of man would I be, to leave her?'

As Lady Mary did for me, Rita places a sympathetic hand on his and expresses her sorrow for him. He pats her hand and whispers his thanks, then walks out to his car, leaving sad footprints in the snow. He has forgotten to pay.

# uncharted waters

Back in the quiet of the *cimitero* I watch the foxes frolicking, scattering snow, and cast my eyes up to the pyramid. Stark and white in halogen haze against an inky sky. I wonder about the story of this tomb and the narcissistic vanity of its creator, lit as it is now to declare its presence as an attraction like a reconstruction outside some Las Vegas casino, except it is real, and in my life every day. It pre-dates Jesus by eighteen years. Maybe before Joseph and Mary were born. I am staggered by this thought, resolving to seek out Caius Cestius. There is no urgency. Urgency is for the living. Caius is probably one of the toga-clad Romans sauntering below. I am privileged beyond my wildest dreams to now meet and talk with people who walked the earth when Jesus was a man, and with those who walked this Eternal City hundreds of years before he existed, when religion was one of multiple gods: of Amazonian spirit gods, Druid rites, and Greek and Roman gods whose forms became the constellations in this broken starry night. This city of Romulus and Remus, rescued and suckled by wolves, who, on 21st April, 753 BC, founded Rome, and, true to their human origins, fought over who should be ruler. If Remus had put up a better fight the city might now be Reme not Rome, but that is not how the tarot played.

I look up to see Orion, sword in his belt as though celestial trouble might not be far away, then cast my eyes down, drifting in thought out to the gully below the wall, until Shelley appears unannounced.

'A penny for your thoughts may seem a rather extravagant payment,' he says, with his customary grin to show his jest.

'Probably worth at least a couple,' I say, smiling. It is hard not to smile at Shelley, whose face so readily expresses mischief, belying genius.

'Let us adventure,' he says, 'for this night is young.'

He beckons me with a finger then drifts up to August, as ever resting on his branch, and says, 'And you, Herr Riedel, do you fancy a stroll into the dark side with our young friend, or are you too busy creating a masterpiece?'

Riedel drops down without speaking, bows slightly, and extends an arm to allow Shelley to lead the way.

'Where to?' I ask.

'To pastures new, young man, and as yet unseen.'

Shelley, sounding mysterious and jubilant, floats before and above us, then settles to walk with us as he steers a passage down through the gardens past the tomb of Keats, who is nowhere to be seen, and out through the cemetery wall to Via Marmorata, crossing Parco della Resistenza dell'Otto Settembre. Then we are out of the park, past the shadowy trees, limbs covered with shining powder, and into Via Annia Faustina. Shelley stops and opens his arms to indicate the bright neon lights opposite. A pink flamingo flashes on and off, and white lights above a green and yellow palm tree pulse rapidly, announcing 'Club Paradise'. The snowy pavement flashes on and off in sympathy.

'Is John not invited?' I ask, curious as to his whereabouts.

'John is with Joseph and Edward, and the children, star-gazing. I fear this may not be to John's particular taste. He sees beauty everywhere, and has little affection for the darker side of life that a night such as this may afford.'

He chuckles to himself, then puts one arm around August's shoulder and the other around mine, so that I feel that by-now-familiar faint sense of warmth as he steers us into the path of an oncoming taxi. The taxi passes through us and pulls to a stop a short way past the club. Two overweight men in business suits climb out and walk back towards us, snow crunching underfoot. They stop to light cigarettes. The older of the two takes out a phone to make a call while the other stands smoking. It dawns on me that I recognise him. He is the fat man from the café. The bastard who beats his wife.

'Ah, it seems we are not the first guests after all,' says Shelley. 'For this, my friends, is opening night.'

I have passed this building many times when it was empty and silent, but the neon signs and gold-painted door are new. A doorman in evening dress, over-worked steroid body bulging beneath a black satin jacket, bow tie straining around his thick veined neck, stares intently at the smokers, assessing them. We stand watching with interest as wife-beater finishes his call, blowing a kiss at his phone, which he then clicks off and drops inside a coat pocket. He fishes about and produces a pink and gold card from the same pocket and hands it to the doorman. I name the doorman Bluto, after the bearded oaf in the Popeye cartoon. Bluto acknowledges them in foreign-accented Italian and opens one side of the double door to reveal a gold metal staircase. '*Benvenuti a Club Paradise, signori. Goditi la serata.*' Welcome to Club Paradise, gentlemen. Enjoy your evening.

They smirk at him like excited schoolboys and pass through the door, which he pulls closed behind them. Throbbing music, distant and low, shuts off into silence. Bluto looks at his watch and breathes in hard, puffing out his chest, steamy breath flowing into the cold night air.

Percy takes the lead and disappears through the door. August and I follow in time to see him drifting up through another door at the top of the staircase. We follow and enter a black-painted corridor where another doorman stands guard. I name this one Brutus. He is thick-set, heavy, but less steroid-pumped than Bluto. Like his fellow doorman, he is unsmilingly confident. He is no Marcus Brutus, though, not the slightest look of nobility about him – but who knows, he too may be a man of treachery.

A cloakroom and hat-check is to our left. A further door announces toilets. A neon flamingo, one leg lifted, stands pink and stark against black, as does a palm tree of green and gold on the opposite wall. The fat men are taking a ticket each from the scantily clad hat-check girl, who is dressed as Cleopatra in a short slit robe of gold silk. She has gold snake bracelets wrapped around both arms and nails painted pink as the flamingo. She is African. She is beautiful. She smiles as though they are old friends, or film stars. They are neither.

Fat man and his friend move to the far door, where Brutus searches them, as though these two could potentially be trouble. They are both breathless from walking up one flight of stairs. The faint throb of dance music suddenly bursts out as Brutus pulls open the door to reveal a dimly lit interior with wall lights pulsing to the beat.

I follow August, who walks through Brutus and the closing door as Shelley lingers, eyeing the Nubian princess.

Music throbs through hidden speakers. The walls are black, as is the ceiling. The floor is gold, in keeping with the staircase and handrails. Light spreads like fine mist from coving around the ceiling and floor skirting. Bar stools set in groups of two are spaced along the gold-topped bar. A barman who could be related to Bluto and Brutus flexes biceps as he bounces a cocktail shaker off his forearm and spins it around his back to catch it with his free hand. He grins with satisfaction. He is a performing animal. There are two small tiered platforms on which semi-naked girls swing and drape themselves around stainless steel poles. A third girl in leather straps and thigh-high boots with a spiked collar around her neck cavorts in an animal cage. Palm trees and flamingos grace the walls. Despite being dead, I feel affronted: flamingos have no place here. A mixture of men of differing ages sit at tables served by topless waitresses. The pole-dancers have elasticated ruffs around their waists so that fat, oily men can push banknotes inside while feeling up the girls momentarily as they pass after finishing their dance. The girls rotate, so that one is always performing while the other collects banknotes, allowing the briefest of touches to be rewarded with a loving smile, and a mock play-slap to a wandering hand, before disappearing through a door marked *Private* to the far left of the bar.

I am immune to embarrassment in my new life, but my sense of what I consider right and what I consider tawdry has not changed. I see bright smiles fade as the girls turn away from their grinning clients' groping hands. What is it about these men that lets them believe that nubile young girls find them attractive in this situation? It is simply about money. Sex as a commodity. Men who control women for profit. Women who are too poor or disadvantaged or drug-addicted or debt-trapped to walk away, or too frightened of unrestrained violence to seek escape. To seek a better life.

I voice my views to August and Percy, who has joined us, perching on the bar counter. Riedel raises his shoulders and shrugs, but Shelley poses an alternative view in response to mine. For some women it is a free choice, he suggests: they thrive on attention, and lust; and so why, when those things are desirable to them, should they conform to the artificial standards of society which are so often set by hypocrites who declare one standard and secretly live another. Why, when they are born free, should anyone live lives of tedium when they have the freedom of imagination to go beyond the boundaries of boredom to a far more enticing existence of excitement and reward?

He grins, and adds, 'Take it from me. A woman's hedonistic fantasy can become her reality, if she dips her toe just one inch into uncharted waters.'

As if to show me that I too am stuck in a gaol of my own creation, he floats across to the cage and cavorts with the dancing girl. The buckles on his shoes glint as he jives. August laughs and remarks that throughout the ages he has yet to see a freer spirit, living or dead.

I think this over, then excuse myself and float through the door marked *Private*. The door leads into a corridor, with three gold-painted doors to the right along the length of it, and a reinforced steel door at the end. This door is painted black and bears the same notice: *Private*. The three gold doors have paintings of exotic birds on them: a flamingo, a pair of love birds, and a white ibis. I float through the flamingo door. I am stunned to see the *bambola*, who is naked apart from see-through pink nylon panties, the waitress uniform, fellating a middle-aged man as he lies on a gold couch, trousers below his knees. There is a smear of dust on a gold table together with a small gold tube.

I slide away out to the corridor. The love bird and ibis rooms are unoccupied. They are identical to the *bambola*'s room. Gold couch, and small gold table. On the walls are prints of exotic birds. A shelf on the wall beside the couch has a bowl of condoms, sex lube, an assortment of dildos and a box of tissues.

I pass through the wall from the ibis room into an office where two men sit smoking cigars and drinking from beer bottles. They are speaking a language I do not understand, but which I guess to be Albanian. They are surly, sour-looking men, both thick-set. The term *gangster* fits them. The only thing that differentiates them is the size of chair they are seated at. There are small packets of cocaine in an enamel box on a large writing desk. A doorbell chimes quietly. The door clicks as the man in the largest chair, after glancing up at a security screen, presses a remote control and one of the dancers enters the room. She is a pretty girl with dyed platinum blonde hair. She looks like Marilyn Monroe. Her hair is well cut to create that impression. The man in the smaller chair throws a bag of cocaine on to a table beside him, having taken the banknotes from her waistband and placed them on the desk. Chairs denote status here. Small chair man counts the cash, then pulls her towards him, holding her tightly by her wrist. He points a finger to her face and tells her, in poor Italian, not to skim money. She asks where she could possibly hide money. He makes a vulgar remark to her about the size of her vagina, saying she could park a Cadillac up there. He pulls her sharply closer, grabs her by the hair, and pushes her head into his crotch. She pulls roughly away from him, massaging her wrist, then snatches the bag of cocaine and leaves. The men share a joke at her expense in Albanian.

I watch them with distaste for a minute. Cocaine-dealing sex-traffickers. *Mafiosi*. Degenerate scum. These people have no belief beyond themselves. Rosary beads lie on the desk. Money and power. They are bullying, controlling, exploitative men without conscience or humanity. The waitresses and dancers in the club appear to be a mix of Romanian, Russian and Nigerian girls, all, I imagine, lured to Italy by these men or traded like slaves with other criminals, who at first shower them with money and cocaine and promises of a modelling career or some other fanciful entrapment, but who now hold them as prisoners, smuggled illegally into servitude as slaves in Rome, with threats of murderous violence to their unsuspecting mothers and fathers should they resist or alert the *carabinieri*.

Sickened by what I see, I float through the steel door to see the *bambola* disappearing through the door to the lounge.

The dancer appears from the love birds room, eyes glazed, wiping her nose with the back of her hand. I follow her and watch as she lights up her smile, brushing past the array of hand stretchers as she heads back to perform. I join August, who is still perched on the bar counter, watching the girls. Shelley is still cavorting in the animal cage. I watch as the *bambola* carries a tray of drinks from the bar towards the table where fat man and his slightly slimmer companion are ogling the dancers. She stands back as fat man's friend hands his phone to Brutus, having been censured for filming the dancer in the animal cage. Brutus erases the recording, before handing back the phone. He leans in to speak to both fat men, with a wagging finger, and points to a sign displaying a camera with a prohibitive cross through it. They look suitably chastised, like two fat, naughty schoolboys. Shelley would be invisible in the footage, but he gave a good impression of a shimmy when he noticed the idiot filming her. A further wagging of Brutus's finger reinforces the rule before he resumes his post. There are security cameras subtly placed and monitors visible for all to see. The obvious message is *behave yourself*.

Percy drifts across to us as the *bambola* places their drinks in front of them. Fatty asks her where she is from, as though she would be interested in a conversation with him. Romania is her answer. He tells her he has never been there, then asks if it is nice. She answers that it is beautiful. He asks where in Romania, as he has a waiter at his restaurant who is from

Bucharest. She replies, 'Galati,' adding that there is nothing there except a steel plant. He hands her a fifty euro note and tells her to keep the change, as though he is Rockefeller or Hugh Hefner. She tells him that she needs another ten: the drinks are thirty euros each. He looks stunned, and fishes in his wallet. To save face he gives her twenty. She smiles and walks slowly back to the bar, her breasts bouncing gently as she goes. She is beautiful. I wonder how long her beauty will last.

I tell August that she lived above Masto but omit to mention Percy's dalliance, as Percy grins at me. August tells me that he has seen her around, and adds that such a beautiful girl is difficult to forget. She hands both notes to the barman, then carries another tray across to a table of younger men, more her age. She stays longer talking to them.

'Seen enough?' August asks.

'More than enough,' I reply.

'I told you, we Germans and English are so alike, Finn. So reserved. Except for Percy, of course.'

He winks an eye at me as he says this. Percy blows a parting kiss to his dance partner, and we drift out together through the wall and down to the snowy pavement. Bluto is checking the tickets of some new arrivals, a group of seven or eight men in suits who look as though they have come from an office Christmas party. One has the remains of popper streamers hanging from his collar.

As we cross Annia Faustina, Percy attracts our attention by saying, 'Well, well.'

We follow his gaze just in time to see the Reverend John Barrington disappear through the side wall.

# baubles and bows

*Vigilia di Natale.* Christmas Eve. A white Christmas in Rome. Truly a once-in-a-hundred-years occasion. Coloured lights are strung along the driveway at Casa di Pace. Cars fill the snow-covered driveway. The orange glow of lights through curtained windows is as warm and inviting a sight as I ever saw. I float through the garden door into a room bustling with life. The chatter of people drowns out Charlie Parker. Two young kids, eleven or twelve maybe, are passing through the room with a tray of champagne-filled glasses and a tray of canapés. A crackling fire burns in the fireplace, drawing a crowd. On the far side of the room Daniela sits on the seat back of a sofa on which August is lying. John Keats is beside her, and Percy is beside him. These people. Always ahead of me.

I wave to them. They wave back. I cross the room to look at the Christmas tree, which has baubles and bows and glittering lights. It is beautiful. It shows an artist's touch. Alessandra pats the boy waiter's head as he offers her a drink. She takes one, and points across the room in the direction of her dead mother-in-law. The boy takes his tray across to a beautiful African woman in a short, tight dress. So tight it follows every contour of her figure, which has Percy's admiring gaze. A gold chain hangs from her neck, carrying a solid gold pendant, the country outline of Sierra Leone. Her dress is neon orange. She is stunning. She takes a champagne glass and smiles so sweetly at the boy that he blushes, his face reddening as though she has read his thoughts. Shelley has read his thoughts too, so he slides off the sofa, glides across the floor on his back and passes between her legs, pausing to look up between them as he goes.

He reaches me, stands upright and says, 'As I suspected, Finn, no underwear.'

I could have told him that from where I stood, from the elastic nature of her dress, and remark so to Percy who, as usual, is grinning in triumph.

'Ah, yes, but, since men of today can see the source of the Nile on maps and satellite photographs, what makes them still adventure there? To see for themselves and to experience the truth of the matter, of course. Your generation are much satisfied with living virtually, are they not, Finn? Watching others climb Everest, racing cars that can be crashed with no one injured, wars waged with casualties who stain nothing with their blood, and sneakily viewing pornography on computers and jerking themselves to pleasure, while losing the joy of the feeling of the softness of skin and the intimacy and excitement of love with another. Tut-tut, is what I have to say to them. Much as you tut-tut my sense of adventure, eh, Finn?'

We laugh together, me shaking my head because there is, as always with Percy, much truth wrapped inside his mockery. The young girl passes with her canapé tray, and pigs-in-blankets draw my eye. Shelley comments that they look like tiny penises. I shall now forever associate them with his observation.

Across the room Vito roars with laughter, and I turn to see him chink glasses with a younger woman who is the image of his mother, Daniela, and who I take to be his daughter. He hugs her tight for an instant, before laughing loudly again at a remark passed by another guest. He looks at her with sparkling eyes, as she again chinks glasses with him. She has his lobeless sharp-tipped ears. Watching them makes me think of the vixen and her cubs, who know nothing of Christmas.

# resplendent in red

I leave Vito and Alessandra to their family, and Daniela and August to Shelley and Keats. A moon has risen and glows iridescent in a starry sky. Clear and crisp. It must be freezing but I cannot feel it. I take up my old post by the bushes and wait. Snow dislodges from shrub leaves as the vixen pokes her nose out to test the night. She comes out cautiously and the cubs, now much grown and less foolhardy, follow behind her. They sniff the air and steam clouds out with their breath. As though reminded of their youth, they spar, rolling over each other in the snow, throwing up sparkle dust. A sharp noise rises, short and cautionary, from the vixen. The cubs stand, attentive now. A cemetery cat, stirred and stretching on a tombstone, alerts them all to food. A short chase ensues and a sudden hiss then a muffled cry announces the end. I walk away down through ranked tombs towards Keats's stone, where Severn, Trelawny and the children are silhouetted against moonlit snow. I wander towards the pyramid to seek out Sanchez, and, finding him gone, decide to go to church.

I turn through streets where people make their way to family or friends with bags of toys and gifts and bottles of drink, trudging through snow, their footprints multiplied over and over to make tracks to follow, like moorland trails lit by moonlight. The air must still be freezing as nothing is slush, just crisp, crunchy snow underfoot, tramped down by the passage of revellers. I head down Via Ginori into Via Giovanni Battista Bodoni and through the closed doors of the church of Santa Maria del Rosario which are shut tight against the cold. Air heavy with incense and candle shimmer. I float up to perch on a horizontal flagpole around which is draped a hanging, reading *Auguriamo a tutti un Buon Natale nella Gloria di Dio*. Wishing all a Merry Christmas in the Glory of God. The hanging has a series of what look like Santa's elves' faces on tennis ball-sized cherries around the border. It strikes me as incongruous within this most serious of buildings, and carries a modernity which jars with the paintings of sorrow and torment that line the walls. Not a lot of joy going on in these scenes, what with Jesus all nailed up, and John the Baptist's head jumping out at me. The Kraafts, Suliman and Barrington are singing along, standing together in an aisle to my right. Sanchez is singing with his eyes closed, away to the left of the pews where the packed congregation stand with shoulders and elbows touching. His joy is apparent. I swear there is a glow to him. A radiance. I think of Ivanov's *The Appearance of Christ Before the People*. Maybe Bernabe is a son of God, or an angel fallen. Who knows? Not me, surely, but hey, if anyone had told me I would drop foolishly and land in a world beyond mine, surrounded by Percy Bysshe Shelley, John Keats, a cast of brilliant women and men and Romans in togas, I would have laughed them out of the bar. For it is only in bars and churches that such conversations ever occur. Chin chin! Bottoms up! *Prost!* Cheers! *Cent'anni! Salute!* I raise an imaginary glass to the citizens of Rome. There is a unity in this gathering which is huge and a thing both untouchable and seemingly unbreakable. Sanchez, eyes open now and glistening, radiating love, sings beautifully. The carol 'Astro del Ciel' rings out with the organ wowing and bellowing and thundering up to the heavens. I decide to join in, singing in English: 'Silent Night'. Sanchez, below me to my left, standing in unoccupied space in the farthest aisle, far from the sanctity of the altar as though he is unworthy of a place of importance, hears me singing in English and turns to look up at me, smiling his joy in the moment. I smile back and wave and continue to sing until he looks away again towards the altar, and to Jesus who is hanging above the glittering gold, looking lost. I decide to leave Sanchez to his God, after looking again at the mass of glinting gold, Old Master paintings, and the hopeful faces of the citizens of Rome, feeling a nowadays rare surge of ill will towards the Catholic church which cut Sanchez and kicked him when he was down. No broken and repentant man deserves to be broken further. Surely no God would ask for that.

There is a beauty to this night that draws me out and on towards the river. A desire to see water carries me towards the Ponte dell'Industria. I walk in a meandering loop, feeling love for everyone I pass, as I did on my last Christmas Eve alive in the packed bar of the Royal Oak, fire blazing, enjoying mulled wine and Manhattans with Hannah before joining her parents for carols at St Stephens' midnight mass. The river surges in the darkness below the bridge. The swell of water rushing is musical. I imagine I can hear the tune of 'The Holly and the Ivy' played by the Tiber just for me. My favourite carol. The steel pavement boards' lozenge studs protrude from ice and packed snow. I sit on a strut high on the bridge, watching Italian families shuffle homewards from church, filled with benign and benevolent thoughts about their fellows. For now.

The walk home from churches throughout Rome signals the fact that it is now Christmas Day. I think of my family, friends and Hannah, and wish them all every good thing, knowing that they will all be thinking of me, the careless young man who tipped their lives upside down.

Thoughts of my lost ones are fewer now, and gone is the aching loss and panic of my initial days dead. My thoughts are of fondness and wishes for peace and relief for them. There is an irony in this. Me, the cause of all their anguish, immune to pain and sorrow.

I float down and stand on a fallen branch which is rushing along to my much-loved sea. I mimic surfing, smiling to myself as I stretch out my arms and bend my knees. Satisfied with my Christmas gift of amusement to myself, I walk across the rolling river to the bank and float up to Lungotevere Testaccio, where I wish the same two Romans a Christmas filled with love, peace and sincere joy. *'Ti auguro un Natale pieno di amore, pace e gioia sincera.'*

Their togas, as bright as new snow, glow as they sit talking, unaffected by cold. They nod towards me and both raise a hand in acknowledgement, and wish me the same. Courteous. I wonder where Caesar is. I am tempted to greet them in Latin. I think of Saturnalia, Roman celebrations and the unimaginable excesses at Trimalchio's feast, and it occurs to me that they must find a Christian celebration incredibly dull. No peacocks roasted, or naked girls feeding lustful men grapes. I decide against Latin. The old saying of *quit while you're ahead* is wisdom.

I walk along past Mattatoio, the guardian of the Tiber. The silver image of a smiling Buddha grins out at me, lit by streetlights shining on the mass of coloured graffiti. I wonder if Carla and Nico are still together, or whether she has moved on again, and he is following Gino in spraying insults. There again, maybe she is not the angel I imagine.

I pass by Gay Village. The place is bouncing. Music thuds from inside, and by the main door two guys in Hawaiian shirts, shorts and winter boots are alternately swinging flower garlands around their heads, smoking and, in between cigarette drags, pouring champagne from hand-held bottles into each other's mouths. As I look to the left of the arched entranceway, I notice a leather-clad man in the shadow of an evergreen shrub in a mouth-to-mouth embrace with Santa Claus, who is resplendent in red. Leather man has his hand inside Santa's fur-trimmed trousers so I stare no more, out of my sense of Englishness. I wonder again what Barrington would make of this. Whether he would call down fire and brimstone and terrifying lightning from the heavens, or simply join in, hoping to be taken for a reveller in fancy dress.

I carry on along Lungotevere Testaccio, listening to the river. A sudden fizzing sound like a zipper quickly pulled races through the night, then a rocket explodes on high, firing out streamers of glittering light, and suddenly the blackness of sky is chased from the world by riotous colour as bangs so loud they echo like gunfire hammer off the solid walls of the eternal city. I sit on the wall and imagine this scene is just for me. For me and John and Percy and Lady Mary, and all my new friends, and all the spirits who make this hidden Rome a joy. Entranced, I watch the display until a final cacophony of celestial orgasms signals the end. I drop down and walk on, satisfied that my fellow spirits will have delighted in such beauty. Apart from love and kindness, the better part of man, I decide, is art and entertainment.

Passing the recesses along the walls, I look for the old man. He is motionless. Snow has collected on his form as though he is bags of rubbish awaiting removal. His fingerless gloved hand is outstretched and protrudes from the shroud of snow. It holds nothing. No cigarette. No aeroplane tickets. No ham. He is dead, although his spirit is nowhere to be seen. I assume he is biding his time, hoping they will take him home to Piedmont or Naples or wherever life was kinder to him. I hope he makes it. My father's parting words come back to me, so I pause by the lifeless mound of ice and snow and, leaning down towards him, whisper, '*Buon Natale, vecchio ragazzo.*' Merry Christmas, old boy.

# creatures of habit

As in life, everything is rolling forward, day by day, hour by hour, second by second. Christmas turns suddenly to New Year and the parties to celebrate the passage of time. Corks popped, flags waved, dancers whirled, trumpets blared, proposals proposed, wishes wished, resolutions made, fireworks worked. '*Felice anno nuovo!*' Happy New Year! Now there will be the inexorable march out of winter towards spring and the promise of the new.

Like a visible sign of the heating planet's silent scream, the last snow and ice melts on New Year's Day, which is bright with winter sun. All trace is gone by lunchtime, as though it never was; as though the city itself had grown tired of it, and shrugged its back to throw off the mantle, not to be worn again for another hundred years – though who knows, in a world so affected by man as this?

I stand in the living room at Casa di Pace where peace, as its name suggests, has settled after a raucous evening. A stunning woman announcer, tanned and glowing, chatters on a television screen, volume turned low, about the highs and lows of the year past and of the expectations of the year to come. A series of clips travel through twelve months. I am drawn to June, July and August, which pan through images of turquoise seas and tilting white-hulled yachts, sails billowing, with tanned, handsome people pulling ropes, then on to a giant cruise ship, huge and stark against blue sky with white gulls wheeling behind its bow, as some B-list starlet waves from beside a turquoise pool; and on then to black bodies drifting in the water as a coastguard cutter slices through dark blue. A map appears showing a dotted line from Libya to Sicily, and the film cuts to a tiny child face down on white sand. Shelley might have had some thoughts of Edward Ellerker Williams if he were watching. The ugliness of these images is brief and the programme skips quickly on to vineyards in Puglia and Tuscany. The presenter flicks back raven hair and leans forward in a practised show, low-cut, enticing, eliciting an approving smile from Vito, which causes me amusement, recollecting Daniela's observation about Vito and his father. Vito is smoking a fat cigar, holding a brandy glass from which he sips occasionally with the look of a man who has it all. Alessandra sits opposite in a high-backed armchair, intent on a magazine, sipping *oloroso* from a delicate frosted glass around which Cupid and Psyche cavort.

August and Daniela are lying on the chaise-longue across from me, chatting idly, eyes engaged. This is a scene of contentment. For the living and the dead. I reminisce for a second or two on the significance, or lack of it, of this day in my former life, the first of a new year. Of how seriously some take it, and of how determined men and women can be on this one day to change forever the things that dog them, and how quickly those well-intentioned resolutions can be forgotten. For we are creatures of habit as well as creatures encoded. An unpleasant or miserable personality could be the unintended gift of a parent who was so gifted by his or her own mother or father, or it could be learned behaviour from a parent similarly taught, or from cruel fates in life experienced, or maybe just the easiest route through the winding, unpredictable journey of life. Give a little; seek a lot.

Trelawny holds the view that men are capable of anything, of depravity way beyond our understanding, and attributes that to their imagination; he says that the worst of men are not evil, as the creation of the devil in a fight against God, but are simply the result of the shifting of boundaries or the removal of limits set within our imagination. He illustrates such views with stories of derring-do and depravity from his travels and unproven adventures. Lady Mary, with her natural optimism and will to see the best in everyone, had scoffed when he'd proposed this to me one starlit evening as we sat around Emelyn Story's angel, calling such talk poppycock, and had wagged a lecturing finger at Trelawny, warning me with her usual twinkling eyes that he was simply stirring a pot of devilment himself. Shelley had cautioned us to believe Trelawny as a man whose word was as truthful as any ever spoken. Lady Mary had exclaimed, 'You do talk such rot on occasion, Percy!' and they had all laughed, except Gramsci, and Sanchez, who had earlier told me of his anguish at seeing news of his country, about 'the descent into madness and the living hell of a country forsaken by good men', to which Shelley had interjected, 'And by your God too, eh, Bernabe?' Sanchez's response was that God cannot form the works of men, but only provide through His teachings a pathway to turn our minds to good. Keats had listened, silent, then added his own view that only men of imagination and belief can create true good. Sanchez, shaking his head, had offered the sad thought that drug barons all too easily imagine acts of evil. He added a confession that he had despaired that God had indeed abandoned the poor of Mexico, whose slaughtered and mutilated bodies were piled high towards the heavens, where entire towns were bereft of men and only women and children survived, until the male children grew to an age where they would be inducted by the cartels, or tortured and mutilated like their fathers before them for their resistance.

In a rare moment silence had descended on our happy group, while we considered Sanchez's words. Gramsci, who had become animated and bounced up and down as he sat, had declared, looking me in the eye, 'A quarter of a million people slaughtered in fifteen years in one single country, Finn. Imagine that. For simply wanting to farm or live a peaceful life. Who could ever truly imagine that? This is a sickness created out of a lack of meaning in this world, where an empty lust for the meaningless lives of others, for celebrity trivia, is all, and where cocaine is God and the poor are disposable, like burger wrappings and cardboard coffee cups. Is it not the most hideous irony that we only truly see this world after death, when we no longer have a voice? Would the thirst for cocaine be the same if cocaine came not like powered snow, but in blackened bloodstained bags with the skin and hair of the slaughtered stuck to them?'

Now, in the living room of Casa di Pace, scene of New Year's Day contentment, I shudder slightly at the recollection of that discussion, and the feeling that my generation, and I personally, have much to answer for. I should have paid more attention to visionary people alive, as I now learn so much from them dead. It is too late for me to change, but I wish for better from my peers who still, I hope, have time to start an unstoppable movement, a swelling wave that will grow to enormous height, with incredible power and force to change their world. To save it. The old adage that *there are those who talk a good job and those who do one* pops into my thoughts. I cast a look in the mirror above the fireplace where olive wood crackles and flames dance, and view my Music Center T-shirt. I shrug at myself reflected. I am powerless to make even the smallest change; New Year resolutions are truly meaningless to the dead. I imagine my family and Hannah's family and our friends all together this day. There is nothing I can do for them either. I shrug again and float through the garden windows to watch the meltwater fall from the trees to ripple the pond.

# worth dying for

The cycle rolls. Even for the dead. Alive, I was wary of the passing of time, and felt strength in the idea of living every day as a precious thing, as a gift. I may be rare in that. This was something my father created in me, that his father had created in him. That time moves only one way. I occasionally look back with some small satisfaction that I was an example for the *live every day and love life* brigade. Whenever Hannah would whine about Monday and express a desire for Friday night, I would wag a mocking finger and say, 'Be careful what you wish for. This is not a dress rehearsal.' She would laugh, but I meant what I said. Why could Monday or Tuesday not be as joyous as Friday or Saturday? Life is what you make it. Bobby Keys knew that. The Rolling Stones' saxophonist. *Every Night's A Saturday Night*. Great book. Until Bobby blew his last after a pretty hefty run of hedonism.

Spring, as it does in the earthly world the other side of the magic curtain, brought everything to the eyes of those who cared to look. Green, gold, red, blue, yellow. One day the temperature suddenly spiked, announcing summer's door-knock, and with every day that followed a fraction more heat added, until Rome sizzled through July and August, and on into September, a fact made obvious from Claudio mopping his brow as he sits outside the workshop sanding filler on a dent repair. A flock of parakeets, green as emeralds, fly screeching by me as I sit watching him from the wall top, startling him to look upwards as they disappear into the fruit-laden tree overhanging his yard. Standing upright and shielding his eyes, he mops his brow again. The birds, flicking and pecking at ripe cherries, oblivious to his fascination, suddenly take flight, disturbed by a burst of Vespa exhaust-pop as Claudia pulls in to park. He bangs his palms together, rubs dust off his hands on his overalls, and, as she reaches him, slips a hand inside her loose shirt as they kiss. She raises one leg, knee bent, so the sole of her shoe faces out towards me. She reminds me of me with my foot flat against the ice cream wall.

'A man after my own heart.'

Shelley. As quickly and silently as he had arrived, he throws himself backwards in a series of flips like a circus tumbler or a man shot at close range, and calls out to me to follow. We make our way, me walking and Shelley floating on his back four feet above the ground, looking for all the world like a man drifting on the sea. Maybe this reminds him of his fateful last day of life. Content with having floated for a time, he stands and walks with me as we pass out through the far wall of the cemetery. I ask where we are going, and he says simply, 'You'll see.'

We find ourselves at Piramide station, Shelley pointing out the most beautiful women. I am in agreement. This was a fine idea. The heat of summer has brought out not only the flowers of the garden and field, but of the city. The flower of womanhood, and the intentionally obvious interplay of handsome Italian men dressed in linen suits with heavy framed sunglasses smiling teeth-white at the women they pass.

'See, Finn? For all that your *femministe* and haters and trolls shout, and the rush of men who wish to become women, there is always attraction and love. It makes no matter whether it be women for men, or for each other, or men who love men, it is all for love and, despite what you people of now would claim as yours, it has always been so, my friend. Take a careful look at some of our toga-clad neighbours at Caius Cestius's little homage to himself. Some there are men who would be women, and women who would be men, and those for whom the only feeling for love is as a mirror, for man to man and woman to woman. It is only a lack of imagination that holds the dead in their tombs, and pins the shackles of restraint to those living who should cast them off. There are many here who know this, even those who would have their names writ in water, choosing to be forgotten by those they loved.'

He suddenly springs forward, and through the doorway leading to the platform, so I follow. A train arrives, and, although we could pass through metal into the carriage, Shelley seems to delight in demonstrating unseen good manners by waiting for the doors to open and passengers to alight before floating into the carriage. Metro Linea B. To Rebibbia. A long way off. Fourteen stops.

The train moves forward, accelerating with rising pitch, then passes out of gloom into sunlight and, rushing forward, rocks slightly as track joints click. We pull into Circo Massimo station, and passengers get off as others join, scrabbling for seats. An elderly man stands to give his seat to a puffing woman, arms heavy with shopping, who probably appears to the old man to be pregnant. Shelley, laughing, says, 'The only child in there is the pasta baby. Did you ever meet a fat nymphomaniac, Finn?'

'No,' I answer, not having ever known a nymphomaniac.

'Sex is the finest athleticism. She would do well to spend more time in between the sheets, and less time in between *gelateria* and *pizzeria*.'

He laughs again at his own joke, amused as he always is at the strength of his wit. He deserves his own accolades. He is a very funny man, and a sharper mind I have yet to meet. I mentally add nymphomaniacs to my list of people of interest.

The train doors slide shut and the wheels turn again. We roll on towards Colosseo. I am starting to feel slightly disconnected, almost light-headed, which is strange as I have felt nothing, other than the faint warmth of touch when a fellow spirit such as Lady Mary should place her hand on mine, since I arrived unannounced on Shelley's tomb. I look at Shelley and see that he is shimmering slightly. I once drove across the Great Algerian Schott for a shoot at a Berber village, the air temperature hot enough to cook a cracked egg, riding on a battered bus whose air-conditioning had broken, its doors and windows open to allow air, hotter than a hair-dryer's blast, to pass through the interior. As we drove, salt as dazzling white as quartz crystal as far as the eye could see, the driver called out in Arabic and pointed across the salt flats to a village on a lake shore, with palm trees swaying, the air bouncing across the salt and the village shimmering and undulating. 'Look!' he had shouted. In French then, he had called out '*Mirage!*' Convinced that what I saw was in fact a village, and that the idea of a mirage was tourist fodder, when this was so clearly houses and palm trees with a small lake in front, I had scoffed. I'd reached for a camera in my bag to provide the lie to add to future dinner party anecdotes. And, as I had raised the camera to the open window, the village, the lake, the trees, had all faded to nothingness before I had time to remove the Nikon's lens cap.

Shelley is grinning at me. He grins a lot. As the train brakes and slows to a stop, he slides out of the door and through the bodies crammed on the platform. We drift slowly out into sunlight, and are met by the incredible sight of the Colosseum towering above. Amphitheatrum Flavium. I follow him as he floats up through hordes of tourists to the high wall edges, which are thick with toga-wearing Romans. I look down to the arena below, where slaves, consuls, beautiful handmaids, senators and gladiators stand chatting. I revel in the spectacle. I turn to Shelley, and, still grinning and shimmering, he holds his hand out and looking quizzically at me, points his thumb down towards the ground then back up again. I raise my hand, thumb pointing towards the heavens, and return his grin.

'Well?' he asks.

'This was worth dying for,' I say, still amazed at the sight before my eyes.

'Let us not outstay our welcome,' he says quietly. 'For this, as you may feel, is where we risk the point of no return.'

We float down to the street, and take a faltering stroll past the Forum and the Triumphal Arch of Constantine, which are evidently still the playgrounds of those who died here. Generals and legionnaires and the finest citizens of ancient Rome are lying around and conversing, like actors resting between scenes on a movie set, with freed slaves and shopkeepers.

An African man approaches us. Fake Gucci and Louis Vuitton handbags looped along his left arm make him appear ceremonial as he waves a Prada bag with his right hand. This reminds me of the ham I waved at Hannah, and of Tariq's last wave to me. We pause and he walks through Shelley then passes through me, smiling at a young couple as he waves his wares at them. I watch him in the hope that he will make a sale. The young man, Chinese and unsure-looking in an Emporio Armani T-shirt, holds up a defensive palm, but his girlfriend, whose hair is the pink of flamingos, the colour of the Nubian cloakroom girl's nails, moves towards the grinning seller as he thrusts the Prada bag outstretched towards her. He speaks in Italian and immediately switches to English when they fail to respond. She looks towards her beau beseechingly, and twirls around, with the Prada bag in both hands. She makes a million little steps like a mechanical toy to turn full circle, which makes them all laugh. The boyfriend agrees twenty euros and hands across a banknote. The seller, sensing an easy target, offers a Gucci bag too, but the boyfriend has started to move away, waving defensively again, when a shout goes up and the seller, and countless others in the square, some of whom roll up their bags in sheets, run to an alleyway and are gone. Two *carabinieri*, smart as mannequins, appear from a side street and stand looking around the square. From the gloom of the alleyway I see a huddle of African men, nervous in their collection.

Shelley remarks on their situation, saying that the quest for a better life is ageless and universal, but that these sellers, like so many, are sold a dream that does not exist. Sold, as he observes, into unsuspecting slavery by those who promote the illusion of a better life. He adds that in his time it was with chains that violent and murderous men preyed on the vulnerable of Africa, but in this present time men without humanity enslave these yearning people with false hope, the worst kind of magic trick.

We stroll on, my feeling of lightness, of a faint shimmer in the ties that now bind us to this other world, making me conscious of the tenuous hold we have here. Eternity can be foreclosed by a will to depart this existence, or simply by an act of reckless stupidity. The kind of stupidity that got me here in the first place. I pause to look at a series of postcards on a stand beside a stall selling all manner of tourist tat, of resin-moulded models of the Colosseum, Roma football shirts and Italian flags. A feast of images of the Spanish Steps, Fontana di Trevi, the Amalfi Coast, multicoloured cliff-side houses of Positano, the turquoise sea, and snow-capped Italian Alps. I will never again ski on a mountain, or swim in the sea.

My sense of wonder peaks when we pass the same man in laurel wreath and Tyrian purple-edged toga to whom I had made my *Hail, Caesar* quip, many months ago. He nods in Shelley's direction and lifts a hand to touch his wreathed forehead. Shelley silently reciprocates. As we walk on he turns to me and says, 'Julius Caesar. Strange fellow.'

The sense of dissipation has left me, and Percy no longer shimmers.

# red, white and green

Keats, as we arrive back from our dance with the limit of our existence, is standing with Suliman, Lady Mary von Haast and John Kraaft's young mother beside the *Angel of Grief*, their attention caught by something hidden from us by the thickness of jasmine overhanging a latticed arbour. Curious, we stroll across to meet them.

As we pass the arbour, I look to where their attention is focused and see a single rose laid on Shelley's tomb. Standing before it is Hannah. Slightly behind her is a handsome man I do not recognise. He is wearing Converse All Star sneakers. Brown canvas. In my earthly days I would have admired his choice of footwear. He moves slowly towards her as she gently dabs her eyes with a tissue, and places a comforting arm around her waist. She has on a white dress patterned with red roses with green stems and leaves. I imagine this is a deliberate match to her thoughtful rose. She is beautiful. She takes a couple of steps towards the cemetery wall, kisses the fingertips on both hands, then touches them against my brass plate. Every moving spirit close by has paused, as they did when I fell. Hannah steps back away from my plaque, then, as though an unseen hand has pressed play, they start to go about their business. Hannah places an arm through his, then they stroll together along the pathway towards the main gate. Gone is the flag handbag I had bought her. She now has a plain white bag, ice cream white, like her dress.

I do not call out. I feel no urge to hold Hannah, to take her away from this man, and make a silent wish that they are happy, and that he will show her the love I no longer can. I watch them as they go. Like the police officers on my first day here, they make a fine couple. It dawns on me that I have an anniversary today. One year dead. As they approach the visitor centre, cemetery lady appears from her office, engages them in brief conversation but remains standing looking towards me as they walk to the gates. Hannah turns briefly in my direction and gives a slight wave of a hand. It is empty of ham. They turn out through the cemetery gates and they are gone.

Cemetery lady then walks up to engage the gardener, who is pruning an overhanging bush. She has on a tight blue dress, and from its outline appears to have stockings below. Shelley has noticed my attention to this and smirks at me. I am imagining what she looks like in her underwear when Lady M appears beside me, places a hand on my arm and pats it gently, as though comforting me. I smile down at her, and raise her hand to kiss it, to show my appreciation for this wonderful act of love.

Suliman, who once told me his name means *man of peace* in Arabic, excuses himself to return to his own garden, his home from home, his sanctuary, and Mrs Kraaft skips away, saying she has things to discuss with her young husband and old son. I suggest we go to Casa di Pace to enjoy the garden there, so Shelley, Keats and Lady Mary, arm in arm with me just as Hannah had been with her beau moments earlier, head off across the gardens. Sanchez, Gramsci, Constance, Malwida and Barrington are perched on tombstones in a rough circle, deep in conversation, further down the *cimitero*. Seeing them, I ask Lady Mary why my arrival in Masto, on that day so long ago, had caused the reverend to point towards me, and Suliman to place his hand up in acknowledgement.

'Oh, John Barrington was just saying to Antonio and Percy that your sudden demise and immediate appearance in this Heaven was irrefutable truth of the existence and kindness of God. The prince was in agreement, but, as usual, our poetic companions denied this.'

Shelley scoffs in mock protestation and vaults the cemetery wall. John, Lady Mary and I pass through the wall in time to see him cartwheeling over parked car roofs up towards the villa. We follow and pass through the garden wall. Lady Mary, although perfectly capable of vaulting, flying, drifting or spinning, always remains dignified and walks. As she walked through my mother that day.

We seat ourselves on chairs below a cypress tree. Alessandra and Vito are under a terrace canopy, drinks in hand, contentedly reading and passing occasional remarks. Daniela and August appear from within the house to join us. Brown bird flits from below our tree to a bird bath filled with water. She drinks, shakes a drop from her beak, then flies to a chair back opposite me. Lady Mary is chatting with the others. Brown bird stares me in the eye, opens her wings, closes them, then opens her beak and talks to me. I cannot understand the language she speaks.

# the sea

As in life I marvel at the days. They roll imperceptibly forward, each as unique as in life. I have taken to sleeping through most nights – well, more resting without thought than sleeping – so that I can experience a sense of awakening to start a new day, although occasional night prowling with Shelley is to be had, when we intrude on scenes of pleasure in shuttered rooms, or visit the cinema to watch whatever takes our fancy, or go to nightclubs to watch girls dancing. As in my former existence, there are days when nothing of great interest happens, and others where sudden jolts or flashes of the new draw attention or exclamation or discussion, such as a boy knocked down by a van outside the *cimitero* gates while he and the driver are both glued to the screens of mobile phones, the child playing a video game and failing to see the van that hits him moments later, and the driver, checking a delivery address with eyes elsewhere as the child steps from between parked cars, a split second late to press down hard on the brake. The result: a child like a good martini, shaken and stirred. Fortunate to escape without breaks, his schoolbooks scattered to be picked up by passing strangers. Ambulance and police. Low-key drama. A sufficient distraction to draw sympathetic murmurings from Lady Mary, and a comment about the triviality of modern life from Gramsci, who bemoans the loss of values, decrying those who are enslaved to technology, 'fed', as he describes it, '*the new opium of the people*' to still their instinct for justice and revolution. The gardener, disturbed by the sharp squeal of tyres on asphalt and the quiet thud of a child hit, had come running, dropping pruning shears as he came. From the gateway he had called to the shop ladies, the same deaf pair I had appealed to in my first hours dead, to call an ambulance. I wished him greater success.

'*Chiama un'ambulanza!*'

Simple dramas. Distractions which provoke similar feelings as in life. Simple dramas which prove that we are as much alive after death as we ever were. Other wonders. Birds singing, flowers blooming. Vito and Alessandra chatting about life and family and art and politics and world events with occasional loving glances over brandies on their terrace. The normality of the day-to-day, punctuated by surprising and unexpected moments such as floating unseen with Shelley through the closed doors of Claudio's workshop to view a change of Pirellis to find him thrusting in time to Claudia's moans as she straddles him on the driver's seat of his Ferrari, which he has removed from the car and placed on the workshop floor. The unexpected and thrilling normally private events which we, the unseen watchers, the voyeurs, can marvel at or laugh about as they bring unexpected joy to our eternal existence.

Keats has wryly observed that we see men and women as they truly are, as we look through windows that open only to those who cannot tell a secret. I think he regrets his *name writ in water* inscription. I suspect he would very much like to hold Fanny Brawne again, if only to have her know that he is well and past illness and despair on this side of the astral plane. Of course, she must now know that for herself, but she may also wonder whether John has released his spirit, or whether he spins in a tube forever, unreleased and unending. That is our hell, I suppose: not knowing whether those we have loved are released after death, or whether those still living are healed from our loss, optimistically believing that we are in heaven or paradise or strumming harps on clouds, or whether they are pessimistically saddened that we are simply dead and gone, like dust blown into the invisible distance, never to be seen again.

The slide of time is as it always was. Slipping through days where the subtleties of change are so slight that each day bleeds unnoticed into the next, until a sudden warm day heralds summer, or a chill wind announces the onset of cruel winter. But to us, the unseen, changes once felt keenly, where a coat was worn or shed, are now things we see but do not feel. Bright green tips announcing their arrival to the seeking eye as spring's trumpet sounds from a distance, or the dark green leaves of mighty trees as they tip with brown and their veins, like those in an old man's hand, stare out through thinning skin to foretell the change from summer's glare to quiet and golden autumn.

Gramsci's caution to me to not hang on to guilt for my generation stays with me, as I watch unseen while young people hold the heads of state to account across the globe. Good for them, I say, but hope, above everything, that perspective, not simply blame, is exercised by those who seek to punish their forebears for this planet's slow destruction. It started with the first caveman who struck flint against dry grass, but few since have shouted to be heard above the noise of progress, or the pursuit of wealth and industry. We call for ever more technology, for advancement, for energy, for television, for computing, for giant aeroplanes, for electric cars and trains, to travel faster, to resolve work quicker, to build more houses, to feed more people, and for medical advances so we can live forever. Now we should all heed the desperate call to save their future, except that the powerhouse nations, the greatest polluters, may well ignore those calls, and turn our beautiful planet into a dying hell. Yet my generation's consumption and demanding obsession with fatuous pleasure is fuelling a cruelty rarely seen since the Spanish Inquisition. What thoughts does the man tied to a chair, with nails hammered through his hands, his bloody tortured screams loud but choked silent as his teeth are ripped from his head, unheard by his butchered wife and children who lie dead and discarded like broken dolls, have about the warming planet? Maybe there is a God who looks down on our lust and consumerism, and the dreadful lecturing hypocrisy of those who feel entitled to tell the masses what they are and how to think, and decides, *It may be better to let these people kill this planet, so poor have they been as custodians. Maybe I should just start again.*

I am sitting in Masto with Keats, Trelawny, Severn, Suliman and Gramsci. After Trelawny tells another hilarious tale of piracy in Greece, I tell them of a time in Amorgos, that most beautiful of Greek islands, when a power cut plunged everything to black, and the stars fell down towards me, as though I could reach up and touch them, as though I could wave a hand through them and make them swirl like a spoon dragging cream through black coffee. Keats smiles and says this is proof of my imagination, that a lesser man would worry about tripping in the dark but my strength of imagination brought the heavens to me, and that is my power, the reason why I am here now, with them.

Smiling with a sense of simple joy in having the freedom to think, in quiet contemplation, in conversation with my friends here, I am silently thankful that I am now free from mobile phone chains and the repetitive endlessness of posting and responding, inhaling and exhaling but never breathing. I am free of technology, of failed batteries and frustration – of social accountability and 'being present' in the modern dialogue where words abound but nothing is said. I am free at last. I belong here.

Keats stands and walks to the door, saying he is off to ask Shelley's view on the falling of stars. He turns as he is leaving and says we must wait to hear the great man's view, all in good time. I stay a while, highly entertained as I am by more of Trelawny's tall tales of Greek adventure, with Lord Byron appearing periodically as his sidekick; then, excusing myself, I stroll out into the day. Everywhere there are colours richer than in life. A seagull, wheeling overhead, calls out to distract my thoughts as I walk, and makes me think of my grandfather, and days by the sea, searching rock pools together at low tide, seeing small crabs startle and run to green shelter, waiting for the tide to turn. I find a new joy in the thought that that kindly man, long gone to me, will be floating high above Lords cricket ground, watching every test match, sitting on the umpire's hat, maybe eavesdropping in the dressing rooms. The seagull calls again, and my thoughts turn to Tariq, to Bengali fugitives escaping to sea, and his sex-ready wife sliding across him, where the sea breaks beyond their parked car, beyond the dunes.

But the views of all here, those who would have believed absolutely, during their worldly life, in a benevolent God's Heaven, and those who believed only in the imagination of man to overcome death, are not changed. Gramsci's accented words ring loud with me. 'This is not Heaven; this is simply the afterlife. We all have our personal purgatory here. For some it is the loss of love, for some it is the loss of power, and for others something so slight as the scent of a flower from their garden. It is just something that ties us to our former life – not a hell, as Dante or the Bible or any good-versus-evil theology would have; it is simply an occasional sense of loss, which quickly fades again to re-emerge at a later date. It simply serves as a reminder of who we once were. Nothing more, my friend.'

My view? I listen to all that is said, and in the morning I see no fault in the arguments of Bernabe Sanchez or John Barrington, but as evening falls I am seduced by Keats and Shelley and every notion these romantics weave before me. I guess I side with John Kraaft, the agnostic, who has reservations as to our presence here; that there may be a God, or that we are our imagination, or simply energy that continues on forever.

Breaking my thoughts as I stroll, someone calls my name. I look across the street to see Percy and John outside the cinema. Percy shouts for me to join them as the show starts soon. I look up at the title above them, in large red letters hung old-style over the cinema doors. *Das Boot*. A German film I have seen before. The Boat. I suddenly realise what I truly miss. I miss the sea.

# acknowledgements

There are times, rare though they are, when someone we have not yet met in person changes the course of our lives.

So it was that some time in 2015 I happened to read an article about an amazing independent publishing house in *The Independent* newspaper. I was struck by the writer's use of the term 'passion' when describing the RedDoor team, and that one word inspired me to submit my novel, which ultimately became *Dust*, published in 2016 by RedDoor in the UK, and later in Germany and Taiwan (officially the Republic of China).

Clare Christian, Heather Boisseau and Anna Burtt received my manuscript, and loved it. I was thrilled. *Dust* was then entrusted by RedDoor to a copy-editor, Linda McQueen, who, despite my long-held belief that every word on every page was perfect, proved me wrong to doubt the need for someone else's take, and transformed my work into something that shone far more brightly than before. Such is the nature of excellence when combined with a passion for literature. Four women whose talent, vision, belief and (that word again) *passion* changed my life forever. I owe a huge debt of gratitude to them all, and will, for the rest of my life, hold them in the highest esteem. Praise and admiration for each of these passionate ladies is really understating their worth, for how can anyone put into words the indescribable gift, and wonderful humanity, of those who change one's life?

It is with grateful thanks that I still find myself accepted and nurtured by the best independent publishing team in the country, Clare, Heather, and Lizzie Lewis, all of whom I now know in person, and the most amazing copy-editor, Linda.

In addition, once again I need to acknowledge the encouragement I received many years ago, and still do today, from my long-time friend Sandy Farmer, who believed in my writing and, from across the world in California, pushed me repeatedly to publish; without her enthusiasm and support, I might not be writing this.

Finally, I need to acknowledge Rita of Masto, and all the passionate women of the world who inspire others.

If you enjoyed *Eternal City*, you may also like Mark Thompson's debut novel, *Dust*.

Read on for a taster . . .

# Prologue

If there's one thing in life that should be considered, I guess it's the idea that we all face a test. At some point. Maybe early or maybe late. Or somewhere in the middle. Who knows where or when? I mean, can you think of one solitary person who has rolled through life without a test of some sort? And I don't mean school exams, or not running screaming from the dentist's chair or having your appendix out. I mean something bigger and deeper than all these things. I mean, look at Old Man Taylor, for instance. He's had his test. He didn't bank on it, but he had it. But I'll come to that...

# – ONE –

It was a perfect summer day as El Greco and I lay on our backs in the rough grass at the edge of the sports field, out back of the old brick locker rooms, gazing at billowing puffs of pure white cloud in the rich blue sky, spotting shapes.

I told him I could see Mount Rushmore, and I could, I swear.

He pointed to the plume of cotton wool that vanished slowly in its margins as I stared upwards and said, 'Yeah, sure looks like it. There's Jefferson, Lincoln and Washington, and who's that other guy? Roosevelt.'

I marvelled at his knowledge for a second or two and said, 'Oh, yeah, I forgot about him,' like I knew.

El Greco was the smartest kid I ever met. He was a sage. He was ten years old.

We lay on our backs for what seemed like an eternity and guessed at shapes while the sun beat down and the long dry grass shimmered in the faintest zephyr of a breeze. Crimson tissue poppies bobbed back and forth with the motion of well-wishers waving handkerchiefs on a distant railroad station. We blew smoke rings as we drew on cigarettes. If we bought cigarettes, we bought Kents. My father smoked Kents, so did El Greco's mom, so if we were caught we could say we found them in the car and were just bringing them in. We also stole cigarettes from our folks.

'Wouldn't it be great if they came in banana flavour?' I said, as El Greco watched a perfectly formed ring lose its shape and drift upwards until it emulated the buckled wheel of some abandoned bicycle. He sat up suddenly and pushed his hand through the ring, smoke gathering momentarily around his wrist. I felt a sudden sadness for its loss.

He turned to face me, brows knitted in consideration. He smiled, nodding. Slowly at first, then rapidly as enthusiasm overtook him. 'Yeah, you got something there.' He nodded again. 'Imagine that? Chocolate cigarettes. Wow.'

I warmed to the theme, basking in the limelight. 'Strawberry and vanilla, pistachio, tutti-frutti!' I yelled, carried away.

'Yeah, you've definitely hit on something there,' he said dreamily, rolling back in the dry grass.

We each used our cigarettes to start tiny fires, watching intently as faint fingers of orange flame licked like tiny gaudy snakes up a yellow stem, suddenly leaping to its neighbour, and then as quickly to its neighbour's neighbour, until smoke was billowing white and grey and flashed with orange as our panicking boots stamped it all into the hard brown earth. The smell of smoke was everywhere as dust and pollen rose like diesel fumes from an old truck just started; we coughed hard as the acrid mixture filled our lungs and clung to our hair.

'There'll be hell to pay if my mom smells smoke on me,' I rasped, as we kicked over the traces of dirt and ash.

'Come on, let's go get some soda or something, it's time to get home anyways,' El Greco said, spitting on the blackened ground. We drank soda, my particular buzz being root beer, but sometimes we drank coffee, just to be different. It marked us out. It made old folks jitter. It was part of our plan.

We stuffed our hands in the pockets of our jeans and jogged across the field. El Greco did his imitation of Bugs Bunny, which always made me laugh, but killed me then because he was wearing his Looney Tunes T-shirt with Bugs on the front. 'What's Up, Doc?' I mimicked. I couldn't do it like he could, but I could do a great rendition of Mickey Mouse shouting 'Pluto!' so I did that too and El Greco laughed like hell. God, he made me happy. He knew all the right things to say, and just when to say them. For a ten-year-old he was one hell of a guy.

We stopped at the top of the field to sword-fight with green twigs we snapped from a willow tree. I was King Arthur and he was Errol Flynn as Captain Kidd. We crossed the roadway into Mister Jeb Doughty's wheat field, passing the broken-down barn that defied wind and rain and always stood half-gone but resolute, despite time and the seasons' relentless assaults of thigh-deep snow and scorching sun. Heading back towards El Greco's house, we heard the distant wail of sirens. We walked back to the fence, hoping to see what all the fuss was about.

There they were, racing up the rise.

We clambered on to the fence to get a better view. Two huge red fire trucks hurtled towards us with sirens blaring and lights flashing like the waltzers we loved to ride whenever Butler's Funfair hit town.

We watched with fixed eyes as dust flew into the air from the sun-baked road.

'Where do you think they're going?'

'Must be a house fire someplace, or Fatty Conway got stuck in the courthouse railings again.'

As the pink dust settled I opened my eyes looking east to see where the trucks were headed. There was a fire all right. A big one. Smoke the colour of an old man's hair pumped up to the sky like whipped cream from the far side of the field.

El Greco saw it as I did, and for once he didn't have to spell it out for me.

'Fuck! Get the hell out of here!'

We hit the ground before my words were done, running as fast as we could across the field. We cursed a lot like ten-year-old boys do, but I outdid my record, gasping, 'Fuck! Fuck! Fuck! Fuck! Fuck!' as we ran. The hollow stems of grass whipped our legs, making them smart. We ran until we were breathless, and collapsed in the shade of a blackthorn tree. I almost didn't dare to look back at the sports field, but fear and curiosity got the better of me and I turned my head. The sky, which had been perfect blue with tufted clouds, was grey-white with huge flashing tongues that leaped into the air. In a few brief minutes, fields of play had turned into a war zone. My heart stopped in sympathy with my breathing as I stared incredulously at the scene before me. I thought El Greco could hear the roaring in my heaving chest. I held my breath in the hope that I could slow my heartbeat down. I once saw a movie where somebody injected this guy with adrenaline or curare or something like that which made his heart race so fast he had a heart attack and dropped dead on an airport escalator. Everybody was fooled by it, except me and the detective who solved the case. I felt like I'd been jabbed too.

'Jesus H. Christ! That's one hell of a fire!' El Greco whistled, and thumped the grassy earth where we lay. When a crisis loomed, he had a habit of sounding like an old man who'd seen it all.

'Let's get the fuck out of here,' I said in a low voice. 'Yeah, let's go, the cops just showed up.'

El Greco's calm tones did nothing to slow the waves of panic that had grown to breakers inside my guts. I felt a hand on my shoulder, jumped like a gerbil and spun around to see El Greco grinning at me. 'Come on,' he said confidently, 'no one knows it was us, and besides, it was just an accident.'

His calm flowed through his fingertips and down my shoulder into my arm. I felt the fear subside for a moment, but as he took his hand away and started to walk, crouched down to avoid detection, it flowed back through me. We'd done it this time. We'd done all manner of crazy things and got away with them, but this was different – this was a crime, and the cops were there, larger than life in their black and white Dodge with the dented fenders and gold badges on the doors.

I prayed to a God I didn't truly believe existed for one last chance. I swore I'd be good forever if only he would take me back a few hours in time so that I could put the book of matches back in the barbecue bin where I found them.

No chance. I looked at the spiralling cloud of smoke and muttered, 'Thanks a bunch!'

El Greco was some ways off, keeping low, so I shuffled faster to catch him up. I wasn't going to be left out on my own in case the cops spied me.

I ditched the matchbook in Horse River, which was nearly dead dry, just a lazy trickle left to mark it on the map. We had not seen rain for what seemed like forever. I tried to look easy as I caught up with him, and, sensing me there, El Greco straightened up and stuffed his hands in his pockets. He grabbed a piece of wheat stem, stuck it between his teeth, and chewed it as though he didn't give a damn for anything, and just for a second I didn't either.

I sighed and said, 'It's only a load of old dry grass anyways. I bet anything could have started that fire. Remember what my old man said that time about the burning bush, and how God put a holy spirit into that bush in the middle of nowhere and it just set itself on fire? I just bet that's what happened here!'

There I was, seeking revenge on God because he hadn't taken me back a few hours so I could put the maniac matches back. Served him right as far as I was concerned. If he ever needed a favour from me he could just go to hell, and that was the end of that. Forgiveness wasn't a strong suit with me. If there was a God, which I truly doubted, he had had his opportunity to make my life a whole lot sweeter, and he'd just blown it.

I started to feel less guilty about opening the little envelopes my father gave me to take to Sunday school, and removing what I liked to regard as a fair percentage, which I split with El Greco and spent on candy and cigarettes.

Of course Mister Schwartz didn't actually sell me cigarettes. He just sold me candy and I fed quarters into the machine at the side of his store to buy the cigarettes, which I stuffed inside my underwear to prevent detection by my ever-vigilant and pious brother, Adolf.

Of course his name wasn't really Adolf. It was Cecil. My mother named him after Cecil B. DeMille. I tried to like him. It was an uphill task but I persevered. He could be almost likeable sometimes, but he was a thorn in my side and he treated my mother like trash. My father indulged him because he saw Super Bowl stardom at the end of the rainbow. They were both sports nuts. My grandfather had fought in France in World War Two, and he said that if Cecil had been around then that war would have been four years shorter. He said that thousands of lives could have been spared, or else all of Europe would now be talking German and driving Volkswagens, depending which side Cecil had been on.

I jumped suddenly from thoughts of God and guilt when I heard the police siren rise from rest. The fire, escalating in the stiffening breeze, crept steadily forward and fanned towards a small group of dormitory-type homes that made up the Green Valleys Retirement Park. The Green Valleys was a group of one hundred single-bedroom bungalows sited around a shallow pond the planners called the Community Lake. In reality the lake was sixty feet by ninety feet and six inches deep so that the folks with dementia didn't drown as they repelled imaginary pirates they thought were invading from magenta-sailed corsairs. The water was dyed deep blue, the shade only ever seen in vacation brochures for sunny Mexico or 'ocean scent' lavatory cleaner.

'Lie down!' El Greco hissed, flattening himself into the stubble as another police car sped along the roadway through swirling banks of smoke.

I dropped to my belly and stuffed my face down in the sharp tubes of cut wheat, which felt hard as drinking straws sticking in my skin, causing me to curse out loud.

'Keep still, for Jesus' sake, J.J. Do you have to make so much fucking noise?'

El Greco cursed a lot when he wanted to make a point.

'I can't help it, Tony. This stuff is stabbing my eyes out,' I said, hoping exaggeration would win sympathy and let me off the hook.

'Try telling that to your warder when you get to Rikers Island.'

His words filled me with dread, and I felt my throat tighten and a lump the size of an eight-ball rose in the barren gully of my throat.

'Only kidding,' he said with a grin, 'we're okay, the cops have gone out to Green Valleys.'

I dared to raise my head an inch or two and saw the blue and red flashing beacons racing away from us on the Green Valleys road.

'Come on, let's get out of here while we've got the chance to save our skins,' I said, sighing with relief, and feeling suddenly and unexpectedly tired.

'Yeah, let's go,' said El Greco, letting the slightest whisper of quiet release fall into his words.

We stuck to an overgrown path across the field to avoid the stream of excited kids running towards the now massive pall of white smoke, which reminded me of the month of February on our kitchen calendar. *Sierra Nevada, and the ski runs of Mammoth Lakes seen from the gentle town of Bishop, California.*

'Look at all these kids! Jesus, we're for it! Someone will guess it was us, I just know it,' I said dismally, thinking of Cecil, and his certain assumption that every bad deed in our little town was perpetrated by me.

'Right, let's slide in with them and go back down there and take a look,' said El Greco excitedly.

'What the hell for?'

'Because if we don't we'll be the only kids for miles who aren't down at the field, and even someone who isn't too bright may find that just a little odd, don't you think?'

He was right. He was always right.

We fell in behind a group of three kids from the local orphanage. You could always tell the orphanage kids: they seemed to dress about eight years behind the times, as though they were in a piece of newsreel footage about some event that had happened not too long after I was born.

You could also tell the orphanage kids because they stuck together in the way that fox cubs follow their mother everywhere; you always saw two or three younger kids with an older one. That was how you knew they were orphans. My mother once caught me making fun of them to some of my buddies. I knew it was wrong to do it even before she caught me, but I did it just the same. Always playing the fool. My group of admirers giggled like girls when I dropped my shoulders down and bent at the knees, holding my head slightly to one side and lolling it about making goofy noises as though I was not right in the head. Bobby Stockton didn't laugh, he knew how wrong it was, but he said nothing; his look said enough. Bobby believed in God and hell; he often steered me away from stuff that I ought not to be heading towards. If El Greco had been there, he'd have told me to shut the fuck up, too.

'Those children hang their heads because they've got the weight of the world on them, because they don't have a mother or father to love them or nurse them when they're sick, and because they know that you all know they wear hand-me-down clothes. Don't you ever let me catch you making fun of those poor children again, J.J. Walsh.'

Her words stung me like icy hail driven by fierce winds. I had never felt such burning shame, as though the ground would surely split and swallow me in a great black gash, down into the very bowels of the fiery hell at the core of the Earth. I tried a goofy grin for my audience to show them I was smarter than my mother, but they all looked as broken as I felt, and I knew the moment was lost forever. I turned to my mother, and I know I touched her with my honesty when I said that I was real sorry, that I'd never do such a thing again. I meant what I said and she seemed to know it. She placed her hand on my head so gently I cried, burying my face in the soft cotton of her summer dress, hiding my shameful tears from view. I never made fun of them again.

El Greco never mocked them. I guess he was only a whisper away from their misery, his old man being what he was and all.

We tagged along behind the orphans down through the scrub grass and across the shiny road to the top sports field. I felt miserable, recalling the day my mother had put me back in my place, and I was doubly weighed down, not just with guilt at starting the biggest grass fire seen in Cranford County since before I was born, but with the iron-clad certainty that we would be caught and punished and put to shame for the entire town to see. I visualised hateful Mister Barr lecturing our school after morning prayers and the proud anthem, telling them all that two of their contemporaries, J.J. Walsh and Tony Papadakis, had been found guilty of wanton fire-raising and were now awaiting their fate, whatever that might be. I could see the fury in his piggy eyes and the small blue veins, all broken in his red shiny too-close-shaved face. I feared and hated that man in a way he could never have understood.

It occurred to me that there might be a possibility that we could go to the electric chair. I'd only ever seen murderers in movies get the chair for crimes too horrific to contemplate, and I had certainly never seen anyone electrocuted for starting a fire, not even one as big as this, but the thought made me shiver.

I got a whiff of singeing pink and blackened flesh and leaped from my daydream with a strangled cry. 'Not the chair!' I screamed, causing El Greco to jump and the orphans to turn around and stare at me. I grimaced with embarrassment at El Greco, who playfully punched my arm, as though he had read my thoughts. I realised with cool relief that the smell was not my skin frying but the acrid tang of a discarded car tyre belching pungent black smoke.

We stood with a group of gawping children by the side of a fire truck and watched as the fire fighters sprayed gallons of hissing water on to the flames. It seemed to me they were fighting a losing battle, for, as fast as they were advancing into the orange frenzy, so the breeze was blowing life into the flames at the far side of the field, and those flames were getting closer and closer to the neat little houses of the Green Valleys park.

'If it burns down the retirement park, we'll get the chair,' I whispered hurriedly to El Greco.

'Ten-year-old kids don't go to the chair, and they don't go to Rikers either. And besides, if you stay cool there ain't nobody apart from me and you who knows,' he said softly.

He was right. Carl Newton Mahan had been six years old when he killed his friend Cecil Van Hoose, who was eight, over a piece of scrap iron on May 18, 1929 in eastern Kentucky. He took his father's shotgun and shot his little friend and even he didn't get the chair. This was another thing we got from the *Guinness Book of Records*. Everyone thought that because we were ten years old we only thought silly things and played like kids, but we smoked and cursed and did all kinds of shit. We never shot anyone though.

'What if Adolf knows?' I panicked again at the thought that somehow my twelve-year-old sadist of a brother would know what I had done. He had an uncanny knack for finding out my darkest secrets. He would sometimes accuse me of them at get-togethers, when there were plenty of people in earshot, and I would blush like a homecoming queen, the letters 'G-U-I-L-T-Y' appearing in trashy neon lights across my forehead, despite my strangled protestations of innocence. I would fold like a house of cards in front of the district attorney, I just knew it.

I watched transfixed as the flames ate the dry grass in a frenzy, reminding me of a speeded-up section in a colour movie I once saw when an adventurer seeking the lost treasure of an ancient Inca people fell into a swamp and was attacked by piranhas in a mass of bloody boiling water. His last horrific scream was echoing around my head when I heard the fire chief barking commands into his crackling radio. Two more fire trucks swung back to the road, sirens shrieking, bells clanging, rolling from side to side as their drivers fought to control the heavy machines. I watched them gaining speed, hurtling along the normally quiet road towards the retirement park. Groups of dogwood trees and gently swaying poplars hid them for fractions of time, and smoke the colour of clouds swallowed them until they reappeared again as determined as before, big red racing dogs coming out of the traps, chasing a flaming hare.

I started to breathe easier when the flames by the park stopped moving forward. We couldn't see them for smoke, but the firemen had control, heroes every one. A bizarre scenario popped into my head, of dozens of old folks in chequered golf pants and sneakers, and housecoats and curlers, jumping for their lives into the six-inch pool. I imagined them lying on their fronts in the lake with their behinds sticking up from the water. It occurred to me that they'd look like dozens of eggs poaching in a great blue pan. The thought of this caused me to laugh out loud. I suppose it was relief that my nightmare was receding and my chances of going to the electric chair were lessening, but I lost control. I stood by the fire truck shaking with laughter. I folded my arms and wrapped them around my body in an effort to control myself. I bent forward and put my head between my knees but it did no good. Streams of tears rolled down my cheeks, causing brown channels to appear through the fine layer of soot that had attached itself to my suntanned face.

El Greco put his arm around my shoulders and patted my back. He murmured something to me, but I couldn't hear what he said over the noise of the engine. I stood upright and turned my tearstained face to his. The look of alarm in his eyes turned to a ten-foot grin when he realised I was laughing. His teeth were dazzling against his tanned face, and he patted me on the back again and ruffled my hair with his hand, much as my father had done when I hit my first home run in Little League. 'Let's go, everything is going to be okay,' he said softly as he turned his head slowly around to check whether anybody was watching us. Nobody was. The fire was diminishing, the way that a pool of methylated spirit does when it burns, shrinking inwards from its circumference, leaving a telltale ring to show its original size. Some of the teenage kids were starting to drift away, making out they hadn't been as excited as the younger kids, but they had been; they just didn't want it known.

That's the thing about kids. When they're young they are excited by everything around them, but when they get older, twelve or thirteen, they become aware of themselves and how they look, and everything outside of that is just bullshit then.

'Look at them,' I said in my own disgusted way, 'they don't even know a good fire when they see one!'

El Greco shook his head, and nodded in agreement. 'Yeah, they just want to be cool, and they're gonna miss the rest of the fun.'

'What fun?' I asked raising my eyebrows, exaggerating my bemusement.

'Why, when the cops start asking questions, of course.'

He looked me dead in the eye, and I swallowed hard, trying to get a peach pit down a drinking straw.

'Oh, Jesus,' I said quietly.

'Tell you what, let's go down to the cops and tell them we saw two kids about so old, one wearing a Bugs Bunny T-shirt, and we saw them start a fire and as they ran off they said they couldn't give a fart if the old folks fried like barbecue chicken. That should take the heat off of us all right.'

I stared at him with my mouth open like the dead cod at Fulton fish market. He stuck his tongue out at me and rolled his eyes back in his head, laughing. Then he saw the strain in my face, fists clenched by my sides, fingers crunched into my palms all white and purple.

'All right, hotshot,' he said, 'let's go for real this time. We're late anyway.'

We shuffled back towards El Greco's house, filtering along with the meandering stream of soot-stained kids. I had the smell of smoke in my nostrils, and when I sniffed my shirt it had the scent of my father in late fall when he burned dead leaves from the maple trees out the back of our yard.

I tried to edge nearer to the boy in front of me, moving close to sniff his shirt. I tripped over a tree root and fell forward against him, bloodying my nose. He turned around and shoved me backwards. 'Hey! What da hellya doin'?' His voice was hard, clipped, nasal. A boxer's voice. He was from out of town and boy, did he look mean. He was probably three years older than me and much bigger, and I didn't want to fight with him, no way. I didn't want to fight with anybody, but particularly not him. For once I wished that Adolf were with me. He would shred him if that kid tried to push him around. Cecil had fast dukes and he liked to use them. Usually on me.

El Greco jumped to my defence. 'He just tripped, that's all; he's blind in one eye, so he can't see straight. He's always falling over. He's real sorry, aren't you, J.J.?'

This guy was probably from Washington Heights or the Bronx and probably had more fights in one day than I would have in my lifetime. I like to think that he wouldn't have hit me because I was a kid, but, either way, I guess El Greco's lie worked. Even a tough guy from the Bronx wouldn't hit a blind kid.

I sighed deeply and held my throbbing nose as the tough kid paced off, swaggering slightly as he went, letting all the other kids know he'd scored a victory without having to throw a single punch. 'Fucking asshole,' I murmured to myself, getting up, making damned sure he was out of earshot.

'What the hell did you do that for? I thought you were dead for sure!'

'I just fancied getting into training for my real contest against Cassius Clay Saturday week,' I said bitterly, dabbing blood from my nose.

Clay had beaten Sonny Liston twice, once in '64 in seven rounds to take the title from Liston, and again in '65, this time in two minutes twelve seconds. I remembered each fight vividly; particularly the fans yelling, 'Fake! Fake! Fake!' as Liston went down in the first round of that second bout.

Nobody would have shouted 'Fake!' if that Bronx boy had put me on the ground. That would have been real enough.

El Greco didn't say anything further. He had saved my skin and I'd given him sour grapes.

'I was trying to see if his shirt smelled of smoke and I tripped,' I said softly, by way of apology.

'Yeah, and you nearly needed Doctor Kesh,' he said giggling to himself. He could never stay mad at me for long, so I laughed too. Doctor Kesh was Armenian and his name was Keshishyan, but that was too difficult to say.

We arrived at El Greco's house, having passed back through Mister Jeb Doughty's field, seeing Jay Baglia sneaking out of the old barn all furtive, until he grinned and waved. We knew he grew pot in there because we hid out there often and saw strange plants growing in a corner where the roof was down and weeds sprouted high. El Greco figured what the taller weeds were, but we never let on. Not to a soul, except Bobby, who came with us to take a look.

We walked around to the back yard to enter by the kitchen door. Nobody under the age of twenty-one was allowed through the front door. It was an unwritten rule and I never broke it; even when rain poured down I always took the long route to the kitchen. The smell of hot charcoal and hickory wood chips charring drifted across the back yard. A welcoming homely smell, redolent of summer evenings and relaxed but excited affairs, when tail-wagging barking dogs gave chase to children playing tag. Any other day I would have breathed the perfumed air, almost able to taste it, but I was somewhat put off by the sight of smoke rising from the vent above the old brick barbecue.

'Late as usual,' said El Greco's mom.

She was pretty. I had no idea how old she was. I never saw a woman since who switched the roles of weary mother-of-two and sex siren as easily as she did. She had a way of smiling as though she knew your innermost thoughts and was relaying them back to you. She made me blush the colour of a distress flare just by smiling that knowing smile, and sometimes I felt like saying out loud, 'I wasn't thinking that!', such was my guilt. Even though I didn't really believe she could read my mind, in truth deep down I had just the sneaking fear that she could. Too much religion and the threat of eternal damnation were weights around me, and, like most who try, I was never fully able to cut those chains.

Missus Papadakis's patterned sleeveless sundress boasted summer flowers and poppies in scarlet, green and yellow on ice-cream white. The loops were empty where a matching belt should have exaggerated her slim waist but she knew it wasn't needed. Her figure never changed, but sometimes she looked nineteen, and then she was older than time itself. I guess the way she held herself told a story of how she was inside. Some days it was as though the weariness of life itself had feasted and sucked the very soul from her; an instant later she would radiate a sexuality that made me embarrassed to look her up and down – though I still did when I thought she wasn't paying attention to me.

I saw her nearly naked once. It was the day after El Greco and I had been looking through her Sears mail order catalogues. We found them in the bureau drawer one hot July day when his folks were out and we were searching the house for cigarettes. We were looking at guitars and bicycles at first then came across the lingerie section. Pages and pages of women modelling underwear. We gawped at them, and in some shots we could actually see the outlines of dark nipples and hairy bushes through the almost transparent material. We spent hours staring at them and getting all hot under the collar. If we heard a car pull up or a door shut somewhere we would slam the catalogues shut and stuff them back in the bureau, red-faced from guilt and passion. After that first discovery, we would spend hours looking at those photographs every chance we got when the house was empty. Busty women in basques and French knickers and stockings and silk pyjamas. So real we could almost feel them, stirring things deep within. Anyways, the very next morning after we first discovered the pictures I called for El Greco early, and, after his mom had made us breakfast of maple syrup pancakes, I went up to the bathroom, and through the part-open door to her bedroom I saw her, reflected side-on in a dressing-table mirror, breasts naked, rolling a stocking up her slim tanned leg to the untanned upper thigh where she clipped it to a black garter belt, stark against her milky skin. I froze, fascinated, eyes glazed and staring. Then she turned slightly and caught sight of me. She wasn't mad, she just smiled her smile and said, 'Show's over, J.J.,' then she pushed the door slowly closed with her foot, still smiling. I ran downstairs, face burning, and took my place back at the table, afraid to let on. Missus Papadakis came down a couple of minutes later, acting for all the world as though nothing ever happened.

I never told El Greco. It didn't seem right to, somehow. She never made mention of that day, but whenever she caught me gazing at her in that way she would give me a knowing smile, and I would cough and ask her a pointless question or wander into the back yard whistling any old tune I could summon into my head.